SPECIAL MESSAGE TO READERS

Tom Vowler is an award-winning writer living in southwest England. His short story collection *The Method* won the inaugural Scott Prize in 2010 and the Edge Hill Readers' Prize in 2011. This is his debut novel.

WHAT LIES WITHIN

Living in a remote Devon farmhouse, Anna's family has always been close to nature, surrounded by the haunting beauty of the moor. But when a convict escapes from nearby Dartmoor Prison, their isolation suddenly begins to feel more claustrophobic than free. Fearing for her children's safety, Anna becomes increasingly irrational and grows distant from her kind husband Robert. And she seems to suspect something sinister of her teenage son Paul. Meanwhile, a young idealistic teacher has just started her first job, determined to 'make a difference'. But when she is brutally attacked by one of her students, her version of events is doubted by even those closest to her. Struggling to deal with the terrible consequences, she must do what she can to move on and start afresh . . .

TOM VOWLER

WHAT LIES
WITHIN

Complete and Unabridged

CHARNWOOD
Leicester

First published in Great Britain in 2013 by
Headline Publishing Group
London

First Charnwood Edition
published 2014
by arrangement with
Headline Publishing Group
A division of Hachette Livre UK Ltd
London

The moral right of the author has been asserted

A catalogue record for this book is available
from the British Library.

ISBN 978–1–4448–1811–6

Published by
F. A. Thorpe (Publishing)
Anstey, Leicestershire

Set by Words & Graphics Ltd.
Anstey, Leicestershire
Printed and bound in Great Britain by
T. J. International Ltd., Padstow, Cornwall

This book is printed on acid-free paper

for Alison

Acknowledgements

This book was made possible by the kind generosity of the following people, to whom I am indebted.

John Pollex, the geezer of ceramics and provider of fine green tea. Louise, whose courage in our interviews was a reminder of human endurance. Lisa Glass and Jennie Walkley-Cox, for matters maternal. Professor Anthony Caleshu, whose initial encouragement sowed the book's early seeds. Arts Council England, for their generous support. Charlie Brotherstone, who quickly became so much more than just a brilliant agent. My wonderful editor, Claire Baldwin, whose belief in and enthusiasm for the book provided its own inspiration. Plymouth University, for its continuing support of literary endeavours. And AVS, who continues to change everything.

Thank you.

The question is not what you look at, but what you see.

Henry David Thoreau

1

It was an exaggeration to term it a media invasion — a couple of journalists from local papers loitered, a man she thought she recognised from the television spoke earnestly to a camera — but the mood of the town had shifted. Anna parked in one of the side lanes and walked towards the post office, where she noticed a group had gathered outside.

Several men and women shuffled about, nodding or shaking their heads at what they heard, breath misting from their mouths. A mother tried to control her two young children as they ran around the small crowd, darting into the road, tagging each other. Those who had been told the news yesterday passed on details to the few who hadn't. The last time anyone escaped, a woman in her fifties told those with a mind to listen, was nine years ago. A couple of burglars, she said. Had a car waiting on the road to Tavistock. They followed her stare, looking across the open moor to the prison, the tips of its proud chimneys veiled by low cloud.

'Did they catch them?' a young man asked before spitting into the kerb.

'No,' the woman said, but was contradicted by another, who was sure they had done.

Anna remembered the news reports. They'd been away for a few days with the children, so only found out on their return. The men were caught — a few days later, she thought — returning with minimal fuss. An official letter came the following week, reassuring them they had been in no danger, that lessons would be learned. A further bid for freedom had occurred a few years ago, the prisoner, having broken a leg in his leap from the wall, managing to crawl fifty yards before capture.

Others in the crowd chipped in with snippets they'd heard about the latest breakout, versions that, to Anna, sounded fanciful. A tallish man in a Barbour jacket and flat cap informed them that the prisoner wouldn't get far. 'That's why they built it here,' he said. 'He'll be halfway down Foxtor Mires by now, if the hypothermia didn't get him first.'

'Natural justice, that,' someone said. 'Saves money.' A few nodded, someone tutted. The cost of keeping a person in prison was raised.

Anna pushed politely through them, avoiding eye contact. The post office door chimed as she opened it.

She didn't watch much television or listen to the local radio station; the first she'd heard was when Robert answered the phone late last night. A colleague had wondered if they'd be asked to help with the search. Anna's husband didn't

2

think so, at least not at this stage. Knowledge of the moor was valuable but little substitute for the tracking ability of the police dogs that would have been used at first light. They had discussed whether to tell the children in the morning, deciding to do so after school, if they hadn't already heard.

The man wasn't dangerous, the news had said earlier, but the advice was still not to approach him. The phrase always mystified Anna; how many people, on recognising a criminal on the run, thought approaching them a good idea?

He'd scaled the wall shortly after dusk, the prison alarm sounding around six apparently. Anna hadn't heard it, despite her studio facing that way. Robert said it depended on the direction of the wind; he'd heard it once, working in the garden, when they used to test it. What were you supposed to do anyway, if you did hear it? Hide in the bathroom? Turn all the lights off? Turn them all on?

Anna had slept uneasily last night — every noise outside and downstairs magnified by, if not fear, then an alertness. At around two, when Robert's snoring crescendoed, she'd looked in on Megan, who was curled up at the top half of her bed, the covers furled in a heap at the bottom. Since starting secondary school, the soft toys had been relegated to the floor, their role as companions perhaps discarded for ever. She pulled her daughter's duvet up, tucked the loose hair on her face behind her ear and watched her for a few moments, envying her ability to sleep deeply.

3

Anna walked to the window and parted the curtains slightly. Moonlight filtered weakly through the cloud, giving an outline of the yard below if none of its detail. The dense woods to the north could just be made out, silhouetted against the sky. As wind gusted, the rafters moaned above her.

She walked past her son's room, pausing outside, trying to avoid the loose floorboard. A faint light issued from beneath the door. He'd probably fallen asleep with the lamp on and for a moment she considered going in to turn it off. Listening closely for the turning of magazine pages or the clicking of a game control, she heard nothing. They'd smelt tobacco on his clothes a couple of times now; Robert was going to talk to him about it at the weekend. They all try it, he said. It's no big deal. But for Anna it was more evidence of Paul's retreat into adolescence, to a place beyond her reach.

She put an ear to the door, held her breath. Still silence. She reached out to the door handle, paused and then withdrew her hand.

Standing midway between her children's rooms, Anna felt the unrivalled ache of parental love, that most visceral of sensations where someone else matters more than you.

Downstairs only the soft tick of the mantel clock disturbed the silence. The fire, long cold, still gave off the comforting smell of wood smoke. In her studio she thought about glazing the last of the bowls, perhaps even working through the night, but decided against it. She checked both doors and went upstairs.

Back in the bedroom Anna took off her dressing gown and nestled into Robert, who grunted and put an arm round her. The bed had hardly cooled. Still sleep didn't come.

Living little more than a mile from a building housing six hundred men who'd lost their freedom had troubled her at first. Driving past it at night, with the children in the back, only the silhouettes of the great tors for company, made her stiffen a little. But over the years it became just a part of the landscape — a grey, austere structure that perhaps belonged in a city or another time, but one that you learned to ignore, such was the surrounding beauty. It became a building that sometimes caught your eye in the distance, the sun glinting off its granite façade. But you could go the long way around, miss it altogether. It wasn't something you dwelt on.

Built during the Napoleonic Wars by French and American POWs, the jail was supposed to improve upon the terrible conditions prisoners suffered whilst being held on derelict ships off Plymouth. Rebuilt and converted for convicts in the Victorian era, its reputation for austerity flourished. And although it had been steadily downgraded in the severity of the criminals it housed, local papers seemed constantly to publish damning reports attesting to its forbidding and wretched environment.

* * *

The post office was empty. The elderly man behind the glass screen half smiled, perhaps glad

5

someone had resisted the scene outside.

'You'd think the world was ending,' he said.

Anna smiled back, unsure what to say. Calculating how much bubble wrap was needed for the next two weeks, she could feel the man's eyes on her. Her face would be familiar in the small town, yet she was probably regarded as an outsider, despite living only a couple of miles away. The pubs were where you ingratiated yourself, she supposed, and she'd hardly been in any of them in the fourteen years of living here. She visited shops when she knew they would be quiet; today's departure from this was exceptional and beyond her control. And so, fairly or otherwise, she was likely thought of as the aloof artist, eccentric and reclusive, one who regarded herself elevated beyond the concerns of the community. That Robert preferred the pub on the road past Postbridge, that the children didn't have friends in the town no doubt compounded their status as *others*.

'I expect they'll catch him soon enough,' Anna said to the man as she approached the counter.

'Dunno why you'd want to escape anyway. They got a telly in every cell. Regular meals. No bills. Wouldn't mind a bit of that myself.'

Smiling weakly she paid him for the bubble wrap and headed back to the car. The sky had darkened and the group had dispersed a little now. One of the older women was talking to a reporter, who scribbled on to a pad. As Anna rounded the corner she saw a man in a suit pointing across to the prison, trying out various spots on the pavement, while a man in jeans toyed with the settings on a large camera. The latter kept gazing skyward, seemingly irritated by the diminishing light and flecks of rain.

Anna kept her head down as she approached them, but could sense the man with the camera pointing her out to his colleague.

'Excuse me,' the one in the suit said. 'Do you live here? On the moor?'

'I'm in a hurry really. Sorry.'

'It'll just take a minute, nothing more. Just a couple of questions.'

And so she found herself standing on the pavement in front of a TV camera and a man preening his hair, while another counted him in on the fingers of one hand.

The reporter told the camera the escaped prisoner's name, how he was halfway through a seven-year sentence for dealing heroin. He then talked about the prisoner's home town and she realised the news people had travelled halfway across the country to cover the story. He introduced Anna, who now regretted being persuaded to represent the views of locals, but the first take was aborted after the reporter sneezed and complained of a cold.

When they started again, Anna was asked if she thought the man was hiding nearby, whether people were afraid living in the shadow of the jail. She kept her answers as brief as possible, which seemed to help terminate the interview in quick time. The man thanked her but couldn't hide his annoyance at her lack of enthusiasm or hint of any alarm. He wrote down her name, checked the spelling, thanked her again.

7

The cameraman looked about for others to talk to — someone more opinionated, Anna supposed — but those who weren't using the shops had left to continue their day.

'What do you reckon?' the man in the suit said to his colleague. 'Have we got enough?'

There was agreement that they had, that the rain was getting harder.

A storm coming in, Anna called to them as she walked to her car.

As she placed the bubble wrap in the back seat, the reporter shouted across, asking if any of the town's pubs served a good pint.

★   ★   ★

Driving home Anna saw a helicopter hovering like a bird of prey beneath the cloud a mile or so north. Its camera would be looking for a hot spot, she guessed, a white mass where you wouldn't expect one, a lone figure of heat huddled in the gorse or the woods. There were endless places to hide, but the man outside the post office was right — you couldn't survive for long without help, not in the winter months. She pictured lines of police with dogs searching the woods and valleys. Perhaps he, too, had a car waiting and was back home, where the TV people were from, enjoying a drink with friends. Or perhaps he was several feet down in one of the bogs.

Nearing home, the outbuildings she passed took on a new significance. She would check the barn before starting work, for peace of mind.

Robert would probably call later to say the man had been found.

As the car wound down the valley towards Two Bridges, the pressure of the exhibition began to push the other thoughts from her mind.

2

The wipers cleared the rain every few seconds, allowing Anna to see the school gates. She'd parked far enough away not to embarrass Paul, but close enough to not miss either of them. She told herself that Megan hated getting the bus, so she'd be half popular.

On the pavement, next to the line of buses, drivers shared words and cigarettes, awaiting the onslaught. The sky, bruised and ashen, seemed to sit barely above the buildings. A pair of jackdaws squabbled around a chimney pot.

She found the local radio station, but there was just an interview with an economist on the recession. Hoping to hear something about the escape, she left it on.

This was an overreaction; Robert would say so later. The bus dropped the children off less than half a mile from the house. And it's not as if there are any dangerous prisoners there these days, he'd say. It's a category C now: drug-related offences, white-collar crime, most nearing the end of sentences and regarded as unlikely to attempt escape. The man would probably be miles away by now, if they hadn't already caught him. All of this she knew.

She looked at the buildings beyond the iron railings. That her children attended the same school she had twenty-five years earlier seemed surreal. There were a couple of new structures, fewer playing fields, but essentially it looked the same. Anna imagined herself a teenager the other side of the gates and a nostalgia for innocence emerged; ignorance that merely frustrated then now assumed a precious quality. All she'd wanted to be then was older, to be able to choose how to live, to escape the clutches of adolescence, fleeing this dreary town on the edge of the moor.

There'd been a boy who liked her, in their penultimate year. His face, florid with acne, came to her as she allowed more memories to gather. Anna had played with his affections, using him to demonstrate her popularity, yet shunning him whenever they were alone and he made his brave and diffident approaches. And then they didn't share a class for a year or so and by that time he was going out with someone else — a frumpy girl, Anna now recalled, yet her jealousy was complete as the two of them clung to each other between lessons like conjoined twins.

One of the wipers grated on the windscreen and the memory faded. A few older children milled out of the gates, jostling and teasing each other. Others ran from the drizzle and on to the buses. Those who didn't get on banged on

12

windows at their friends. A male teacher near the gates shouted a rebuke but was ignored.

As she watched, boys her son's age swaggered by, feigning assaults on each other, whistling at a group of girls across the road, some of whom shouted or gestured back. Anna avoided their faces, happy the rain on the windscreen hid hers. As they passed, one of the boys was pushed into the car, knocking the wing mirror back. An apology of sorts came, before retaliation was sought and a chase ensued.

The argument of a few nights ago replayed in her mind, its form consistent these days, phrases like clichés. Tension could build hours before they went to bed now. It's just a phase, she would say as they went upstairs, her husband's face disconsolate or cross in the half-light. It always passes, she'd continued, still kindly, not yet defensive. He was loving enough not to say how long it had been. Four months this time. Maybe five.

Anna considered how she'd feel if he had an affair. Whether it would change something, prompt a reaction in her. There could be little blame if he did. She knew he wouldn't, though — as much as you can know — which just intensified the guilt.

And so after arguing as quietly as they could, they had fallen asleep, backs to each other, the hurt and rejection following them into their dreams. Just hold me, she sometimes said, but Robert would be asleep. Or too hurt. They usually woke in each other's arms, which was something.

At either end of the abstinence they sometimes made love when she'd rather not. At what point, she wondered, did Robert realise this? Because you could always tell when someone was withdrawn emotionally, there in body alone. A lessening of movement, the cessation of sounds that signify pleasure. Eyes almost vacant, the mind elsewhere. He stopped if she asked. Always. But those times when he knew he'd lost her but carried on anyway, carried on until the end: what went through his mind in those frantic few minutes when only he was participating?

★ ★ ★

From the gates Megan appeared with a friend, their hoods up. Anna pushed the wipers on full, staring hard through the rain. She tooted once, flashed the car's headlights and her daughter looked over. Megan said something to her friend and then came over to the car, getting in the back as Anna turned off the radio.

'Hey, darling.'

Megan mumbled a response.

'Good day?'

'Hmmm. It was OK. Why are you here, Mum?'

'I was out this way. Have you seen your brother?'

'I saw him this morning.'

'Yes, I know. I mean after school.'

'No.'

Anna considered going now; her son would be fine. Perhaps just watch him get on the bus.

14

She thought she recognised one of his friends as he walked past the car. Megan was talking about a girl in her class who stole things, how nobody liked her, that they were all a bit afraid of her.

Some of the buses pulled away now, children's faces pressed against rear windows, distorted and comic. One boy threatened to expose his backside to those outside, but lost his nerve.

There was hardly anyone coming through the gates now. Maybe she'd missed him in the rain. She asked her daughter which bus they normally got on, but Megan couldn't tell from the car. Perhaps he came out another way; there were a few other exits beyond the buildings. They waited until all the buses had finally driven off.

'Did Paul say anything this morning about going to a friend's after school?'

'I don't know, Mum.' Megan said this in a sarcastic voice, as if remembering detail that far back in the day was unreasonable.

He was to tell them if he wasn't coming home. That was the rule allowing him to have a mobile. She checked hers. Nothing.

'Stay here, love. Just going to see if I can see your brother.'

The rain had eased a little. She stood by the gates, checking the car in between scanning the doors of the buildings. The exodus had all but finished, a few last stragglers in ones and twos.

From the far side of the main playground, a man on a bike headed towards her. Trousers tucked in socks and a pink cycle helmet gave him a farcical air. As he neared, Anna recognised

15

him as one of Paul's teachers. History or geography, she couldn't be sure. But definitely one from the last parents' evening.

He slowed to pass her, smiled.

'Hello,' he said.

Anna half smiled back. He was almost out of earshot when she said, 'My son, Paul. Paul Curtis. He's not come out.'

The man stopped, putting a foot down, looking back. He thought for a moment. 'Paul Curtis.' He considered the name. 'No, he wasn't in class today.'

'Oh.' Anna tried to hide her surprise. She thanked the man and walked back to the car.

3

I run ungainly along the corridor, cursing the squeak my shoes make on the wooden floor, while remaining grateful they don't have heels. A few papers fall from the wallet folder that's pressed to my chest and I scramble about the floor gathering them, praying the corridor remains empty. My pace slows to a brisk walk as I pass each door, before speeding up again. It's almost silent until I turn the corner and near my classroom, where a clamour awaits me. Pausing for a moment outside, I straighten my blouse, tidy my hair, get my breath back. I fling open the door to ironic cheers.

I'm never late. It took a catalogue of mishaps to arrive on my third day in this job ten minutes after my class.

'Have a seat,' someone says. 'The teacher's not here yet.'

Howls of laughter.

'You're late, Miss,' a boy at the back says. 'See me after.'

I avoid any eye contact, walk to my desk and

try to compose myself. I consider if any colleagues saw me, whether another teacher's been in here on hearing the noise. Scanning the room I try to exude confidence but they see I'm flustered, from running, from embarrassment.

I remove my jacket, leaving them to carry on in small groups, some merely catching up on last night's TV, others whispering, perhaps scheming. A few will be prepared to test the new teacher, see how far they can push me. There's a group of four boys at the back that I immediately identify as the ones I need to win over, dominate even, if I'm to gain their respect.

From my case I take out material for the lesson.

'Got a note from your parents, Miss?' one of the group of four shouts, referencing my age as much as my tardiness. They'll be used to someone of a different generation standing in front of them.

I remember a teacher at my own school, a biologist. He clearly loved his subject but certain classes walked all over him, throwing chewing gum at his back, coming and going as they pleased. It made for an uncomfortable spectacle if you weren't part of it, watching this crestfallen man trying to be heard, pleading with the moderate ones, incredulous that the science couldn't win them round. You'd see him slowly boil into an unconvincing frenzy, his beseeching shouts becoming crazed and high pitched, serving only to enhance his subservience. It always ended the same way, with him scuttling next door, fetching Mr Davies, a brute of a man

18

who undoubtedly mourned the passing of corporal punishment, a man who only had to look at you to instil fear and silence. You could sense the lack of respect even he had for his colleague: *You're a scientist, not a teacher*, a sideways glance said.

Everyone knew the near-comic routine. Davies would enter to an orderly but chuckling room, glower sufficiently, make a token example of someone. But his contempt was obvious, impossible to hide, and as soon as he'd gone the mayhem resumed with renewed vigour, as if the class had been betrayed by the vicarious chastisement.

I vowed during training not to allow this, to never be feckless or lose control. Being late today had weakened my position but it wasn't terminal. I let them continue as I finish unpacking my case before rounding on the most vocal one.

'Up here, now,' I say.

The group pretend not to hear me.

'You, in the corner, blond hair,' I say, a little louder. 'Up here.'

'What, Miss?'

'You heard me, up to the front.'

His friends goad him, cheer. 'She wants you,' one says.

'Now,' I say firmly.

The boy stands, pushes his chair back with as much disdain as he can gather. It's all done in his own time, a posturing gait, an act perfected. He ambles towards me, grinning at each row as he passes. There's a wolf whistle from the back, a giggle from one of the girls. He stands in front of me, an inch or two taller, stocky, total confidence in his physicality. A few awkward tufts of stubble sprout from moderate acne. His clothes and breath smell of cigarettes, a couple of fingers yellowed from the habit. The nails on some of his fingers look painfully bitten down.

I imagine he has to work hard to maintain his alpha-male status when in possession of it. A slightly weaker physique, a few inches shorter, and his looks and appearance would invite bullying.

Academically, with the exception of one or two, this class is not expected to threaten the higher grades. I've been told my predecessor did the minimum required to achieve a quiet and early retirement. A frustrated writer, he found the restriction of the syllabus and the increasing disinclination of children to read anything, let alone literature, demoralising. His lessons, apparently, involved the class silently 'reading' Hardy or Steinbeck, while he wrote chapters for a novel that — as far as anybody here knows — has never seen the light of day. The homework he set was formulaic and usually unmarked. And so while not expecting miracles, the school wants me to push them a little in their final year, to break through, to help arrest a run of poor Ofsted reports.

'What?' the boy says to me with something nearing aggression. The room falls silent. They'll be familiar with this, their classmate jousting with a new teacher. Their excitement lies in gauging his opponent, assessing where I draw the line, the extent of my armoury.

'And you are?' I say.

'On time, Miss.' Laughter breaks out behind him and he turns to lap it up. It was a good line, I'll give him that.

'Your name.'

'Jamie.'

'Jamie . . . ?'

'O'Sullivan. Two Ls.'

'You can spell, I see. Well done. Not all hope lost then.' My tone, a little barbed, surprises me. For the first time he looks unsure, gauche even, and a frisson of power sweeps through me. I step to the side, leaving him standing there and address the class, introducing myself. I tell them what we'll be doing this term, ignoring Jamie, who's shuffling from side to side, emitting sporadic sighs. He looks to his friends at the back and I tell him to face the blackboard, which he does with a theatrical huff. I set the class an exercise, an ice-breaker to be completed before the bell. When I finish addressing them, Jamie goes to sit down.

'Where you going, Jamie O'Sullivan with two Ls?'

'Sit down, Miss,' he says.

'Oh, but we've not finished yet.' He stares hard at me before skulking back.

I have an anthology in my bag for my afternoon class. I tell him to face the front while I flick through it.

'Hands out of pockets,' I say, handing him the open book. The class remain quiet, engrossed by what's playing out before them.

21

'Will you read page forty-three please.'

'What?'

'The poem. Will you read it. To the class.'

'Out loud?'

'Well, they're unlikely to hear it otherwise.'

'No way.'

'So you can spell, but you can't read.'

He looks up at the others, feigning indifference. 'I ain't reading no poem.'

'Might be better than a detention.' He looks at me, checking for intent, estimating what he's up against. 'Go on,' I say. 'Or you can read the entire book to me at four.'

This prompts muffled laughter from a few of the girls at the front. He shuffles about, looking to his friends again, his neck reddening. Another glance to me tells him there's only one way to end this. He coughs, nervously, then begins.

''Had I the heavens' embro, embry . . . ''

''Embroidered,'' I say.

''Embroidered cloths, en . . . '' He looks at me again, genuine panic in his eyes.

''Enwrought.' It means woven.'

'I know that,' he snarls.

'I'm sure you do. Carry on.'

He stutters through each line, murdering the cadence with a staccato drawl and more coughing. Each time he struggles with a word, more giggles come in front of him, which I should quash but don't.

The last line is spat out. ''Tread softly because you tread on my dreams.''

He hands me the book but I remain impassive. I want there to be no ambiguity, no repetition.

'Now read the last line again,' I say. 'But this time slowly. And Jamie, try to give it some feeling, as if you mean it.'

There's a sense of dread from the others, an intake of breath at my persistence. I know I'm pushing him and for the first time I consider whether I've gone too far. A reputation as a maverick with pupils or colleagues will be unhelpful. He takes the book back, scans the class, silencing the giggles, and reads the line again, all of his stuttering and diffidence gone. This time there's menace in the words, a calm anger that spreads out into the classroom.

He places the book on the desk, walks slowly to his chair and sits down.

'Thank you, Jamie,' I say. 'Perhaps now we can get on with the lesson.'

4

I go back into the bedroom where Nick is rolling a joint. He looks almost smug, sitting up naked against the headboard, as if he's beyond reproach. What a few weeks ago had still felt exhilarating has become trite — a headline: Head of Humanities cheats on wife with younger colleague.

Until now I'd contained the guilt, tucked it away in some cordoned-off part of my mind as I settled into the job. Disorientated by his seduction while it masqueraded as friendly support, I let my guard down, fooled myself.

The used condom lies on the floor next to his clothes. I frame the scene in my mind, my decision suddenly made easy.

'Does your wife let you do that in bed?' I say.

He inserts a conical piece of card, licks the gummed paper and sticks it down. Lighting the twisted end, he inhales deeply. 'Our bed's strictly for sleeping, I told you that. You want some?' He offers me the joint, its smoke tendril curling upwards, filling the room with a piquant fug.

25

'No thank you.'

'You had a bad day or something?'

'Or something.' I open the window. A thin breeze has traces of winter on it.

'You work too hard,' he says. 'Stop trying to make a name for yourself. That place takes your soul if you're not careful.'

'Has it taken yours?'

'Years ago, baby.'

'Please don't call me that.' I put my skirt and blouse back on, before piling Nick's clothes on the end of the bed.

'Not very subtle,' he says. 'Kicking out time?'

'I have a lot on tomorrow.' I point to the floor. 'You going to dispose of that?'

'Fuck, I thought it was men who were supposed to wrap things up quickly. Come and go, as it were.'

'It's nearly six, Nick. How late can you be working at school?'

I watch him smoke, this man who must be at least twenty years my senior.

'OK, I'm going. Just let me finish this.'

Was I so lonely that a little charm from a married colleague was all it took? Other teachers weren't unfriendly, yet three months into the job I still felt on the periphery, somehow unconnected. I think back to life at university, the friends I made there. How we promised to stay in touch. And then moving here, excited by all that lay ahead.

At the start I told myself Nick's ring might mean nothing. That a divorce could be imminent. Not because I necessarily wanted anything of more substance, more that I wasn't some wrecking ball. But then came the revelation of children, two girls, and a content if not blissful union. And yet I was happy to take what was on offer, slipping seamlessly into something I knew to be wrong.

'Does she know about me?' I once asked, thinking there might be an arrangement between them.

'She doesn't ask,' he said, which somehow gave me less legitimacy.

'Are there others, then?'

'Of course not.' He almost looked hurt by this.

'But there have been?'

'Come on, why all the questions?'

Because I'd hoped there was more than this. Because this isn't how I see myself. I don't want to hurt anyone. I don't want to be hurt.

As I pass the bed, Nick grabs my arm, pulls me towards him. He lifts my skirt up, puts a hand between my legs, fingers clumsily rubbing me. 'Come on,' he says, 'I've still got some time.'

I wriggle free, out of his reach and continue tidying the bedroom. 'I'm tired, Nick.'

'Your loss.' He leans back, focuses on smoking again. 'We good for next week?'

'I can't Tuesday.'

'No?' Again the hurt, but this time it's affected.

'My little project, as you call it. One of the boys can't do Thursdays now.'

'I told you you're wasting your time with the likes of O'Sullivan.'

'Yes, you did.'

'You can't get through to kids like that.'

'You said that, too.'

'Well, I've been doing this a bit longer than you.'

'Which makes you an expert.'

'It means I've seen boys like them, the homes they come from. The worst combination of nature and nurture.'

'What's nature got to do with it?'

'They're delinquents; their parents were, and theirs before them. Their path is already set. Concentrate on the ones who want to learn.'

'So, just give up on them?'

'They get given the same as everyone else, it's their choice what to do with it. You can't force-feed them.'

He offers me the joint again, which I ignore.

'People learn at different speeds,' I say. 'Jamie and Simon need more than the others. And not because they're stupid; it's their home life that's the problem, that and the labels we give them.'

'So it's our fault?'

'Partly, yes.'

'I'm just saying, a few sonnets aren't going to stop them stealing cars and setting fire to them. You watch too many films.'

'Fuck you. This isn't middle-class white woman takes literature to the ghetto.'

'No? What is it, then?'

'They need some extra attention so they can make informed choices and know what's possible. I know I can get through to them. Especially Simon; our first session went really well. They just need someone to take an interest in them.'

'You're a teacher, not a social worker.'

'And I want to teach all of them.'

'So they learn what? You think everyone can be inspired by Orwell's dystopian warnings, or poets moaning about the futility of war? That some great epiphany will occur? That they'll think, yes, I see now that I must study harder, stop shoplifting and vandalising the town and ingest the world's literature? And if they do want to learn, then it's in the syllabus. A bit of after-school tuition with you isn't going to change anything. It's naïve.'

He relights the joint, studies its tip as he exhales. His eyes, impossibly blue, fix on me, a last plea to end hostilities.

'I think it's time you went, Nick.'

He tosses the duvet back, stands and pulls on his trousers, joint in the side of his mouth like a sixties hearthrob. I watch as he gets dressed in my flat for the last time and make a more considered guess at his age: early forties, if I'm generous, though he wears it well. Still two decades apart. Almost a generation. And yet, as I look at his body a last time, I know I'll miss this, however snatched these late afternoons are, however complete my guilt.

'You take it all too seriously,' he says, doing up his shirt. 'You'll see I'm right.'

'I hope not.'

'You have to separate the two. Leave work at work.'

'If I wanted nine to five, I'd have worked in a bank.'

'You've been doing this job, what, a few

months? You'll burn out. Running around trying to save everyone with the power of words. Maybe some people don't want to read the classics. Fuck knows I didn't at school. Some people are meant to work in factories. Or end up in prison. It's the natural state of things.'

'You've always been so supportive of this. Anyway, it's not about literature per se. It's about leaving school *with* something, believing that things are possible.'

'I'm just trying to save you some heartache. The ones who want to learn, do. We offer the knowledge and they can ingest as much or as little of it as they like. The ones who don't — the likes of O'Sullivan and Phillips — well, as long as they're not stopping the others.'

'You're being elitist.'

'No, that would be telling those two to go home, that they're not welcome.'

'We might as well tell them to go home if it's not getting through.'

He uses the long mirror to finish his tie, re-creating this morning's appearance.

'Why's it so important to you?' he says.

'Because knowledge can change people's lives, give them hope where there's none.'

'You still believe that?'

'Yes.'

'You're sounding like an incoming politician now.'

'Those two, they go home to arguing and misery and crime . . . '

'So did I. So do most kids around here. Education isn't a panacea for everyone.'

'It's a way out, once you know the rules. Once you have options. You do well at school, you can do anything; you fuck up, it's hard to ever turn it around. As teachers, I thought it's what we all believed.'

'I did. Give it a few years, you'll see.'

'I'm still going to try.'

'What do you think can be achieved in an hour a week?'

'Are we talking about students now or us?'

'Funny.'

'Goodbye, Nick.'

He puts on his jacket, grabs his case. The joint is left to burn out in the ashtray.

'I'm doing that, am I?' I say, looking at the condom. He huffs, picks it up with a thumb and forefinger and takes it into the bathroom. The flush goes.

I stand there motionless as he kisses me on the cheek. 'Mondays and Wednesdays are still difficult for me, baby,' he says.

'They're all difficult for me, Nick.'

5

Smoke coiled from the chimney up into the drizzle. Megan, having regaled the day's detail to her mother, ran inside the cottage using the key under the plant pot. Anna looked up to the hills beyond the river, the regimented conifers aligned on their upper slopes.

Inside warm, dry air from the kiln filled the downstairs. She flicked the switch on the kettle and shouted up to her daughter, 'He didn't say anything to you on the bus this morning?' No answer. She tried her son's phone again. The message started before it rang: Yeah, busy, leave a message, her son said.

She tried Robert, who answered eventually. 'Hi.'

'Paul didn't come out of school.'

'What do you mean?'

'I went to pick them up, but he didn't get on the bus.'

'How do you know?'

'I watched until they drove off.'

'You might have missed him. Why were you there?'

'I was passing. A teacher said he missed a class.'

'Well, they do. He's almost finished for the year. They all skip a few. I'll talk to him later.'

'I'm going to walk along when the next bus passes.'

'Anna . . . '

'Has there been any news on the prisoner?'

'I've not heard anything. Stop worrying. I'll be an hour or so.'

Anna took Megan some squash and a plate of dried fruit. She was drawing the shells they'd collected on Wembury beach last weekend, her face intense with concentration.

Paul's room was the usual mess. Unmade bed. Clothes strewn everywhere, left where they'd fallen. Posters of near-naked women, perhaps celebrities of sorts, had increased in recent months. Anna insisted they were taken down initially; an angry scene followed, a compromise reached the next day.

'He's going through puberty,' Robert had said. 'Let him have his space; he'll grow out of it. They're just posters.' But they revolted her. Her son appeared to enjoy looking at the most clichéd form of soft pornography. Ridiculous breasts, their size and shape a tribute to silicone; lascivious pouts that suggested a ubiquitous availability. She pictured her son looking at them, desiring these women, if only for a few intense minutes at a time. They'd got him to agree to no actual nudity, yet the images in front of Anna remained just as sordid.

There had been little sign of interest in girls before this; no mention of dates or would-be girlfriends. Anna had been more than happy to leave whatever passed for domestic sex education to her husband, a talk that apparently dispelled none of its truisms.

'Where do I start?' Robert had asked her, squirming as she imagined Paul would once it began.

Anna teased him before replying, 'Try to gauge where he's up to and go from there.' Her son, she later learned, affected an impressive indifference, remarking that *the little chat* was not only superfluous but also years late. Barely a minute later Anna heard a relieved Robert vacate Paul's bedroom, issuing a you-can-come-to-us-with-anything closing statement.

And so Anna suspected Robert was relieved when the posters started to appear; that at least some interest in such matters was apparent, that Paul's *development* was on track despite the absence of any significant parental input.

Perhaps her husband's own bedroom as a teenager had been adorned with similar images; perhaps every boy's was at some time. She thought back to her own adolescent crushes, but the posters of wholesome pop stars seemed innocent, somehow removed from lust and desire. If her memory could be trusted, looking at them had merely brought fantasies of romantic gesture, maybe a lingering kiss. Or perhaps time had just sanitised her own prurience.

She wondered whether Megan noticed them — these ridiculous and insulting parodies of femininity — on the rare occasions she was in her brother's room. And if so at what age she would start to realise she resembled them in no way. There had been one such visit to her brother's room a few weeks ago that Anna knew of. For all her son's bravado and aloofness, he had a near-disabling fear of spiders beyond a certain size. Small ones could be coped with, thrown from his window with the aid of a mug or glass. But anything larger meant vacating the room swiftly and reluctantly asking herself or Robert to remove it. And with both parents out one day, in order to remain in his room he was forced to ask his little sister for help. Describing the event at dinner, with almost no smugness, Megan had described cupping the creature with her hands before releasing it at the back of her cupboard, much to Paul's disgust.

★　★　★

As Anna walked up the lane, the last of the day's watery light was waning. The cloud had dispersed a little, allowing the first stars to shimmer. The lambent glow from a distant farm flickered. She listened to the waters of the West Dart resound through the valley. It should be the perfect place to grow up, she thought: nature's chords, its hues, abounding; exploration of a wondrous landscape filling days, the children wandering home across sun-bleached plains for tea. But for Paul adolescence contaminated the beauty; living here was a burden to him, forever reliant on his parents to take him anywhere a bus or skateboard couldn't. Occasionally friends came to stay, but he was generally out of the loop, always on the fringes of peer activity. And the isolation was something to rally against, a stick to beat her and Robert with.

The flashes of rage were a recent development, though — perhaps the last six months or so — his temper flaring with minimal provocation these days. Anna forced herself to stand her ground each time, refusing to ever be afraid of her own son, even as his face, inches from hers, blazed with fury. Robert remained faithful to a non-confrontational approach, with the children at least.

The worst of these outbursts had come a month ago. Robert was still at work, Megan listening to music in her room. Anna had a fire going but there were no more logs inside. Knowing Paul still had his shoes on, she asked him to fill the basket up and bring it in, which after some huffing he did. A minute or so later she could hear him trying to open the back door with his foot, so that he didn't have to put the logs down. The door finally opened, but he must have lost his balance, spilling the logs on to the kitchen floor. She listened, waiting for the swearing to start, but after a moment's silence the house was filled with an explosion of violent crashes. Anna ran through to see Paul lost in a blind frenzy, kicking the wood as if it weighed nothing, smashing it into cupboards and appliances again and again, malevolence billowing from him, distinct from him. She shouted at her son to stop, but he was oblivious to her words, to anything else. When at last he did stop, the kitchen was silent apart from his panting.

37

Slowly he surveyed the carnage around him, as if checking every log had been subjected to at least one strike. Finally looking up at her, there was a hint of confusion in his face, the anger dissipating by the second. Anna thought he might even start to cry. Torn between shouting more and holding her son, she merely began placing the logs back in the basket. With only a few left, Paul slowly bent down and helped her gather them up. When they finished, Anna placed a hand on his shoulder, before Paul headed to his room. By dinner he seemed himself again and the incident was never mentioned.

Megan, though, still flourished in the landscape's wonder, Dartmoor her oversized playground. Friends, for her, were found in unseen creatures and imaginary playmates with whom she would talk for hours. When real friends visited, they were initially fascinated that Megan lived in the place their parents occasionally came for epic hikes, where you could go for hours without seeing a building or a car. But the novelty soon faded with the absence of modern forms of entertainment, and Anna watched her daughter's doleful face as they asked if they could go home early.

Up until a few years ago her children had even played together on occasion, but now the four years between them was the greatest it had been.

★ ★ ★

Nearing the end of the lane, Anna heard a vehicle climbing the hill before she saw its lights.

The cattle grid clanked as the bus passed across it. She pulled her coat tighter, blew into her hands. She could just make out the driver in the interior light. Four or five passengers were dotted about. It climbed through the gears, gaining speed down the hill, each change an event of silence. She watched it pass Two Bridges. There was still time to stop, to let Paul off. The engine rose momentarily as the clutch went in, but the driver was after speed to climb out of the valley. As it passed, Anna made out the people's faces, heading on to Princetown and beyond.

Back inside she thought of friends Paul might be with and whether she knew any of their numbers. She rang her parents, the last place she imagined him being. No, they'd not seen him. What was wrong? Nothing.

She trawled the last few days for arguments, the conflict that had become commonplace whenever Paul was asked to do something — to pull his weight, as Robert termed it — but there had been nothing of note since the incident with the logs. No real explosions of temper, none of the cold stares that could possess such antipathy.

The home phone went. Anna rushed to it.

'Is he home?' Robert asked.

'No.'

'He's probably gone to a friend's. He should have said, yes, but there's no need to worry.'

Anna put a couple of logs on the fire and went into the studio. The exhibition was ten days away. It was her first solo showing, the gallery allocating her space for an entire month. The opening would be a necessary evil, the effusive gallery manager fawning over everyone, topping up glasses. Canapés and sycophancy in abundance.

The promotional aspect troubled her at times. Having to sell herself, push her work. If people liked the pots, fine; that was what the website was for. There was some passing trade as well, although the pottery was difficult to find without directions.

She shipped a few pieces to Europe, one Dutch collector in particular regularly bought her raku. And a couple of galleries in the south-west carried some of her work all year round. But in a couple of weeks she'd wear a dress for the first time in years and force smiles as people sipped cava and asked her ridiculous questions. She'd suggested to the gallery that it might even work without her, but her presence was a condition of the slot. 'You have to put yourself out there more,' the manager had said. 'People like your work, but they want a face to accompany it.' There'd been pressure for a photograph on the website, which she'd resisted until recently.

She heard Megan go into the living room, turn the TV on. Anna checked her phone but there was still nothing.

The shelves behind the wheel were full of pots for the event. They were more audacious than usual: her art had become more decorative over the years, less functional, more individual. It was strange to think of what she made contributing to someone's collection.

Tall pieces, anaemic and lifeless, waited to be glazed after their biscuit firing. She remained loyal to the earthen colours she began with: cadmium and terracotta, sienna and vermillion, inspired by the seasons and flora of the moor. The exhibition was titled Winds of Change. It sounded affected now she thought about it. It was supposed to capture the impermanence of the moor, its threat from man, from climate change. The gallery had asked her to write an aesthetic statement for the accompanying booklet. In it she talked about the Bronze Age settlers who made pots on the moor before her, the materials they'd used from the earth and rivers around them.

It was still difficult to regard herself as an artist and she wasn't sure she did. Selling functional slipware at markets had brought in a moderate income over the years, supplemented by working in the studio in Plymouth. That, and being a mother, having a family, had been enough. She didn't need anything else. But then a local reporter did a piece about her last year and her sculptural pieces began selling. Shops and galleries asked for more.

Her work seemed to capture a mood of sustainability: her pots were all handmade, she only used materials found on or near Dartmoor. Clay came from a quarry to the north; her glazes were fashioned from gravel, china clay and feldspar; water came from the West Dart or the nearby spring. She even had a traditional momentum wheel, powered by a foot pedal, giving her pieces a subtly different finish to an electric one, due to the wheel slowing a little when you shaped the clay. People took home a small piece of the moor when they bought her pots, she remembered the reporter writing. The only incongruous aspect, as far as Anna was concerned, was the electric kiln, which ran off their generator. Second-hand from the potter who taught her, it served a purpose but lacked the authenticity she sought. The following spring had been pencilled in to build a wood-fired kiln — hard work as you had to stoke the fire every fifteen minutes, night and day, during firings — but its alchemical appeal remained. The thrill of opening the door once it had cooled days later, seeing for the first time the patterns the ash deposits had left in the clay, would be unrivalled.

Outside, a day that had barely seemed to get started was now cloaked in darkness. Anna checked her phone again, went into the kitchen and began peeling the vegetables.

6

To the south, beyond the hills, the last hint of indigo had faded from the sky and the main road could only be seen from the studio when an occasional car traversed it. The last public bus of the day would pass soon. Anna went into the kitchen, checked on dinner and came back, taking her position by the window a full ten minutes before the bus was due.

Megan wandered in, bored. 'Can I help unload the kiln later?' she asked.

'Not today, darling. It's all for the exhibition. I can't risk breaking any of them.' Her daughter looked hurt by this, unused to being patronised. Anna attempted to rescue it. 'Saturday. We can finish your bowl then.' Her daughter skulked upstairs, unimpressed.

Anna's thoughts returned to her son. How many classes had he missed? Were there more issues at school they would soon be made aware of, another letter asking them to come in for a chat? Was this the start of an even more difficult period? Fifteen was an age when you took stupid risks to ingratiate yourself, to save face or impress. You rebelled without really knowing why. Authority of all kinds was to be resisted, quasi-radical ideologies tried on like a jacket, before moving on to the next. Conversing with adults (who were regarded as another species) was something you had to do to acquire the materials necessary to exist — money, lifts, permission. And the person who refused any of these could expect a volley of invective aimed their way, the slamming of doors and a punishing silence.

It was, by most accounts, a horrendous age to be as a boy — a heady brew of hormones and pubescence tugging you one way then the other. And yet, on occasion, there were glimpses of another teenager — the one or two erudite books she noticed by his bed, a passing remark at dinner when the angst dissolved and a forgotten warmth broke through. A hint of the young adult to come, she hoped. There were artistic sensibilities within him too — mostly musical — that could be encouraged from a distance. As a twelve year old he'd shown an interest in pottery, watching Anna at the wheel, learning techniques, even making some interesting pieces. Together they would gather feldspar upstream, splashing each other until drenched. He would help her mix glazes, stack the kiln, ask questions. But his promise wasn't matched by any sustainable enthusiasm. Boredom came too easily, a teenager emerged, impatient, withdrawn, and now angry.

A beam of light appeared over the hill, its line

sweeping into the valley, illuminating the surrounding fields. Anna watched the vehicle weave down, disappearing behind a line of beeches, then emerging again. It was moving too fast to be anything other than a car. She followed its progress anyway as it headed east towards Ashburton.

She thought of the prison a mile away. On clear nights the sky above it glowed crimson from its lights. You could see it for miles, a red mist shrouding the jail below as if a fire raged.

She tried to picture the prisoner, imagining him cold and hungry. Desperate.

The lane was suddenly lit up, the high headlights suggesting Robert's Land Rover. Megan came down to greet her father, Anna put some water on to boil. As he came through the door, Anna turned to say that she'd not heard anything but was met by the sight of her son, Robert just behind him. Sodden through, Paul's uniform clung to him like skin. His hair was like a wet rag; droplets of rain hung from his fringe.

'Paul!' Anna said. His eyes met hers, full of defiance rather than guilt.

'Passed him walking through Merrivale,' said Robert. 'Hitchhiking.'

'Paul. What were you doing?' He looked hard at her but said nothing. 'Why didn't you go to school today?'

'I did. Just left early.'

'Why?'

'Got bored.'

'Paul, what's the matter? Why were you on the moor in this?'

45

'Perhaps we can talk about it later,' said Robert. 'Go upstairs and dry off.'

'No, hang on,' said Anna. 'Why were you hitchhiking? You could have phoned one of us.'

More silence. Anna noticed there was skin missing from Paul's right hand, a couple of his knuckles badly swollen. His left eye looked puffy, the beginnings of a bruise surfacing.

'What happened to your hand?'

'Fell over,' he said without looking at it.

'Go upstairs, Megan,' Robert said softly. Megan just stood there, staring at her brother.

'Now,' Anna said, less kindly, and Megan did as she was told.

Robert put a hand on Paul's shoulder, but he shrugged it off.

'Where did you go after school?' said Anna.

'Nowhere. What's it matter?'

'Are you in trouble?'

'No.'

'It's dangerous out there in the dark.' She wanted to make her case without reference to the escaped prisoner. 'Cars can't see you.'

Paul sighed. 'Fuck's sake. I used to do it with Cadets.'

'That's different. You weren't on your own.'

Anna wanted to say she'd hated this as well; not the exercises, the playing at soldiers, but where it might lead, what it said about her son. You have to let him do what he wants, Robert had said. He'll grow out of it. But she didn't want him playing with guns, learning how to kill. He left anyway, when the rebellious phase found momentum.

46

'Can I get changed now?' Paul said.

'I just want to know — '

'Anna.' Robert's eyes pleaded with her: *Leave him for now*.

'Go on. We'll talk about this later.'

★ ★ ★

Dinner passed in near silence, the only noise the staccato of cutlery chinking against plates. If someone spoke, it was to ask for something to be passed. Paul didn't look up for the entire meal, and, like Anna, merely pushed food around his plate. Megan watched everyone's face in turn, understanding only that something was wrong. Robert smiled at her unconvincingly.

'So,' said Robert, 'did you two hear about the escape?'

'Yeah,' said Megan. 'A boy in our class told everyone. His dad's a policeman at the prison.'

'A prison officer, you mean,' said Anna.

'Mmm, and he said the man poisoned all the guards by saving his medication for weeks and crushing it up in their tea so they fell asleep, and then he took their keys and broke out, and that he killed a horse on the moor and cut it open and took out all its guts so he could sleep inside it without getting cold.'

'Don't be stupid,' said Paul.

Megan looked at her father.

'That's probably not what happened, darling,' he said.

'Anyway,' said Anna. 'There's nothing to worry about. They'll catch him soon.'

47

'Who's worried?' said Paul.

'No one,' said Robert. 'We just want you to be a bit more careful. Use your phone.'

'It was out of battery.'

Robert looked at Anna, as if to say, see, before turning back to Paul. 'Can you not skip any more lessons please?'

They finished the meal in silence.

'Sorry,' Anna said. 'There's no pudding tonight.'

At this, Paul slid his chair back and went upstairs.

7

Anna watched from the kitchen window as the children ambled along the lane. Megan stopped to inspect something in the hedge, before running to catch up with her brother. Breakfast had passed with small talk, the tension of last night deferred.

She had gone up to Paul's room after dinner, entering after her knocks were ignored. He was massacring some alien life form on the computer screen.

'Paul.' There was urgency to the killing, his index fingers and thumbs frantic. 'Can we talk?' She sat on the end of the bed. 'Is there something wrong at school?' He let out a tut, moved closer to the screen. 'If you're in trouble . . . You can tell us anything, we're here for you.' He stopped pressing buttons, his character on the screen static as bullets rained into him. 'Please, Paul.'

He paused the game. 'There's nothing,' he said without looking at her. She offered to fetch something for his hand and eye but was told it was fine, not to fuss. Standing outside his door, Anna listened for the game to resume, but it remained quiet.

The children rounded the corner and were out of sight. She waited until, five minutes later, the bus appeared over the hill.

Upstairs she turned the computer on. Paul's monitor wallpaper was an animated woman, scantily dressed in leather and draped over a lustrous motorbike, whip in one hand, cigarette in the other. Impossibly proportioned, she posed unambiguously.

There was a password prompt. She hadn't thought of that. Anna looked around the room, considered stopping. She typed her son's full name. Nothing. Some of the posters above her were of bands. She tried them one at a time, but without success. The football team he'd followed as a child failed also. Between the musicians, the woman who featured most on the walls was a blonde called Viktoria, the spelling, Anna supposed, an attempt to stand out. She typed the name and the password box disappeared.

Tens of icons greeted her from the sides of the screen. She got by on the family computer — a friend of Robert's had set up her website, shown her some basics — but nothing more. Anna brought the internet up and clicked the history icon.

She had no real sense of what she was looking for, although the posters around her suggested what she might find. They could have put blocks on what he could view, but this wasn't their parenting style. She couldn't even admonish her son's use of a password without giving herself away.

She went through each site Paul had visited in the last few days: some guitar shops, a band's home page. Email. Social networking sites. And then the expected. Plastic-looking, near-naked women faking lust, promising extreme pleasure if you signed up. She thought for the first time about the legality of her son's activity, regardless of its morality. The text suggested the women were over eighteen, though many didn't look it. She went through a few pages, following his trail. Paul seemed to have a preference for blonde women — petite, large breasted.

As she clicked through the pages, the thing that struck Anna the most was the near total absence of pubic hair. She had seen men's magazines, as they were euphemistically termed, once or twice by accident, but these images were more disquieting than any she remembered. As she went from model to model, it was clear you had to be shaven to feature. Even the older women had sexual organs that resembled young girls', though the effect was more of a game bird that had been plucked.

She tried to remind herself that most boys his age did this, the curiosity inevitable. It was important to guard against an overreaction, to resist her worst fears. It occurred to her that Paul might have signed up to some of the sites, downloaded things he shouldn't have, paid to access restricted areas. She made a mental note to check credit card bills.

Curiosity drove her on.

Promises of guaranteed satisfaction were made. Join Today icons blinked everywhere, drawing the eye, only pence a day, the claim. Anything could be catered for, whatever your requirements. The enumeration to the side of the images revolted her: pussy, anal, group, fetish, fisting, hardcore, teens, bondage, S&M. Was this where her son's view of women would be formed? A teenage rite of passage, where you learned that women were vacuous sex objects, paraded merely as providers of corporeal pleasure. As carnal entertainment.

But something else had happened as well. Pornography, far from being the guilty preserve of seedy old men, now seemed to have permeated mainstream culture. Television, billboards, magazines (even those aimed at Megan's age group) were laden with raunchy caricatures of female sexuality. Women, regardless of age, were all now girls. Female bands shouted about empowerment and sexual liberty as they performed erotic dances on stage or coiled themselves around poles. Pre-pubescent girls wore T-shirts emblazoned with the Playboy bunny or the words PORN STAR. Women went to see female strippers out of irony. It didn't feel much like liberation to Anna.

On the screen there were allusions to more extreme sites. Words such as torture, abuse and asphyxiation seemed to make the case for censorship, something she'd have rebelled against at university. She told herself Paul hadn't necessarily visited these. That it meant nothing. That he would grow out of this. But for now it was all available, any time of day. You might live in complete isolation but the internet could still bring every sordid facet of the world along a phone line and into your home in seconds.

Clicking on the homepage icon, Anna was taken to a band's website. Back in the history column she saw there'd been a visit to her own site, which surprised her; Paul hadn't even been in the studio for years and a nostalgia rose for such times. There was little else she recognised. She closed the internet down and looked for a file that might be a diary, anything that would give her a glimpse of his thoughts, of trouble at school, but there was nothing. In the bottom corner of the screen was a photo album, which she opened. The pictures surprised her; she'd hardly seen him use the digital camera that was a birthday present last year. There were a few of friends playing guitars, lager cans and ashtrays distributed among them. But it was the ones in a file marked 'Me' that were unusual. Taken surreptitiously, they featured Robert and herself mostly, the occasional one of Megan, performing unremarkable routines in and outside the cottage. Some had been taken through windows, others from the far side of a room, the subject only ever side on, obliviously attending to something else. Where he'd tried to zoom in, the quality was poor. Despite the title of the file, it contained no photographs of her son. Robert appeared most frequently, chopping wood in the yard, cooking, asleep in the armchair. There were hundreds. Although not clear, one looked as if it had been taken in their bedroom as they slept.

The gloomy light meant she couldn't be certain.

Perhaps they were a project for Art. Again, she couldn't ask him about them without giving herself away, risking a scene.

The thought caused the guilt to amplify. She shut down the computer and went to start work for the day.

As she prepared some clay, the home phone rang. As a rule she ignored it once in the studio, but the gallery was keen to pin down the precise details of the launch, anxious nothing was left to chance, and so called frequently. Her greeting — terse, a little annoyed — was met with silence and, a few seconds later, the dialling tone. She swore at the phone.

Back in the studio Anna put some music on — Rachmaninov — hoping the stirring melodies would distract her mind from itself.

8

I've stopped shaking for the first time in hours.

The parts of me beneath the water are a fierce pink, as if I've been dipped in a dye. I contemplate the pain, as someone might a picture or a memory, studying how the burning makes me feel. The cadence of falling water is hypnotic, its permanence a balm, drowning out the noise in my head. The water level rises imperceptibly, bringing with it the line on my body that distinguishes burning from not burning. Steam surges upwards. As I lower my legs slightly, water laps over my grazed knees, the mottled pinpricks of blood washing away to nothing.

A minute or two pass.

I must have turned the tap off, though I don't remember doing so. As the adrenaline ceases to loop round my body, more localised pain makes itself known. Arms. Scalp. Breasts. Each hurts separately yet the hot water blends them until I *am* pain.

I stare at the glass of vodka by the taps with only the vaguest memory of pouring it. Sitting up, I drink it in one. It tastes of nothing, though I appreciate the brief burn as it surges down my throat.

Exhausted by the effort to move, I slink back down.

The phone rings in the lounge. As the answer-machine clicks, a voice follows. It's Nick. He'll be drunk, heading home to his wife. Come on, he's saying. Forget what I said the other night. I was upset. What we have is special. I need you. Let's not throw this away. Other clichés follow in a slur. Our last conversation replays itself in my head. His mocking me, almost paternally, as if I'd agreed to take in a pair of stray dogs. Pick up, I'm running out of change, he's saying. The message stops.

Several times I close my eyes tightly until specks of light fire across the back of my eyelids like shooting stars. Coloured blotches bob around. When I open them the reality is the same.

Thoughts slowly play themselves out to nothing and I'm barely aware of the trance my mind has embraced. Time is static, or passes regardless of me, I'm unsure which. My breath becomes rhythmic and I imagine focusing on it for ever, as if in meditation: soft inhalation, release, a cycle I can control and trust. And then the front door buzzer sounds, a little longer than is normal, someone making a point with their finger. My heart does a jig. Time returns. The panic, almost subsided, returns and I'm hyper-alert, primed like an animal. Ready.

I stare through from the bathroom to the flat's

front door, hoping the man who lives below doesn't let the person in. My breathing is short and rapid once more. The buzzer sounds again, twice more in succession, staccato and familiar. Nick again, I think — jumped in a taxi after telling his wife he's having one, maybe two more. A minute passes and the phone goes again — the box across the street, I figure. There's no message this time, and I'm spared declarations of love that will be forgotten by morning. I calm a little. Please go, I hear myself saying.

Once I'm sure he's gone I allow my legs to part properly for the first time, anticipating the ferocity of the sting, yet wincing all the same when it comes. Small skeins of blood, like threads, float in the water, before dispersing to nothing. I touch my face, my cheek still sore. I lie there, willing the trance to return, but it doesn't. The plug, not a perfect fit, allows water to seep indiscernibly away. Whenever I feel the burn lessen, I turn on the hot tap until finally water slops over the side of the bath, forcing me to pull the plug out. I do this for what must be an hour, maybe two.

Perhaps it didn't happen, at least not as I remember. My brain is playing a trick. Too much work, overtired. Some sort of delusion, a hazing of reality. It feels important to remember it correctly, but for now I can't.

I go through the day again, retracing it from the start up to the session after work. Then home. A snatched dinner; a glass of Rioja. Music. I'd put some music on. Neil Young. And then the buzzer.

Unable to continue, I take the pumice stone my mother brought back from one of the Greek islands and begin to draw its flat surface up the side of my right calf. It catches the tiny hairs of my leg, scritching. I continue with slow, rhythmic circles, again observing as if from above, as if someone else is both initiating the action and experiencing it. An out-of-body experience. The phrase fascinates me momentarily. Occasionally the stone elicits pain and I find myself pressing harder here, forcing it deep into the muscle or scraping it against my shinbone until I wince and cry out with the throbbing. The noise I produce makes me self-conscious now that I no longer wish to be heard.

I cover myself in soap, every inch of skin above the water, even my face and hair, until a lather adorns me like a frothy coat. The pumice is frustratingly smooth. I wonder what else there is in the flat, but the brushes are all soft. I want a wire one, like the ones used to clean metal. Like the one my father uses to remove flaking paint. I want to feel the tips of it tear into me, removing layer after layer until what is left is me.

I persevere with the stone, scrubbing with fury that becomes desperation, as if I've been exposed to radiation or a deadly virus. An image appears in my mind, of men in nuclear protection suits with powerful hoses, blasting me from every direction as I cower polluted in the corner. Don't stop, I say, get it all off me, but the water runs to a trickle and they stand there laughing.

The top of the pumice is less smooth and hurts more, but still it can't go deep enough.

And there's a spot on my back I can't get to from above or below. Anger rises. It should be easy to cry but no tears come.

Another layer of soap. This time I push some into my ears, up into my nostrils.

I submerge myself below the water's surface, holding my breath until a ringing sounds in my temples, my lungs burning. I fantasise about swimming down, emerging in an underwater world where I am something else. A mermaid perhaps. Or a stingray lying unseen on the ocean floor. I open my eyes, the soapy water smarting. I recoil and splutter until I'm sitting up. I think I'm going to be sick.

More hot water, only now it's barely warm, the tank cooling.

A car horn rises from the street below. Someone shouts back.

I try to remain completely still, challenging myself not to make the slightest tremor in the water. After a minute I become aware of my heartbeat, my ears pulsing to the da-dum da-dum.

I lose time, the water cold again. I sit huddled, chin resting on my knees.

Finally I pull out the plug and find myself in an empty bath as the last of the water gurgles away. I sit there for several minutes, wondering what happens now. Perhaps nothing. How long could I stay here, sitting like this? Days? Weeks? You can live off water alone for ages, don't they say? It occurs to me to remain here for ever, until, finally, the landlord finds my skeleton lying cold against the enamel.

I count the tiles around me. There are thirty-four whole ones. I count again — thirty-five. Next time there are thirty-three. I count in twos and reach thirty-four again. I could definitely stay in here if he hadn't used the toilet.

Eventually I start to shiver.

Exhausted and weak, the effort needed to climb out is immense. The vodka, whilst leaving my head clear, still causes me to stumble, and I almost fall back into the bath. Avoiding the mirror, I put on my dressing gown. Nausea sweeps through me. I rush to the basin, retching several times.

Brushing my teeth feels ridiculous — the mundanity of the act, its everydayness absurd — and I almost laugh. I brush and brush them before using the mouthwash. Habit draws me to the mirror but again I resist.

The living room seems to have changed. I can see its familiarity draining away, its new significance growing by the minute, claimed by tonight. I look at the phone, its little green light flashing from Nick's message. I think to call someone, my mother perhaps, but instead unplug it at the wall. I check again that the door is locked.

In the middle of the room, lying where he flung it, is the Harper Lee. It looks awkward, perched up like a tent, out of all context, like a piece of modern art. I pick it up, placing it back in the bookshelf I'd slid it from earlier. Some of the books protrude slightly so I push them back in until they are flush. The sound system emits a low hiss. I turn it off.

A siren sounds in the distance and for a moment I expect it to grow louder but it fades to nothing. Standing by the living-room window, I imagine Nick pressing the buzzer below, blowing into his hands before giving up and returning to the warmth of the family bed. A few voices, the last of the locals to leave the pub on the corner, drift up from the street. They take an age to pass, stumbling, singing, laughing. I want to pull the curtain back a little, to see another person, but I can't bring myself to.

I remember his tongue.

More nausea. This time I am sick a little and the smell threatens to provoke a vicious cycle. The water is still not hot so I boil the kettle to rinse out the sink. I brush my teeth again, the mirror catching me out this time. Just a glimpse. A flicker of someone I don't want to see.

Two wine glasses stand on the lounge table — one half full, the other empty. I take them into the kitchen where I wash them in water, again as hot as I can bear. I dry them, place them in the cupboard. The wine left in the bottle glugs to nothing as I pour it away, a little burgundy whirlpool, the smell overpowering, repellent. Hot water from the kettle follows it.

I curl into a corner of the sofa, holding a cushion tight to my chest. The trembling returns although it's still warm in the flat. I click the TV on, press the mute button. I'm aware of the shapes on the screen, their colour and movement, but nothing else.

A thought forms. Becomes a voice, looping like a mantra: *Why did you let him in?*

9

The woman behind the counter takes my details — name, age, dates, GP — while giving vague assurances about confidentiality. I'm shown to a small room where I sit and wait alone. Piles of leaflets and fading lifestyle magazines adorn the only table. After ten minutes a nurse enters and tells me there are no female doctors on until later today and do I mind a male doctor. She says she'll accompany him. I nod. About thirty minutes, she tells me.

'Can I get you anything?' she says before leaving.

She's the first person to be nice to me and I struggle not to cry. The receptionist at school had been pragmatic on the phone when I called to say I'd picked up a virus, that I hoped to be back in a few days.

Every time a door closes in another room of the building I flinch in my seat. Sound seems to magnify and skew as it passes through the walls around me. Voices resound. The air, dry and synthetic, reminds me of childhood visits to the dentist.

Finally the same nurse calls me through to the examination room, which although cooler, is stark with artificial light. The sterile, antiseptic smell almost makes me retch. Across the room, reading from a clipboard, is a man in a white coat. He motions to me to take a seat. It's still sore to walk and I sense the nurse following my tentative steps. The doctor offers me the beginnings of a smile in between reading what I assume are my notes. I sit down.

'Hello,' he says. He introduces himself. 'It says here you were attacked on the sixteenth.'

Unsure if this is a question, I force a smile back.

'Tuesday, yes?'

I nod, knowing what's coming.

'And today, Friday, is the first time you've told anyone?'

'Yes.'

He looks at me, before looking back down at the notes. 'And you've not told the police?'

I thought my last answer had made this clear, but shake my head anyway.

'Do you want us to report it now? We're not obliged to, but we can. They'll send someone to interview you.'

I shrug my shoulders, the nausea worsening.

'Well, you don't have to decide now,' he says.

I can still go home, I tell myself. I don't have to do this.

'The purpose of the examination,' he continues, 'is to check you medically and to collect any evidence there might be left, in case you decide at a later date to report it.'

The nurse hands me a gown and shows me to a panelled screen in the corner.

'Pop that on,' the doctor says, 'and we can start.' He carries on talking even though I'm out of sight. 'If there's anything you don't understand, just ask. Any time you want to stop, we can do that. Some of it is unpleasant, I'm afraid, but necessary.' I wonder which are the pleasant parts.

The nurse tells me to stand on the paper sheet when I undress and to leave my clothes on the floor. There may be evidence on them, she says. I think to say that they're not the ones I wore on Tuesday, but don't. The plastic gown is cool on my skin. I secure the tie behind my back.

I emerge from the screen to their stares, as if I'm trying on a dress in a shop. My head bowed, I walk across the room.

I'm told to sit up on the examination table, feet over the side for now. The doctor offers me a tranquilliser — mild, he says — but I decline. Numbness is not a problem.

The nurse walks over to the screen where she starts to put my clothes into separate bags, which are then sealed.

'Now,' he says, 'much of the evidence will be gone or contaminated after a couple of days, but you never know.' I consider myself as evidence. As contaminated.

'Have you bathed or showered?' I nod, causing him to tut, seemingly from frustration rather than judgement. 'More than once?'

'Yes.'

He looks over his glasses at me. 'And brushed

your teeth, I'm guessing?'

He ticks some boxes, scribbles something.

Surgical gloves are snapped on to his hands. He takes a small comb from its wrapping and starts to draw it through my hair. His other hand rests on my head, the first person to touch me since Tuesday. He smells faintly of disinfectant and his breath, as his face passes inches in front of mine, has a trace of mint on it. The nurse is by my side saying something about always wanting hair like mine, how lucky I am. My scalp is still sore. 'Sorry,' he says, seeing my face, and I feel like a little girl. He seems to examine the comb after each sweep. 'Have you washed it?'

Endlessly, I say to myself while nodding.

He tugs the comb through the occasional tangle, constantly apologising in a way that doesn't mean sorry.

'Just going to pluck a few hairs,' he says. He drops them into a clear bag held by the nurse. 'Now, if you lie back for me and pop your legs up in the stirrups.'

I wince doing this and the nurse touches my arm. I can think of few less dignified postures, feet pointing to different corners of the room.

He begins with the same comb, making little staccato sweeps through my pubic hair, examining anything he might have gathered like an archaeologist. 'Hmm,' he says a couple of times. To stop myself being sick I study the patterned ceiling, following the whorls of Artex, imagining they are maelstroms dragging me into another world. Deeper and deeper into the white water.

'Again, just taking some hair.' The voice brings

me back to the room, the pricks of pain barely registering. I begin again, plotting entire worlds above me, the white ridges now mountain ranges, the grooves valleys cut with rivers.

'I'm going to take some samples from your vagina and bottom now.'

I picture a vast wilderness of snow-peaked hills unspoilt by human settlement. Tall pines populate the chaste landscape.

'Do you know if he ejaculated?'

I invert the view in my mind, so that I'm looking down on it now. I'm an eagle soaring through the cloud. Wind rushes through me as I dive. Everything is beautiful white.

'Miss Jacobs, do you know if he ejaculated?'

The words pull me away from the ceiling. They seem ridiculous, beyond comprehension. The nurse takes my hand, says something about how brave I'm being. The ceiling returns to Artex.

'I don't know,' I say. 'I think so.'

More note-taking.

'Did you bleed much?'

I nod.

'I don't think you'll need stitches,' the man says. 'It'll be sore for a while. Try not to do much.'

There's more probing. I hear the words 'sample of discharge'. A cotton swab is taken. The same is done inside my mouth. I gag, remembering his fingers there.

The doctor then scrapes under my fingernails with a little tool before clipping them and tipping the cuttings into a clear bag, which is sealed. I wish one of them would say something to break the silence.

A tourniquet is tied above my elbow, a needle pushed into a vein in my arm. I watch as the blood is drawn upwards, darker and more viscous than Tuesday's. It's divided into two containers, which the nurse writes on. The doctor removes the tourniquet.

'Are you sore anywhere else?' he asks.

I point to my other arm. 'And my knees.' I try to locate the sites of the pain, but it still feels as if I hurt everywhere. He looks me over, presses, prods.

'There's no obvious bruising. If you tell the police tonight, they might want to photograph your knees.'

I tell him I've never bruised, even as a child.

'We'll give you some antibiotics, in case of STIs. The tests will tell us. HIV infection is extremely unlikely, but we test for it anyway.' The acronyms are both familiar and strange. 'Are you taking any contraception?' he says.

I'd been on the pill until two months ago, when my GP advised a break. I shake my head.

'The chances of pregnancy are small.'

I smile because I want something to be grateful for.

'It's too late for the morning-after pill but if it's something you're worried about we can fit an intra-uterine device — '

'A coil,' the nurse interrupts.

'This can stop the egg fertilising, but . . . ' he counts the days, 'Tuesday, Wednesday, Thursday, today . . . there's no guarantee.'

He asks more questions, about my next period, future tests, my options, but my head is swimming, the room spinning. He asks about the coil again, but I shake my head, the thought of more invasion too much.

'You should buy a test kit, find out for sure as soon as you can.'

There's a psychiatrist on call, I'm told, who is on his way. Again the doctor asks about the police.

I'm shown to the shower in the room next door. The nurse gives me a towel and says she'll find me some clothes. I fold the gown neatly on the chair and let the water fall on me. It's cool at first and I resist the urge for heat. I didn't tell them how many baths I'd had in the last three days because I couldn't remember. They've merged into one long unsuccessful purge, the water, just as now, unable to cleanse me.

When the nurse returns, she finds me sitting on the tiled floor, huddled in the corner.

10

I wake just after six. The sodium glow from the street lights filters through curtains that haven't been opened for more than a week. The occasional car passes outside in that other world; I've glimpsed it on television, heard it discussed on the radio, yet I am no longer a part of it. It must have rained, or be raining, as I can hear vehicles sluicing water into the kerb as they pass. Snippets of conversation rise up from the street below as deliveries are made. There's a hint of baking bread from the shop a few doors along. Denying the world to one of my senses seems to have heightened others. I listen for birdsong, but hear none.

The man in the flat below turns over, his bed creaking like old bones. His alarm will go off at twenty past, though he won't hear it for several minutes. If I'm perfectly still I'll hear him get up, urinate, then start the percussive hiss of his shower. Sometimes he whistles, hums a little tune. At six fifty his door will bang shut and the building will be mine alone.

In the months I've been here, I've met him only twice; the hours we keep are disparate — lives lived feet yet worlds apart. We nod, half smile, content to remain atomised. I consider this man I share nothing but a front door with: his weekend visitor, the sporadic bursts of inoffensive music, muffled telephone conversations. I consider the women in his life, how he regards them. I wonder whether he's ever thought about coming upstairs, trying his luck. He's not unattractive. As I think back to last Tuesday, I picture him out at the pub, visiting friends, walking the streets. I picture him, because I need to, anywhere but at home that night. I need to believe that the noise wasn't ignored, that the cries weren't dismissed as none of his business, or as shrieks of pleasure.

The days fuse, barely distinguishable from each other, their advent marked by the jolt of exiting a few hours' fractured sleep. Where possible I control their content: the phone remains unplugged, television is allowed to come and go at my behest. The buzzer has sounded several times, likely men and women selling windows or religion. Maybe Nick was one of them — off with a virus, still the word at school. I don't breathe until I sense they've left.

There it goes, his alarm, rousing my neighbour from slumber. I realise I don't even know his name, other than what appears on the post I place on the communal shelf for him. Mr S. Turner. Shaun. Stephen. Stewart.

I bath two or three times a day still, although the need for a fierce temperature and endless scrubbing has eased. Instead I soak in the water until it has wrinkled and blanched the skin of my hands and feet, giving them a ghostly aspect.

Apart from the school and the surgery, I've rung no one.

There's a sense of being outside time, of occupying a half-life where twilight is a constant. I like to think of my body shutting down as if hibernation neared. Not dead, but not wholly alive either.

Unremarkable hours are spent on the sofa, staring through the TV, its banal shows indistinguishable from each other. I've got to know the safe channels and times. I rarely turn it off, though, maybe muting the sound for a few hours, which satisfies both my need to be alone and not to go mad from isolation. I find myself observing women in particular. Their clothing, their hair and make-up, their posture. There's a homogeneity I'd not noticed before, a code to being a TV woman. I'd expected it on game shows: the manicured, unblemished, pouting clones, supposedly there to embellish proceedings. But I see now that it's ubiquitous. Newsreaders, politicians, presenters, all hidden behind a fascia of insincerity. And then there are the advertisements in between that suggest there is no need to tolerate what they call symptoms of ageing. Imperfections could, and should, be treated, removed.

I think about how long it took me to get ready for work each day; how much make-up I put on; the clothes I chose. How I decorated myself, not out of symbolism or ritual as ancient peoples might have. More because it was unacceptable to let the world glimpse the unmasked me, as if a woman needed enhancing, making prettier, beautifying. Not to do so is to be plain, frumpy, unfeminine.

And when I walked through the gates, was I seen as a teacher first or a woman? Did boys look at my legs when I wore a skirt? What about colleagues? Yet when I sensed Nick watching me in the staffroom, didn't I take longer to get ready the morning after? Didn't I wear tops I knew to be flattering? I was seduced but I was complicit in this dance; I flirted, adjusted my posture to suggest availability, parading myself like a peacock. I returned his smile across the room, though mine was mock coy, hoping to convey sweetness, an innocence, but again interest. His approach a week later was confident, my inexperience in the job his leverage. He looked me up and down, boxes ticked or left blank. A lunchtime drink was suggested, the dance choreographed by cliché. He pursued me and I enjoyed the attention. By the time I learned of his marriage — over in all but a legal sense, he said at first — the momentum seemed unstoppable. And when we ended up in my bed, I was somehow both virgin and temptress.

★　★　★

Listening to the town as it stretches into life, the bustle of rush hour comforts me now that I'm not a part of it. I like the promise of calm beyond the clamour. Throughout the day I watch the

74

light change in the flat, guessing at the weather, the colour of the sky. Later, shadows extend into the room, another rush hour and the town yields to a wintry slumber once more.

Apart from the examination, I've left the flat only once. For hours I just stared at the door, willing myself to venture out. The ten-minute walk to the shop felt insurmountable. My biggest fear, apart from the event itself, apart from seeing him, was being locked out, of not being able to return to my sanctuary. I chose a time that was quiet but still light. A woollen hat came down to my eyes. Tracksuit bottoms and an old raincoat completed the look; I imagined a frumpy appearance would reduce the chance of it happening again. I held the door keys tightly in my pocket the whole way. Rows of parked cars and shop windows offered me my reflection but the thought of seeing it sickened me.

I bought cigarettes for the first time since I was a teenager; I tried one later that day but felt sick. The bread remains unopened; soup is all I can manage without retching. I could feel the woman's eyes on me as I paid, though I didn't meet them. She probably thought she knew someone who looked like me, a woman who came in regularly but didn't buy cigarettes, who didn't look so dishevelled. In the chemist next door I bought several things I didn't need, a mild anger rising in me at my shame.

I walked tight to the wall all the way back, as if this lessened the distance, but also because I needed the buildings to prop me up every few hundred yards. When I reached my front door I noticed my knuckles were white, the keys only released in the shops. A film of sweat clung to me, cold and pungent. There was some post in the letterbox but I left it there.

★ ★ ★

My dressing gown on, I go to the drawer in the kitchen. The box, if you ignore the wording, looks much like any other. It could contain any type of medicine — tablets that heal, that ease pain, cream that soothes. The words say that it's easy to use; results are promised in three minutes; it's the brand most doctors recommend.

I read the instructions on the back. They are strangely simple. A child could follow them.

I go into the bathroom, the light seeming more harsh than usual. Despite all the cleaning, I still think of him being in here. How he used the toilet afterwards. How he didn't flush it, that I had to hours later when I could bring myself to move. I used a whole bottle of bleach the next day, throwing the brush away once done. I have flushed it a hundred times since.

I open the box. More instructions fall out. I tear open the foil and look at the stick. It resembles a pen. Something you could write the future with.

I look at myself in the mirror for the first time in days. This is just to make sure, I say to the person I see but don't recognise. It will be OK. You need to check, then you can begin to move on. As the nurse had a few days ago, I tell the woman in the mirror she is brave, but she doesn't believe it.

I remove the cap and squat over the toilet. Five seconds, it says. Hold it in the stream for five seconds.

And now I wait for two minutes. A hundred and twenty seconds to see the colour of my future.

I watch the clock in the kitchen, the second hand sweeping slowly but inexorably round. A car horn sounds in the street below. Someone shouts. Still there is no birdsong. I give it two and half minutes before looking at the result window.

11

They missed the flash of bronze on the hillside beyond the river. Anna was distracted by nostalgia for a time when her son joined them on walks before she lost him to adolescence; her daughter was busy searching the sedge and fern for deceased specimens to add to her collection. Anything would do: grasshoppers, beetles, a damselfly if she was lucky. As parents, Anna and Robert had watched helplessly as Megan's fascination with insects and wild creatures — alive or dead, but mostly dead — grew from the books she asked them to read as a toddler to the hours spent foraging in the garden and beyond, before running in excitedly cataloguing another corpse. She would then glue them to pieces of card, identifying them underneath in a child's scrawl. When the collection reached double figures, Anna insisted it be moved out of the house, and so now, when you opened a drawer in the dilapidated Victorian chest in the barn, you were greeted by dozens of exoskel-etons that, Anna had learned from her daughter, could take years to decompose once the insides had dried out. Each year that passed, the realisation that Megan wasn't going to grow out of her macabre hobby anytime soon sharpened.

It's not what a little girl should be doing, Anna's mother would say once or twice a year. That Megan was never going to be sugar and spice and all things nice was fine with Anna. Her only concern was others, Megan's friends especially, not accepting it. Perhaps if her daughter could curb the eccentricity long enough at school, being different could even ingratiate her, if she kept the right side of it. But it was a fine line.

The flash of bronze, its heart and lungs working to their limit, wove skilfully about the gorse, heading for the conifers to the west. Depending on the observer, the lightness with which it moved was either balletic or terror-struck.

Anna called to her daughter, who would otherwise stay out here all day.

As siblings went, Paul and Megan showed fondness and dislike for each other in inconsistent bursts. A genial interaction could become a battle a moment later. Equally, skirmishes were forgotten the next time they encountered each other, the slate cleaned by distraction. Both were at awkward ages — a son battling a whorl of hormones, angry, misunderstood; a daughter whose otherness could render her first year at secondary school an ordeal.

It seemed a tired debate, trying to discern the origin of a child's behaviour — something innate, early experience, a blend of the two — but as a parent such reflection had an inevitability about it. Last week Anna had read about a combination of genes that determined how left- or right-wing you were likely to become; that how liberal or conservative you were was mapped out from before birth, which seemed fanciful to her.

But whether nature or nurture made her children themselves, she had come to value in them anything that undermined the stereotypes of gender. At the start of the summer Megan came home claiming to have seen a dragonfly devouring a bumblebee. She described the golden rings of the former as being slightly brighter than the fur of the latter. She said, and Anna had learned to believe her utterly, that she had been so close that she could hear the slurping and crunching as the dragonfly slowly ate its prey head first. Anna wondered if she'd ever seen a child as content.

And so there was still something absurd in having the moor for a back garden. Anna felt no bourgeois guilt — their land was modest, the barns renovated over two decades, firstly by her husband alone, then the two of them together.

Looking ahead she could see the cottage now. The pots would be midway through their second firing. If it stayed dry all weekend she would finish the last of the raku for the exhibition.

Paul's curtains were still drawn, mornings an anathema to be slept through at weekends and holidays. She had rung the school yesterday morning, spoken to the year head, then to Paul's form tutor. There was little out of the ordinary to report, the latter had said. Paul was still aloof, a little rude, but often just withdrawn. There'd been no repeat of last term's playground brawl, the cause of which remained a mystery. Both boys had maintained a code of silence as letters were sent home, warnings given. Anna chose not to mention the recent marks on her son's hand, the bruised face. His grades had slipped slightly, the teacher said, but no, there were no issues they knew of. Did she want him to talk to Paul? No, said Anna.

Unremarkable at any subject, Paul had always done just enough to get by, comfortable in middle-set anonymity. An initial flair for art and music hadn't materialised into genuine academic pursuit, as they had thought it might. Sciences and languages had been shunned where possible. Computer programming remained a possible career path, but only by virtue of ruling out others. Anna thought back to a parents' evening a couple of years ago, before her son had chosen his final subjects. His English teacher asked her whether Paul read much, outside of school.

'The occasional magazine,' Anna had said. 'Computing, guitars.'

'No, I mean fiction. Novels.'

'No, not really.'

Apparently, the class had all struggled with a piece of homework the previous term, with the exception of Paul, who handed in one of the most original, insightful answers the teacher had seen. They had wanted to enter it for some award but Paul had refused.

'It's something you might want to encourage,' the man had said.

They tried, a novel or two as presents for a while, but the books' spines remained creaseless, the outstanding homework apparently a one-off. As for the future, a college prospectus and application form lay untouched in his room, and although there was still time left, it was anyone's guess what her son would be doing this time next year.

* * *

Up ahead Anna could see the Land Rover wasn't outside the cottage; Robert would be home for lunch if he could get away. She acknowledged to herself the possible over-reaction with the prisoner, how she'd allowed the media tumult to affect her. The moor was so vast; there was room for a man on the run as well. This feeling of being watched, of the tors bearing down on her, would pass.

The late autumn sun, its warmth of a few weeks ago gone, barely touched the garden now. Three wet summers had left the valley verdant. These were Anna's favourite times of year: the seasons between seasons, the transition from one state to another, when the old held on as long as it could, affronted by the onset of the new. Birth, death, rebirth.

Megan finally caught up.

As they walked along the side of the valley, a heron tracked the river south, its wingspan majestic, more redolent of a condor's. They watched it fly beyond the cottage and up over the larch plantation. It was then that Anna saw the flash of bronze as it disappeared into the trees. She wasn't sure what it was until, half a mile or so north, at the edge of her vision, the first horse and rider appeared on the top of Beardown Hill, like some scene from a film. Others followed, their silhouettes rising like targets at the fairground. As they moved south, she could make out the red in some of the riders' jackets, the lustre of their boots in the sunlight. A few hounds appeared on the horizon, between the horses and the trees. Megan followed her mother's gaze, aware something unusual was occurring. After frantically circling for a minute or two, the hounds — now in their tens — headed at pace along the crest of the hill towards the trees, their wraith-like cries carrying across to the other side of the valley. As the horses speeded up, one of the hunters sounded a horn, a noise Anna had only heard on documentaries or the News, despite living on Dartmoor for fourteen years. The hillside was now alive with hounds and horses sweeping southwards. As they reached the conifers, the hounds disappeared into the woods, leaving the hunters at its edge. The silence was only broken by the occasional muffled keening of the hounds rising out of the trees.

Since the ban, the hunt were only allowed to use two hounds to kill foxes, but as many as they liked if they only chased a scent. Quite how you were supposed to rein the hounds in when scent became cornered creature, Anna found puzzling, suspecting ambiguous legislation was exploited at this point.

A minute or two later, from the treeline nearest the cottage, the creature bolted, sped down the slope and crossed the river at the shallows, heading for the stone wall that marked the cottage's boundary. She felt exhilaration that the fox might escape, the hounds left baying in the woods, the riders oblivious around the corner. Anna and Megan watched until the animal disappeared behind the wall, so they could only guess which way it had gone. A few seconds later they saw the old gate in the corner of the garden fly open and then the flash of bronze streaking across the vegetable beds towards the barn. After a few moments of panic, it forced its way between a gap in the sheets of corrugated iron and was gone.

'What will happen now?' said Megan.

Anna didn't know. The fox hadn't shown any interest in the chickens gathered at the other end of the garden, consumed as it was by its own plight. But it couldn't stay there; Megan would try to befriend it, take it food or something. Perhaps it would just creep away later, after dark. She took Megan's hand and walked a little quicker.

With several hundred yards still to reach the cottage, one of the hounds burst from the treeline halfway up the hillside, its pitch higher, almost demented. As the others emerged, tearing down the hill like a wave, the hunt came around from the side of the woods, following at a canter.

The hounds could be heard crossing the river, before one at a time they jumped on to the garden wall. For a moment they seemed confused, their heads shifting from side to side, sniffing the air for scent. Then one leapt into the garden, seeming to grant permission to the rest, and they were soon yelping in a frenzy as they scrambled around the barn, the gap just too small for them to get through.

As Anna and Megan reached the house, the riders were lined up along the wall, as if waiting to begin a race. One of the men in black called out, something polite, Anna thought, though she couldn't make out what.

'Go inside,' she said to Megan, who ambled to the front door without actually going in.

Anna crossed the garden, where twelve or so hunters, mostly men, waited for her on horseback. One of the riders in red offered a blithe apology.

'Think our prey has gone in your barn there,' he said loudly over the symphony of whines.

Anna watched as the hounds continued to circle the building, scratching furiously at possible entry points.

'Can you get your dogs out of my garden,' she shouted.

The man looked hard at her, gauging the best approach.

'They've got a scent, love,' he said. 'Best let them finish the job.'

'I don't care what they've got, I want them out of here. This is private. Call them off now.' She turned and saw that Megan was still standing by the front door. 'Go inside!' she shouted.

The man's face was rich with disgust, his eyes conveying the contempt of every hunter ever thwarted by a defiant landowner. Looking down at Anna, he patted the neck of his horse, as if to demonstrate he understood more than she the rights best afforded to animals. She could see he regarded the moor as his, or as belonging to his kind — people who knew the order of things, whose love of tradition and resistance to change united them. She could almost hear him saying, this is how we do things here. If you choose to live among us, you must assimilate accordingly. Anna wondered whether resistance from a woman was harder for him to endure. Whether he was nostalgic for a time when leaping the wall and trampling her aside would have been little more than a footnote in the regaling of the day's sport. The other riders bunched up behind him, but he seemed to know better than to protest further, instead dismounting and signalling to a few of the men. They were about to climb over the wall, when Anna said, 'Can you use the gate, please.'

The four of them walked along the wall, came through the gate and started dispersing the hounds with shouts until the pack realised their entertainment was probably over for the day. A vitriolic blast on the horn and the hunt rode back up the valley in a defiant procession.

Anna stood by the wall, watching until the last horse was out of sight. She would check the fox had gone later. As she turned back to the house, Megan was watching from the kitchen window, her face a picture of excitement. Above her, sitting in his bedroom window, her brother surveyed with disdain the scene that had woken him.

12

'You could have come out to help,' Anna said to her son at the dinner table. 'Didn't cross your mind?'

The morning's spectacle had been relayed to Robert, who seemed more concerned by possible damage to the wall and garden than anything else.

'There were hundreds of them, Dad,' said Megan.

'Don't exaggerate, darling,' Robert said. He looked at Anna. 'I'll ring them later, make a complaint. They've never come this side of the river before.'

'You knew your father was out,' Anna continued.

'It's only a fucking fox,' said Paul. 'You should have let them just kill it.'

'Paul . . . ' Robert said as Megan giggled. They'd given up admonishing the profanities unless their daughter was present, and even then Robert's rebukes had a beseeching rather than berating tone.

'They do it for fun, Paul,' Anna said. 'As sport.

People fought for years to get it banned.'

Her son shrugged his shoulders. She noticed the grazing on his knuckles had scabbed into iron-coloured crusts, the bruising of his black eye now only apparent by comparison with the other. Looking at him, the images on his computer appeared in her mind and she strained to repel them.

'It's no different to fishing,' he said.

'Of course it is. Foxes are . . . ' Anna paused to choose her words carefully.

'Mammals,' said Megan, pleased with herself.

'So?' said Paul.

'They have bigger brains than fish.' Megan again.

'That should help them get away better then,' said her brother.

Megan looked to her mother for support, who in turn looked to Robert. Let them make up their own minds, Anna could see him thinking.

'It's different from fishing,' Anna said, 'in that fish aren't torn apart alive.'

'You said they're not allowed to do that any more,' said Megan.

'They're not, no.'

'So what's the problem?' said Paul.

'They didn't have a gun with them as far as I could see; how else were they going to kill it? You can hardly whistle a pack of hounds to heel just before they catch a fox.'

'Dan's old man lets the hunt on his land,' said Paul. 'He says foxes are pests.'

'That's rich coming from Dan,' said Robert.

'I'm not saying they don't ever have to be

90

culled,' Anna continued, 'but it shouldn't be done for sport. Anyway, cars take care of more than enough.'

Robert looked up, as if about to join in, but thought better of it. Anna knew he'd say that, from a farmer's perspective, cars didn't kill enough on the moor, and that while he didn't particularly support it, there were more important threats to the landscape and its wildlife.

After a silence Robert tried to defuse the tension, asking Megan what she was doing at school next week.

'We have to dissect a frog, which means cutting it open.'

'Urgh,' said Robert in mock disgust. 'I presume they provide one.'

They'd had a letter stating it wasn't compulsory, that those who didn't want to participate could leave the class. Megan, they knew, wouldn't be one of them.

'What's the difference between that and killing a fox?' said Paul.

'The frog will be dead,' said Anna. 'And it's for science.'

'If it's for science, why do they need to do it every year?'

Anna went to speak, but wanted the perfect answer, one that rendered her son's arguments impotent.

'Did you know,' said Robert, perhaps sensing this, 'if you put a frog in boiling water, it'll jump straight out? But if you place it in cold water and then slowly heat it, the frog will just stay there and die.'

91

'That's horrible,' said Anna. 'How do you know that?'

'Someone's done it, I suppose.'

'But you don't know.'

'I read it somewhere. The point is we don't notice subtle change.'

'Did they really do that, Mum?' asked Megan.

'It's probably just a thought experiment. Like the one with the cat.'

'It's hardly quantum physics,' said Robert.

'What cat?' said Megan.

'They didn't really do anything to the cat, love.'

'We're not talking about cats,' said Robert.

'What did they not really do to the cat, Mum?'

'Nobody did anything to the cat or the frog,' said Anna.

'Course they did it,' said Robert. 'It's only a frog.'

'They wouldn't be allowed. Not these days.'

'Perhaps it wasn't these days.'

'Did they boil the cat in water, Mum?'

'Of course they didn't, darling. It was in a box.'

'How did it get there?'

'It's not real, Meg.'

'They poisoned it,' said Robert. 'Or not.'

'Did it die, Mum?'

'Yes and no,' said her father.

Anna gave up and went to the kitchen to bring the casserole in.

'Mmm, beef,' said Robert.

'Don't,' said Anna, casting a look his way.

Robert winked at his daughter, who smiled

conspiratorially without really knowing why.

Anna served the food. 'Next time there are hordes of dogs tearing around the garden trying to rip a fox to bits,' she said to Paul, 'I'd appreciate a bit of support.'

He grunted whilst loading his plate with potatoes.

This brief engagement by her son was preferable to his usual monosyllabic discourse. Unpalatable views were better than none at all. And it would only take some influential new friend, infiltrating his world with precocious guitar skill and anti-hunt sensibilities, to see Paul adopt a contrary belief. That was what he needed to sweep away the apathy: something to focus the anger on, narrowing it to a single target instead of the world in general. Perhaps it would be a girlfriend. He would announce he was bringing someone for tea, a friend, he'd term her. A vegan or something, so she couldn't eat what they normally did. The soft porn posters would be swapped for crude political sentiment; his appearance would change overnight. Stickers embracing slogans would appear on his guitar, loyal to the cause of the month. It seemed far-fetched for now; maybe in a year or so.

Megan, she felt, would be more consistent, her relationship with animals neither sentimental nor indifferent. She'd already announced to a teacher, and presumably a class of bemused children, that she wanted to be a palaeontologist when she grew up. Anna wasn't convinced her daughter knew entirely what this meant, or even where she'd learned the word, so last summer they'd bought her a kit from a museum, a piece of clay in which a replica dinosaur fossil had been entombed. It came with tools and various brushes. Apart from meals, they didn't see her all weekend. On the Sunday evening she came down to announce she'd excavated part of a stegosaurus.

There was something both omnipotent and helpless in watching your children's lives form. At times you seemed the supreme architect, conducting the orchestra of all they experienced. Other times you watched with impotence, scarcely able to comprehend the complex machinations at work. You took the credit when things went well: *look, world, at what I've delivered you; look at what's been achieved by the sum of my virtues.* And, when they didn't, you nodded in the direction of every extraneous influence you could think of. Responsibility: absolute one moment, absolved the next.

Paul and Megan's disparate temperaments, though, were, if the science was to be believed, fixed pre-experience, determined in the womb, during the vagaries of pregnancy. And their contrasting births offered prescience to this end, clues to the personalities that would emerge. While Megan entered the world almost serenely, her face content, tranquil from her first breath, Paul emerged from a long and difficult labour to produce an ear-splitting wail that Anna could still hear today. Coupled with this was an expression of torment, as if being born was some punitive act. As a baby he cried more than his sister would do; he slept more lightly, woken by the slightest noise. Megan had fewer colds, while Paul caught everything going around, his symptoms always more severe, his complexion more pallid.

The arrival of a sibling, when Paul was four, saw him display curiosity and resentment in equal measure, though the former soon lost this particular battle. It was, Anna's parents pointed out, to be expected, as the firstborn adjusted to the halving of attention. But she found it increasingly upsetting, particularly when Paul's behaviour appeared malicious, beyond that of a jealous toddler. At first he would just hug Megan too hard or attempt to pick her up in an ungainly fashion.

'He's just copying what we do,' Robert said.

But then he began throwing things at her, toy bricks, a tennis ball — trying to teach her to play catch, Robert's take — the objects often hitting her squarely in the face.

Sometimes Anna would see Paul administering little pinches to his sister's legs and arms, his face on being admonished full of impish delight rather than contrition. Again she was assured this wasn't exceptional.

On one occasion Anna entered their bedroom to find a four-month-old Megan in her cot beneath a pile of blankets, her face smothered by the weight, still breathing but more by luck than design.

We were playing hide and seek, Paul's explanation. Again Robert played it down, while Anna fretted, assumed the worst.

And so Anna stopped leaving her children

alone together until Megan was at least old enough to protest verbally, by which time Paul had begun to accept her presence was permanent, the resentment finally subsiding, allowing a bond to emerge between them.

The next period to trouble her was years later. Her son's treatment of small animals — snails, worms, insects — again seemed, to others, little more than typical boyish conduct, as Paul, with a single stamp, dispatched them with apparent glee. Bees were snared in a net, boiling water poured on them. But such blithe cruelty, albeit a supposed mandatory phase of boyhood, unnerved Anna and she fought its implications.

Later, in bed, she found herself imagining the fox again as it hid in the barn, its body in overdrive, the hounds circling, desperate to get in. Its fear was merely a series of chemicals, she told herself. Nothing was reflected upon, no detail that could be recalled later. Inches from death, it knew only to remain still. To accept its fate.

She wondered how far the prisoner had got, whether he had spent a night or two on the moor. It was possible he, too, was huddled in the corner of a barn, alert, listening for his pursuers.

★　★　★

Anna had meant to check the barn yesterday, but the day had got away from her, darkness drawing in before she'd remembered. Now, opening the wooden door warily, she looked around inside, checking possible hiding places, but could see no trace of the animal. The gap in the wall, affording succour to anything smaller than a hound, had spots of drying blood along the edge of the corrugated iron where the dogs had tried to force their way in. She pictured the scene inside the barn, tried to imagine the sounds had the hole's circumference been a few inches greater. Anna wondered how long the fox had waited before emerging from the barn, certain its pursuers had departed.

Turning to go back inside, a shape by the log pile in the far corner caught her eye. Its colour next to the wood, the barn's half-light, perhaps explained why she'd missed it initially. She walked over to it. There were no obvious wounds, no bite marks, just a thin line of blood trailing from its open mouth. Its eyes were still open, glazed yet holding the vestige of a life not long ended. Teeth almost a perfect white issued a final grin.

There was something unfair that, having evaded the hounds with skill and cunning, the creature should die of shock, and anger with yesterday's hunt rose again.

Anna found some old gloves and, lifting it by its brush, carried the fox down towards the river. She crossed at the shallows, walked a few hundred yards up into the gorse and placed it in a small clearing where the carrion birds could see it.

13

The buzzer sounds. It still cuts through me, even this time when I'm expecting it. I'd heard the car pull up, its doors open and close, my mother's footsteps on the pavement below. But still, like a gag reflex, my body shudders at the noise, adrenaline flashing through me. I look out of the window, check the car, confirm that it's them. I press the button to let my parents in, remove the chain from the flat door and look in the mirror.

I've tied my hair up, even put some make-up on for the first time since two Tuesdays ago. I want to resemble the daughter they'd seen in the summer. The one who got the train to Devon, thrilled by a new job, in love with the world and all it could offer. I try to evoke courage, to protect them from this thing.

They'd driven up to collect me once before, during my last year at university. Glandular fever had felled me a few months before exams and Mum insisted I recover at home, the train too exhausting to consider. She enjoyed having her little girl back, someone to fuss over again, to draw out the maternal instinct. She made soup, brought me magazines in bed. We played Scrabble and canasta endlessly. But as I recovered, we annoyed each other in equal measure, as I became desperate to return to friends and my relatively new world. Being home confirmed how right I'd been to move away from provincial life, to make the leap to something more ambitious. You could get trapped growing up in those rural backwaters, oblivious to the rest of the world, entangled in small-town mentality. School friends had stayed there, had children, got the kind of jobs you resented forever. It was such a fine line.

An embittered old teacher, obsessed with Larkin, had piqued my interest in studying further. After class one day, we went through a poem I'd written. It was clumsy, affected, but showed some promise, he said. He asked about my plans after A-levels; I told him I didn't have any. There followed something between a speech and a lecture, the kind made in films where the maverick teacher tells the bright but cloistered pupil to make something of their life, to escape the small-town clutches before it was too late. 'This is somewhere you come to retire, to escape at the other end of life,' he said. 'There's nothing here for the young. Nothing but having babies and fighting outside pubs.' He brought some prospectuses in the next day and suddenly the world opened up.

★ ★ ★

I open the door to my mother. Her eyes are red from crying. She looks me up and down as if conducting a stocktake, before forcing a smile and hugging me. 'My baby,' she says over and over, sobbing into my shoulder. 'My baby. We're here now.'

Behind, my father stares at the floor like a child who thinks reality disappears when you don't look at it.

'Dad?'

He looks up slowly, his face haunted, full of shock. There's anger there too, I think. Just a trace. He puts a hand on my shoulder but says nothing. I look at him, trying to gauge his thoughts. I realise he'll be the next man to enter the flat. Eventually he moves forward and holds Mum so that she's sandwiched between us and we stand like this in silence for several minutes.

I called home this morning. Almost two weeks had passed. I'd fantasised for days about them not knowing, about nobody knowing. I would hand in my notice at work, citing family illness, a parent that needed caring for. Nobody at work knew much about me, not even Nick. I could move away, start again. It would be fine. Even after the examination I thought nobody need know. The doctor talked about the police, reporting the attack, but somehow I couldn't bring myself to open that particular door, inviting in further horror. This happens to lots of women, I told myself. In some ways I was lucky: sore for a few days, but otherwise uninjured. And surely better to have known him, for it not to have been a stranger in some alleyway. That was something else altogether. This was a different kind, not like that at all. I would just move on.

I tidied the flat endlessly, cleaning, scrubbing. My secret. I could contain it. In a month or so, it would seem like nothing. I was lucky.

But waking today I had to share it. It had become too big for one person: I needed to give some of it away.

Dad had answered the phone, plunging straight into small talk — weather, the garden, news from the town, from my brother. I kept it together, my responses monosyllabic. His repertoire used up, he finished with a rhetorical, 'How are you?' before putting Mum on. She talked but I remember none of the detail. I just focused on her voice, its familiarity, its association with the past, with an innocence I was once part of. I let her continue, gifting her a few more minutes of ignorance before introducing her new daughter. For an hour before I'd practised euphemistic revelations, but there seemed no words other than the real ones. As I said them they seemed to fall like a guillotine blade, cleaving the past and future cleanly and for ever: *Mum, I've been raped*. There can be few worse sentences. Few things more terrible a parent should hear. And yet, because of my desire to soften the blow for her, they came out untailored, as if I was telling her I'd applied for a job or had a bad cold.

Something between a gasp and a scream came down the phone. Then silence. I heard her shout to my father before she fired off some questions. Was I OK? Were the police with me? Again she called to another part of the house. Was I sure I wasn't hurt? What had happened? Had they caught the man yet?

I played down everything, gave little detail, stressed I was free of injury. I said that it happened a while ago, which seemed to confuse rather than comfort her. Then her voice was muffled and I realised she'd covered the phone and was telling my father, or at least saying that *something bad* had happened; it was impossible to imagine her repeating my announcement verbatim.

'Mum,' I said. Their voices were barely audible. 'Mum.'

'Darling, I — '

'Mum, can you come and get me?'

* * *

They would be four hours, five if the traffic was bad. They would put some things in a bag, leave as soon as they could. I'd be fine, I said, holding back tears.

For the first time in two weeks I opened the curtains. The day was sufficiently grey not to boost the room's light much. It was strange seeing the town after only listening to it, watching its events play out in my mind. Nothing was different. Dogs were walked. People stood and chatted. Others were at work. At school. I felt no more part of it now that I could actually see it. Using the curtain as cover, I watched for some minutes, fascinated by small detail, things unnoticed before. It was like a television screen. Nothing was real.

I sit on the sofa with my mother. She won't stop holding my hands in hers, her grip both tender and firm, as if she were cupping a rare butterfly. I study her wedding ring, finding it almost absurd that my father would have placed it there the best part of thirty years ago. He paces around the flat, shuffling on the spot for a while. He can't look at me for more than a second. No one speaks. He walks over to the window, looks out, then draws a finger along the black line of damp. 'Landlord not forked out for double glazing,' he says. 'Must be freezing in here this time of year.'

My mother looks at him, a beseeching glare that means do or say something useful. They are doing their best. I offer them tea but am glad when Mum asks if I'd rather just get off home in a bit. The word has a warmth the way she says it, like a place where nothing bad happens.

After the next silence I try humour. 'At least Gran will have something other than Michael to tell her neighbours about this month.' My brother, cleverer, more adventurous than me, calls my parents once in a while from some far-flung corner of the globe, relaying his latest adventure to them.

'We haven't got hold of him yet,' says Mum.

'You don't need to,' I say, the shame shared enough for now.

We sit in silence a while longer. I notice Mum's gaze moving around the flat, studying its layout, her imagination cruelly busy.

'Where . . . ?' she starts.

'It doesn't matter,' I say.

'I'm sorry. You're right, it doesn't matter.'

Our exchange gives my father the courage to speak of it. 'You have to report this later today,' he says. 'It goes without saying. I can't believe you haven't already.'

Again my mother glares at him askance, eyes pleading with him to shut up.

'I knew him,' I say, immediately wishing I'd waited.

My parents look at me, then at each other, then back to me.

'It wasn't some stranger, waiting in the dark for me to get home. I let him in. I knew him.'

This seems to change things, their faces lurching through degrees of bewilderment.

'We thought . . . ' says Dad. 'So he was a boyfriend?'

'No.'

'But you asked him in? A friend, then. Someone you work with? A teacher?'

'He's someone I teach.' Unlike this morning, I get to see their expressions at this latest revelation.

'What do you mean, someone you teach?' says Mum. 'You mean . . . a pupil?'

'Yes.'

Dad makes an incredulous snort. 'A boy?'

'A young man, yes.'

'But . . . '

'He's fifteen,' I continue. 'His name is Jamie O'Sullivan. Remember I told you I'd asked to teach two of my pupils after school, ones

105

struggling in class?'

'You said something.'

'I've being seeing them, for extra lessons, an hour a week.'

'Fifteen!' Dad says. 'How can — '

'Shut up, David. This isn't the time.'

'But I don't under — '

Mum doesn't let him finish. 'Let's get you home, darling. Have you packed everything you want for now?'

I nod. I've put some clothes in a holdall. A couple of books, a washbag.

'I'll put it in the car, then,' says my father, pleased to have something to do.

Once he's gone, Mum tells me to ignore him. That I can tell the police in my own time. She sounds confused. 'I'm sure . . . ' she starts but doesn't finish.

I collect a few last bits, look around the place, wondering if I'll return.

Dad appears at the door. 'Have you turned everything off?' he says.

My mother puts an arm around me as I get into the back seat of the car. It makes me think of criminals with blankets over them being shepherded into a vehicle by police. I don't imagine anyone is looking, taking any notice of this unremarkable event, but I can't look up to check.

And then we flee. Heading west to the place I grew up, where I regarded innocence as a failing. Back to where nothing ever happens.

The journey is silent for the most part, save my mother asking how I am every once in a while. An hour or so in, she tells me how the woman next door complained about their leylandii. About a fire at the pub. She tells me the Laceys are divorcing, an affair. That Michael won't be home for Christmas again. I don't respond, but she carries on.

As the car leaves the M5, the silhouetted hills of Dartmoor rise up. The setting sun leaves a golden slit of fire between them and the low cloud, like a seam of lava in rock. The vastness of the moor makes itself known; long walks in childhood gather at the edges of my mind. The very thing I escaped from now brings some comfort, as I imagine miles of wilderness, valleys, tors.

The rhythm of the road is soothing for the first time; a background drone, like white noise. After a while I ask Mum to put some music on, doesn't matter what, I say. If there's any more silence I fear that I'll tell them. A trio of terrible disclosures in one day would be unfair. I won't tell them yet that they're taking home two people, one inside the other.

14

Mum fusses around me, asking if she can come as well, saying that we could go in the car, have lunch somewhere.

'I want to be alone, to just walk. I'll be back for dinner tonight.'

She finds me some gloves and a hat, tells me I need better walking boots, that she'll buy me some in town tomorrow. Stay away from the firing ranges, her last words.

She stands at the front-room window, her face taut with worry. She's wondering whether I'll come back. She'll watch the clock all day, fretful, powerless — the irony being I *have* given today to contemplate life, *a* life, just not my own.

I walk out of town, the sun low and pale, still giving a hint of warmth to my face. The scent of wood smoke rides the air, the breeze barely apparent. Within minutes I'm aware of the sounds of nature, as if they'd been muted for years. Birdsong accompanies me along the lanes. In the distance the waters of the Tavy carve inexorably through the land.

I'm guided only by a vague sense of the moor being to the east, of Dad driving us there as children on Sunday afternoons, until I was old enough to decline, preferring to meet, at first friends, then later a boyfriend.

I walk through small villages where passers-by smile or say hello and I manage half-smiles in return without making eye contact. A mother walks her two young children, the son kicking a stone that falls to rest near my feet. Unconstrained by the convention of strangers, he stops and stares at me, wondering if I'll play, before running on.

The road winds upwards and I try to remember the last time I came up here. Ten years ago, maybe more. Fields seem alive with crows, their squawking and cawing like malevolent laughter. Others circle above them. I remember a line from a poem, describing their airborne song as having two cronks to each circuit. A lone pheasant nervously patrols the field's edge.

The countryside soon becomes moorland, with granite rocks scattered among the sedge and rushes, rising to giant stacks in the distance. Wild ponies graze on the lower slopes. Several sheep eye me keenly, their red identification marks like gunshot wounds.

In the three weeks I've been back a pattern has emerged. I go to bed first, lying there listening to the sounds of the house. To say I'm afraid of the dark would be simplistic, but I leave the lamp on all night. In the mornings Mum brings me breakfast, which I usually leave. I mask being sick as best I can. If she hears, I connect it to the trauma of that day. Baths are still long and hot. Time plays tricks on me.

One evening Mum announced Michael was on the phone, from South America. There was something staged about it, but I welcomed not having to start at the beginning. We took turns crying before settling into some sort of conversation. I can remember almost nothing of what he said, just that his voice had a calming quality to it, and that, for the first time since that day, I wasn't being judged. He told me to get on a plane, to visit for as long as I wanted. The idea both excites and terrifies me. He told me to stay strong, that he would try to come home sometime. I made him promise to call again soon.

Most afternoons I read vacuous lifestyle magazines, then the three of us watch television in the evenings as a family. Mum guards the remote control for when anything upsetting or inappropriate comes on. Some nights we hop from one channel to another, in search of banality. They've become more sensitive to it than me; at the first sign of anything remotely violent, the channel is changed. Same with anything sexual. Even an extended kiss raises tension in them.

Nature programmes and wildlife documentaries are deemed the ultimate safe ground, my parents' posture visibly relaxing when one comes on, as if humans, somehow, were outside of nature, that the behaviour of animals was removed from our own. Ducks rape, I wanted to

111

say. In gangs. As do dolphins. Male wolves lock on, their penises swelling once they've ejaculated, making sure no other male gets a look in. We're all animals.

They want to speak of it, of their incredulity, but the inadequacy of language prevents them.

Last night we watched a programme about birds. A cuckoo flew down to the nest of a reed warbler, pushed an egg out, before laying one of its own. It chooses the warbler as the eggs are similar in appearance. The whole procedure takes about ten seconds. The warbler returns none the wiser. Once hatched, the cuckoo chick began evicting the other eggs, one at a time, heaving them out over the edge. If the host eggs hatched first, the cuckoo, once it broke from its shell, again forced the other chicks out. We just stared in silence at the screen as the cuckoo slowly, determinedly, used its back to shove the others up the side of the nest and out to their deaths. Once out of the nest, the fallen chicks are ignored by the mother, which instead brings food for the cuckoo as if it were its own.

I walk on, setting a course for the highest point of land, wondering if rising above everything will bring clarity.

My father leaves for work each morning before I'm up. I hear him pass my room, feel him holding his breath, pausing for just a second outside my door. Later he tells me about his day. He fires words into the air, chronicling mundane events in his monologue. He controls the conversation as best he can, choosing topics he can cope with.

Looking north, on the horizon, I can see Brentor Church balanced on its rocky outcrop. The wind has picked up; I lean into it, imagine it cleansing me, airing my soul as if it hung on a line. A few cars pass, leaving me feeling self-conscious, out here with no dog or companion, not even a bag. A stile over the drystone wall offers further solitude and I leave the road behind.

I watch a buzzard spiral in the thermals, perhaps a prelude to a violent act, its prey oblivious to the danger above, unaware of its selection. The wind starts to bite at my face and I pull my hat lower. I remember warnings given, about people coming up here unprepared, how the weather can turn in an instant, trapping the unsuspecting. All the seasons in one day, the cliché went.

I think of the cuckoo chick, what it does to survive, how it's programmed to murder, to trick its new parent. How the warbler arrives back at the nest to find a lone chick, one that doesn't resemble itself. And then it feeds it unquestioningly, again and again returning with food, until the chick is the same size as its foster parent.

I consider what is inside me. For a week or so I told myself it could be Nick's, however unlikely that was. I rehearsed how I'd tell him, what his response would be, whether he'd try to influence me one way or the other. Perhaps his children would play with it. But one morning the denial had gone, the cold reality brushing it aside, leaving only horror.

That it is mine too has hardly crossed my

113

mind, and I pause at the realisation. Mine, I mouth to nobody.

I push on. Questions rise. Are you a person yet? Does your violent conception change what you are? What you would become? A violent end might be apposite, the briefest of existences, sandwiched by two brutal events. Nobody would know.

And the alternative? What part of him would be you? You, this thing that grows in me, the result of hate and anger, the produce of humiliation. Can you be anything other than wicked? Than a reminder?

There is still time, weeks I've read, yet by the end of today I hope to know.

A sign alerts me to the danger of the firing range. Of soldiers using the moor, practising violence amid the beauty. I walk and walk, through shallow peat bogs that belch with each step; past gorse, its few remaining yellow flowers protected by furrowed spines. Lichen-covered stone circles are a reminder of ancient settlements, of a time I can't imagine, when survival dominated everything. You grew and farmed and mined and herded and raised a family. You put your faith in the land, you worshipped it.

There are few trees now, save the plantations in the distance, and I try to picture the moor as it once was, under its wooded blanket. I climb higher. A lone hawthorn, slanted by the timeless wind, clings to life amid the rocks. The tor I'm heading for looks both near and far. Boulders lay strewn around it as if spewed from a volcano.

My pace is furious now, slowing only when the soft ground claims a boot and I almost topple over. For a moment I imagine I'm the last person alive, that I'll just walk forever along these sun-kissed trails.

A story, a myth, comes to me from childhood and I try to recall the detail. A girl's grave, somewhere on the moor, where flowers mysteriously appeared each morning. And something about a cloaked figure sitting mournfully on the grave some nights. I try to think who she was. A young girl, a socially unacceptable pregnancy. A suicide. Custom wouldn't allow her to be buried in consecrated ground, so, in death, she was banished to moorland. I wonder if it's nearby.

Other myths of the moor come to me. Dad's brother used to try to scare us as children on days out. There was a part of the moor where hairy hands appeared on your steering wheel, forcing you from the road. And he told us of the rock at Dewerstone, more than a hundred feet high, where the devil would chase sinners over the edge, his phantom hounds waiting at the bottom.

For the first time today a fatigue sweeps through me and I recall a restless night. I had woken, gripped by terror, my sheets sodden with sweat. I dreamt I'd been giving birth, Jamie pulling the baby out. I couldn't see it, pinned as I was by paralysis. I was desperate to know if it had any of my features, if people would say it had my eyes, my mouth, but he held it away from me, the nurses only saying how beautiful the child was. You can't keep it, was all I said. It's

115

mine. And then he walked around the bed, revealing the bundle in his arms, and I saw that its face was a mirror image of his.

Occasionally, a walker appears on the horizon and I alter my course slightly to avoid them. Despite eating little today, I feel I could walk all day, climbing tor after tor, restrained by nothing. Another drystone wall defines my route, as I follow it out of the valley. Halfway up I'm aware of a pied wagtail chirping a few yards ahead on the wall. As soon as I reach it, it flies on a little, then seems to perform a dance on the wall, incessant in its frenetic trilling. After a minute of this, I wonder if it's trying to lure me away from its nest, from its young — I've read they do this — but it's the wrong time of year. I alter my course a little, cutting across the heather.

Yesterday I was interviewed. You have to tell them eventually, my mother had said repeatedly, without referencing what. I rang the school first, left a message for the head to call me back, which he did an hour or so later. He didn't seem to understand what I was saying, and I had to repeat it. His stupefaction reached me as silence. Finally, he asked if anyone had been told, which I took to mean the police. It was the next call I would be making, I said.

They drove down, the detectives, a man and woman. He was older, forties perhaps. I didn't like him. She was pleasant enough, younger, smiling awkwardly as he took notes. I'd practised telling them in the morning, keen to get the order right. They asked questions, pausing as my mother brought in tea and biscuits. So you had

116

arranged for the extra lessons? You were teaching him after school? You let him into your flat? The boy's parents knew? I wished they didn't keep calling him a boy. And then: I'm sorry, but we have to ask. Did you give him the wrong impression? Was there any physical contact before? Did you make it clear you didn't want to have intercourse? I said that we didn't have intercourse.

I began to float away then, as I've learned to, drifting to a safe world I'd crafted, images from childhood, playing in fields, exploring the few residual ancient woods of the moor, feeling tiny yet secure.

I was brought back by their silence. They said they'd check the physical evidence from the examination, interview Jamie. They asked if photographs were taken. I said there was nothing to see, which brought faint surprise to the man's face.

Even if evidence was found, the woman said, it could come down to who was believed.

'And what with all the time that's passed,' said the man.

The woman smiled uneasily, the plate of biscuits untouched.

'And he's fifteen?' the man asked again, without looking up from his pad.

'Yes.'

'Do you know when he's sixteen?'

I said I didn't. I told them I was pregnant. It seemed to add weight to my claim: a boy cannot do what he did; a boy cannot produce a baby. The woman asked if I'd been sleeping with

117

anyone else at the time. The man wrote down Nick's name. A colleague, I said. Married. Oh, the man said. I asked them to contact him at school. I owed him that.

There were tests, if I wanted them. To show whose it was. It's not Nick's, I told them. I asked if they could not tell Jamie; they said they wouldn't, but it would emerge the further proceedings went.

A watery line of cloud has appeared, as if drawn, on the horizon to the west. The late sun turns the fern a rusty orange. I place a hand on my stomach. What do you expect me to do? The warbler knows no different; nature overrides, maternal instinct flourishes. If I could eradicate the event from my memory, I could look at you with nothing but love. But you will always be a connection to that day, a living reminder of what he did to me.

And you will have his blood — blood carries everything. There will be codes, genetic instructions, forces I can't repel. There will be a blueprint to replicate his behaviour; the inheritance of wickedness. The capacity to be the same. Like father, like son. Better to sever the link; better to give up on you now, when you're not really a person.

Or I could let you grow in me, then give you to others. Perhaps they wouldn't know. You wouldn't know. I'd become a vehicle, transporting life. Our paths would never knowingly cross again. I would hear none of your triumphs, none of your transgressions. Either way, your eyes would never see into my own, echoing a malevolence I want to run from forever.

I reach the top of the tor and walk round the granite stack looking for a way up. A few ponies graze on the slopes beside me, their distended stomachs, their squat legs, giving them a comical gait. As a teenager I remember being upset on hearing that the Dartmoor pony was a delicacy in France.

I climb one of the giant weather-worn slabs, its surface unyielding, timeless. A sheer face at the top takes all my strength as I stretch up, hands and feet searching for fissures. For a moment, as I can't seem to go up or down, I feel some small exhilaration for the first time in my new life. The rock, cold on my cheek, rises calmly above me.

I writhe myself up over the final section, standing up into the west wind. Miles of Dartmoor stretch in every direction, verdant and fertile. Looking out I trace the route I'd taken as far as possible, back to the serpentine road that unspools into the distance, specks of occasional cars the only reminder of human life. The light, soft and diffuse, picks out the pine trees and valleys to the north; to the south the last of the sun splinters through gaps in the cloud and dances on the surface of the reservoir. I feel as though I'm at the heart of the moor, its rhythms and pulse emanating from this spot. I imagine a Bronze Age settler standing here, surveying her world, watching over cattle, over children. I envy her lack of choice, her marvelling at the miracle of birth. A gift from the heavens.

I start to shiver. Gusts threaten to unbalance me. Inside, you fight for life.

15

Megan ran into the kitchen.

'There's a police car,' she said. 'Coming up the lane.'

Anna watched from the window as it drove slowly around the house to the back and parked next to the Land Rover. A man in uniform got out and spent a moment or two scanning the yard and outbuildings. He looked beyond the house, up to the conifers and the tors, before turning full circle to take in the valley and Wistman's Wood in the distance. Robert put on his fleece and went out to meet him. Anna told Megan to stop staring, but was ignored. After a minute or two she asked her daughter what they were doing.

'Dad is pointing a lot. The man is blowing into his hands and nodding. Now they're going over to the barn.'

Ten minutes later Robert was back inside. He told Megan to go upstairs as they needed to talk about something. She huffed away, life apparently unfair.

'A few people have reported someone hanging

about,' said Robert, 'near the end of the lane, down by the river, looking suspicious. They think it might be the prisoner.'

'Not much of a getaway,' Anna said, 'if this is as far as he's got in a week.'

'I know, but it's the only possible sighting they've had. We checked the barn. I said I'd keep an eye out. They're going to move the search back this way.'

She tried to match her husband's calm tone. 'I'll meet Megan off the bus when Paul's not with her.'

The only other time a police car had been in the yard, they'd just returned from a weekend at Robert's parents. As they drove up the lane, they could see a man in uniform peering in through the cottage's windows, one by one. As they parked he approached them. A call had been received by the post office, the man said, worried about all the mess on the windows, seen by someone on their morning round.

'What mess?' said Anna.

They walked over to the side of the house. On the inside of the kitchen window were great swirling patterns of what looked like dried blood.

'It's like it all the way around the ground floor,' the policeman said.

Robert told the children to get back in the car, but was ignored. Anna unlocked the back door and they went inside. All the downstairs windows were like it to some extent, a spectrum of hues ranging from a few days old to the relatively fresh. Some of the whorls were laced with black feathers, looking like clumsy modern art.

Walking around, more feathers could be seen on the floor. Much of the furniture had been defecated on. They went from room to room, eventually finding it in Anna's studio.

'Looks like a jackdaw,' the policeman said. 'You must have left a window open somewhere.'

They hadn't. It had come down the chimney, they later worked out. Despite the gore, the children, Megan especially, had been fascinated.

'Why didn't it just fly back up the chimney?' she said. 'It must have remembered how it got in.'

It took three buckets of soapy water to get the windows clean. For weeks Anna pictured the bird flinging itself again and again at the glass, uncomprehending of the invisible obstruction, until, exhausted, it had given up.

Robert secured a wire cowl to the top of the chimney later that week.

Her husband's words of a few moments ago repeated in her mind. *Someone has been seen hanging about.* It made her think of the phrase 'loitering with intent', something people didn't say these days. She went over the last few days, trying to work out if the feeling of being watched had any substance to it or was merely the work of an overactive mind, one whose default was distrust and suspicion. *Someone seen hanging about.* Movement in the corner of an eye while out walking, previously attributed to some marvel of nature, now assumed a malevolence.

She would wait until the man was caught before walking up the valley again. Just to be sure.

123

It was perverse that on such a great expanse of moorland you could begin to feel claustrophobic, trapped. Perhaps living so close to the prison when you had children was irresponsible, foolish even, reliant as you were on the thickness and height of a few walls, on the vigilance of a handful of staff. This thought led immediately to another: how the ratio of prisoners to guards seemed negligent, an escape inevitable. And why weren't the police doing more?

'What about an alarm?' she said to Robert. 'And another security light, at the front?'

'Bit excessive. Come on, he's not going to stay in one place for long. They said he's not dangerous.'

Robert called up to Megan, whose covert listening at the top of the stairs lacked sophistication. He asked if all her homework had been done as she scuttled back into her room.

Anna tried to remember where her son had said he was, what time he was due back.

'Come on,' Robert said, pulling her into him. 'Focus on your show. It'll be fine.' He kissed her forehead softly and went to light the fire.

From her studio she watched as the police car disappeared down the lane.

16

Robert watched the woman pulling his pint. The knuckles of her right hand blanched as it gripped the long handle, making three complete pulls before topping up. He was her only customer, as he often was at this time of day. She smiled warmly as she gave him his change, perhaps a gesture all regulars received, though he liked to think not. He made some comment about the greyness of the day, which, after her agreement, led only to silence, save the occasional crackle from the fire.

He took a long sip of his pint. 'Had many in?' he said.

'A few. Nothing like last week. I think everyone on the search came here for lunch.'

'Not found him yet, then?' Robert knew they hadn't but was keen to prolong the exchange.

'Not that I know of. Last I heard, they'd moved north, up around Fernworthy, before heading back this way this morning.' And with this she attended to something further along the bar.

He took a guess at her age: early thirties, perhaps older. Not as attractive as the girl who did Friday and Saturday nights, the one only a few years older than Paul. But the thought of her top rising slightly up her back as she stretched to reach an optic, revealing the contours of an elaborate tattoo, drew him in for one or two drinks after work with increasing frequency. He almost asked her about the artwork once, a polite inquiry as to the meaning of the Celtic symbolism, before catching himself in time. Rehearsing the question later, it sounded clumsy at best, lecherous at worst, especially as their conversations barely evolved from the ordering and serving of alcohol.

But looking was harmless enough, he told himself. It hurt nobody and, as long as he wasn't spotted, offended no one. Assuming her ring wasn't a prop, a tool of the trade, he wondered what her husband thought, whether he considered that men might frequent this place longer just to look at her, comparing notes from a distance, even trying their luck if the chance arose. Did he watch her get ready for a shift, observing the clothes she selected, the time taken with her hair, with make-up? Perhaps he drank here, watching the watchers, possessive and proud, ready to move in when lines were overstepped.

The woman — he had no idea what her name was — was tending to the fire now. He watched her drop two logs into its centre, before she manoeuvred them side by side with the long poker. He was about to compliment her on the

126

heat it produced, on her attention to the most effective arrangement of the wood, but a couple came through the door, led by an excited Labrador. Robert smiled at them, grateful that the silence would be punctured by something other than his own awkward ramblings.

In a way these moments, this snatched voyeurism, was the extent of his sexual pleasure these days. He'd always been aware of other women, even before his marriage had entered this passionless phase. But in recent months, as the advance of midlife taunted him and Anna's frigidity took an increasingly entrenched residence, this observation of women he found attractive became compulsive, his subsequent detailed fantasies fuelled by the hour or so spent here on his way home.

During the day, as he toiled hard in solitude, Robert at least allowed the disgust, the vestiges of self-loathing, to register, the guilt lingering beside him like an unwelcome colleague. But it was what this early evening ritual said about him that he battled all day on the moor, vowing to go straight home before again yielding to the weakness, almost miserable at what he appeared to be becoming. The image of turning into, if not a dirty old man, then a middle-aged Lothario was an affront to who Robert believed he was. He loved his wife, a fact he presumed would insulate him from infidelity, even the kind only dwelt on. It felt like the worst cliché: a husband, denied the spontaneity or routine of lovemaking, turning his attentions towards other, usually younger, women.

And what would he do if the opportunity arose to do more than look? Nothing, he knew. A reassuring nausea would rise whenever he allowed a fantasy to lose its surrealism for a second. Picturing the hurt in his wife's eyes, on his children's faces, was also unbearable.

There'd been a colleague who flirted with him, shortly before Megan was born. They'd visited a couple of primary schools, long hours spent together, their remit to inspire the children with local nature, promote the moor. He'd chosen to ignore his thoughts at first, as if they were someone else's, instead enjoying the ease the two of them had around each other. He pretended the teasing was harmless banter, the rapport of workmates. He convinced himself the eagerness to get to work was merely affection for someone who shared a career as well as a love of Dartmoor.

Within a few weeks spouses were barely mentioned. They developed nicknames for each other, using them in emails. It felt safe, partitioned from reality.

Dropping her off after work one day, she sat in the Land Rover a few seconds longer than needed, allowing a moment to gather momentum in the silence. She went to open the door but instead leaned over and kissed him softly on the mouth. He pulled away, but not immediately, as if not initiating it allowed a moment's inertia. They both apologised, exchanging awkward emails the following day, and Robert found a reason not to work with her whenever possible. For weeks he told himself he hadn't kissed her back, or that if he had it was so as not to embarrass her. She suggested they meet one evening, to discuss what happened, but he declined.

A few months later she moved on, a post with another National Park. He never heard from her again. That night, after the kiss, he had looked in on Paul, sufficient moonlight spilling into the room to illuminate his face as he slept. Robert stood there in the doorway for several minutes, listening to the rhythm of his breath, knowing that something had almost been lost. Later, in bed, he held his pregnant wife tightly, perhaps more in love with her than ever before, the evaporation of lovemaking still years away.

And so because he knew he was incapable of unfaithfulness, it was safe, this window of lasciviousness he allowed himself between work and home.

In the toilet Robert checked himself in the mirror, wondering what others might regard his strong points these days. Although not old, it had been years since he could, by most measures, be termed young. Forty had taken care of that. But he'd not lost his hair. Working outdoors gave his face vigour. And the body still stood up to most demands, boasting a paunch half the size of most men his age. Yet his wife clearly found something in him that repulsed her. She was charitable enough to deny it, always stressing the issue had its origin in her alone, that he'd done nothing wrong, in behaviour or appearance. At first he'd accused her of having an affair herself, getting it somewhere else, his primitive suspicion. But as the months passed he realised that some part of her had shut down, like a mine sealed off, its seam of jewels exhausted. Whatever it was she had once found arousing about him had slowly receded to almost nothing, the extent of her passion reserved for the endless hours shut away in the studio, her art the closest thing to a rival.

He would try to tease out details of her previous partners, the extent they had tolerated her lack of sexual interest, if indeed they had to. But the subject remained impregnable, always skated over, dodged like a seasoned politician. They were of little consequence, she told him. Never serious or worthy of recollection, which only served to bolster their potency in Robert's eyes. Nameless, faceless, they taunted him from their bastions of anonymity, untouchable, unaccountable. And the more his wife dismissed her past, the life she had had before him, the greater his resentment of it became. He could, he realised, be with her for the rest of his life but this part of her would always remain hidden, entombed in the depths of her mind.

In many ways, when she did finally relent in the bedroom, it was like sleeping together for the first time, especially after the more prolonged gaps. Perhaps in that sense the unfamiliarity retained lovemaking's edge, keeping it fresh. It was, if he chose, easy to imagine she was a stranger, someone he'd picked up that evening and knew nothing about, her body to be discovered anew if she could bear it. Perhaps this was the closest he got to the other Anna.

* ★ ★ ★

Driving back to the cottage, Robert opened the windows of the Land Rover, letting the cold air rush in to claim the warmth of the fire from his face, purging the remnant prurience from his mind. He shouldn't have two pints and drive, even out here where traffic was almost nil at this time of day in winter.

His mind returned to happier times, when he first saw Anna on the moor, how he'd cursed himself for not prolonging their exchange as she disappeared up the slopes of a tor. How, months later, when he'd seen her again in a nearby market, he forced himself to ask her out, groping clumsily for words like a teenager. The first kiss. That first night in the cottage. How she'd shivered when he touched her.

As his headlights swept across the terrain, sporadic standing stones were lit up, their tips shrouded by a mist that rolled silently and quickly by. To the east he could just make out the stone circle, the silhouetted slabs like giant dominoes waiting to topple on to each other. He thought about the prisoner. They'd been told he wasn't a threat to people, but little else. Despite the police visit, Anna's response seemed an overreaction, missing the point that the man would be desperate to avoid anyone, would risk even hypothermia to evade capture. So what if he'd spent a night in their barn, scavenged for food; he would have been long gone before first light, most likely moving at night, hunkering down by day.

He tried to imagine the taste of freedom gained after years of incarceration, how even the uncompromising moor must feel like Elysium after residency in a prison that had barely been upgraded since its construction two centuries ago. What would the man have missed most? What luxury would he have craved night after night, its detail painstakingly recalled by a mind barely able to? Simple things, Robert supposed. The smell of fresh coffee. A favourite pint. A forgotten view. His children. But as his mind returned to his wife's coldness, Robert suspected that he and the prisoner, at this moment, shared the same primal desire.

★   ★   ★

Once home he found everyone in the lounge, watching the television keenly.

'Look, Dad,' said Megan. 'They've found him.'

The local news report detailed the timings of the capture, before a man in uniform praised the cooperation between police forces, reassuring the public there had been no danger.

The prisoner's face looked gentle to Robert, almost serene — more that of someone who taught yoga than a seasoned criminal. He didn't seem like the sort of person who fared well inside. As cameras flashed, two burly men ushered him into a van, to begin the journey back to the moor, the reporter said. He'd been arrested in a flat in the Midlands, a cousin admitting to harbouring him for a few days.

There was then a shot of the prison, grey and dank in the mist.

Robert wondered how the man had felt during his week of liberty, whether the possibility of an increased sentence was worth it. The governor spoke to the camera now, reading from a statement, a hint of embarrassment apparent as he promised improvements in security. A debate about public safety followed in the TV studio.

They watched it as a family, their part of the moor having its little moment of prominence, getting both national and local coverage. Megan asked if the man would be in trouble for escaping. Even Paul seemed roused by the story.

There would be a group of locals outside the post office in the morning, wondering if their children were safe. Too soft on them, some would say. A reporter would do a feature, there would be calls for a new governor perhaps. And then it would be forgotten.

Whatever it was the prisoner had felt most deprived of, Robert hoped he'd experienced a little of it before the knock at the door came.

Looking at his wife he could see the relief in her face, causing him to wonder whether the drama's denouement would mark an end to the current abstention.

17

The man blew into his hands as he watched the lights flicker in the house below. It was completely dark now, the steep sides of the valley barely visible. Each step he took sent a soft crack into the night until he emerged fully from the woods. He felt less exposed here now, in the darkness, when there'd be no repeat of the incident yesterday.

From start to finish it had lasted little more than ten minutes. He had heard the dogs before they were upon him, but the tumult once they entered the woods still caused him to panic. A person on the moor with binoculars was commonplace enough, he'd reasoned, but he was hardly dressed like a rambler. He'd returned today to the shop that had sold him the binoculars and bought some walking boots and a fleece.

Once he had realised the dogs weren't attacking him he just stood still, letting them rush past. They circled, frenziedly sniffing the ground, their barks making his ears throb. After a minute or so they'd gone, tearing out from the trees as quickly as they'd entered. A horn then sounded and the man finally understood what was happening. There was a thunder of galloping horses forty or fifty yards to his left, accompanied by more horn blowing. He'd waited until the noise faded before continuing to the edge of the woods, where he hoped the house would be visible in the valley below.

The cottage, he'd discovered yesterday, was several hundred yards up a private lane. The end that met the road bore no sign, so he'd parked and walked along it. There appeared to be a right of way for walkers, though it was hard to be certain; an old man with a rucksack had passed him, but could easily have come from the house. That the man smiled reassured him a little and he continued on. He saw that the lane went right up to the building but that walkers were directed along a rudimentary path to its side, which snaked into the distance. He'd pulled his cap down a little and followed the path. As he continued, there was movement in one of the upstairs windows, but when he looked he could see no one. It wasn't until he was level with the building that he saw a wooden sign on the open gate. *The Barns* — the name he'd eventually found online two days ago.

Yesterday, standing at the edge of the trees, he'd watched the scene unfold as twelve or so horses lined up along the wall, their riders dressed in hunting attire. Beyond the wall, in the garden, the hounds circled a barn, their barks echoing up to him on the wind. His gaze traced

136

the lane back to the main road and he'd congratulated himself on his navigation. Having parked almost a mile away, he'd headed along a track before approaching the woods from the other side.

As he watched, a woman had appeared from behind the cottage, walked towards the riders and began remonstrating with them. It seemed to take an age to get the binoculars to focus and he adjusted them to little effect. In the end he closed one eye, which allowed him to see better. The woman was pointing, probably shouting, though he couldn't hear her from here. Little clouds of breath rose from her mouth. He tried to focus in on her face, cursing his inability to hold the binoculars still enough. Leaning his arm against a tree allowed some stability. It was impossible to tell, although it looked like the woman he'd seen on the local news a few days ago. There was a piece about an escaped prisoner on Dartmoor, a local man who'd got over the wall and fled into the night. He was only really half watching it. And then there she was, talking to him through his television.

Drug offences, the man interviewing her had said at the start of the report. A dealer; hence the tenancy of a Cat C. You didn't get much stick inside for that, unless you tried to bring your livelihood in with you. You could just keep your head down, respect people's space and you'd be fine. The escape would even have brought him a certain kudos, as long as he didn't go on about it when he was caught.

These prisoners had it easy, thought the man.

137

They didn't spend their sentence fearing attack, having to put in requests to the authorities for protection. They got to swagger about, sharing their gallows humour: old lags who knew nothing else; the young ones who resisted everything until they were slowly broken down by the system. There were scuffles for power, mostly over heroin, but one thing above all else united them — the possibility of getting at people like him. To find a way to the so-called cucumbers. The nonces. Rapists. There were others they wanted to harm — debtors, grasses, thieves — but it was this first group they'd do anything to gain access to.

And even when you were safe from them, there were the guards to worry about. You can forget us and them; the screws hated sex offenders as much as the regular prisoners did.

But that was all behind him now, the man thought. He wouldn't return to a place like that. He was better now. That's why he'd been allowed to leave. They'd taught him how to control the urges, to spot them early. How to avoid triggers that left him vulnerable, at risk of doing the thing he enjoyed doing. The treatment, as they called it, became increasingly bizarre throughout his sentence. A friend he made inside knew someone they'd operated on, removing the relevant tissue for good. But, he was glad to discover, they didn't do that any more. Chemicals were another option, and lacked surgery's permanence but, he was told, as sexual gratification itself wasn't his main motive, these would have little impact. And so it was amusing watching them try to find something that worked. They used something called aversion therapy once. He had to tell them things he absolutely hated, one of which was yoghurt. Not all yoghurt, just the stuff with small lumps of fruit in. (As a child his father had once made him sit at the table for a tearful five hours until he'd finished the entire pot.) And so, with his permission, they fitted a tube into the side of his mouth, the other end of which had some sort of pump. They would then play recordings of some bloke making a woman do it against her will, while feeding him the yoghurt that he said disgusted him the most. After weeks of this they would test him on the machine again. (He couldn't recall its name, something with a load of Ps in it.) They'd clip it to his penis and show him various scenes from films. In some of them the women were up for it, others they weren't. The machine would then measure how much he was enjoying the second lot, which he wasn't supposed to at all. After giving up on the yoghurt, they got him to talk about his childhood, his first girlfriends. How he felt about women, especially his mother. Although it wasn't unpleasant like the yoghurt, he soon got bored of it. Talking about his fantasies with them, though, passed the time more quickly, but sharing the detail of how he masturbated seemed over the top. Some things should be a person's alone.

And then there was the room they all sat together in. Group work had the advantage of being able to listen to all the no-hopers sharing their particular depravity with everyone. These sessions always left him feeling normal by comparison.

The people in charge seemed so disappointed when their methods didn't appear to work. But whilst it was fun watching them try, he realised he wasn't ever going to be released unless he helped them, showed them the progress they wanted to see. And so he did.

The segregation had at least allowed him time to reflect on the woman it all began with — not the girl in the park, but the first one. The one, as they say, you never forget. None of the other times had captured the thrill of that one. That sense of power, of revenge.

As darkness fell yesterday, he'd made his way down the slope of the valley, walked round the barn and slipped in through its door.

Waiting for his eyes to adjust he'd stood as still as possible. After a few moments there'd been a curious scratching to his left and he'd braced himself for an assault. Realising there was nobody else there, he'd walked over to the sound's source. The animal, smaller than a dog, seemed to hiss at him and he remembered the scene he'd observed from the edge of the woods earlier that day. A single heavy kick to the fox was all it had taken, a muted yelp and he was alone again.

And now, as he watched the house below, a sense of power surged through him. He trained the binoculars on to the windows. Occasional shapes passed by one of the downstairs ones. He studied those on the floor above, watching for movement. Higher still, smoke rose from the chimney stack into the night. In the yard a car was parked by the barn.

He rubbed his hands together; the drop in temperature the elevation brought surprised him. Sleeping in the car was no longer an option; some of the local pubs probably did rooms all year round. He'd try one later.

As he made his way down the side of the valley towards the house, a wave of excitement rushed through him at the thought of seeing her again.

18

The Poulters are here. Mum knows them from the church, she said, as if this provided the necessary context. I've not met them before, but I could have drawn a reasonable likeness from the snippets I'd heard. Conservatively attired, iridescent with faith, they sit adjacent to each other on the edge of the sofa, chinking bone china cups on saucers in unison. Their hair matches in style and hue.

When my mother talks about church events she's involved with, the impression I get is of a hobby — quaint gatherings absent of doctrine or dogma. I picture lots of baking, fundraising — more a lifestyle choice than a calling. It was offered to us as children but never forced. But when the couple in front of me start to talk, their posture, their manner, is one of pious caricature.

I had tried to slope off upstairs but Mum was wise to it, handing me a plate of almond slices to take in.

I introduce myself. 'We've heard a lot about

you,' the man says, as if I were barely out of primary school.

I sit down, resigned to the situation.

'Our son is training to be a teacher,' says the woman. 'Works so hard. Never any time to himself. It's such a virtue, passing on knowledge to others. Your parents must be proud.'

I can think of nothing to say, so grin inanely.

'We hardly see him these days,' she continues. 'He never stops. Lesson plans, marking, meetings. Of course the admin takes over these days. Too much filling in of forms if you ask me, not enough actual teaching. And the children are allowed to do what they want now, the staff afraid to even tell them off. If they brought back a little more discipline, there wouldn't be the problems there are.' She raises her eyebrows at me, as if a great wisdom had just been shared.

'At least the holidays are long,' says her husband, crumbs of cake speckled in his beard. 'He's hoping to get a post back this way soon.'

Teaching isn't something I think of fondly now, but I nod anyway, still ignorant of why my presence is required. As recruitment drives go, it lacks subtlety.

I wonder if they know. My parents would have had to say something about my indefinite return home during term time; poor health is convenient for only so long.

It's my turn to speak but small talk seems beyond me. I try to think of something that could need my attention elsewhere, but then Mrs Poulter nods in the direction of my belly. 'And your mother tells us you're expecting . . . '

144

Flushed, I look to see where Mum is, but she's hiding in the kitchen. I aim for a genuine smile but it won't form, and I end up grimacing. I hadn't actually told my parents not to tell anyone outside of family; I just assumed they wouldn't.

'It's OK,' she says. 'We won't say anything.'

I try to form some words, unsure if I want to shout or just walk away.

'Martin's goddaughter has just had her first,' the woman continues. I presume Mr Poulter is Martin. 'A wondrous gift.' They smile at me in harmony and I get some sense of what this is about. The woman talks about the glory of childbirth, the privilege of bringing another into the world. The fulsome phrases stack up like a queue of circling aeroplanes. They continue like this for a few minutes, alternating like some double act, before allowing me to speak.

I work hard to compose myself. 'Are you worried I'm going to have it flushed away?' I say.

Mr Poulter almost chokes on the last of his second almond slice.

'Well, there are always alternatives,' his wife says, unmoved by my choice of words. 'All life is sacred. God loves all his children, however they come about.'

My mother has outdone herself. 'Come about?' I say.

'Yes.'

'You mean conceived.'

'Yes.'

'Then why don't you say that?'

Mum hears the rise in tone and comes in from the kitchen. 'How are we doing for tea?' she asks.

145

I stare at her, but she avoids my eyes. Taking the teapot, she returns to the kitchen.

'I haven't decided yet,' I say, which isn't true but I find the words empowering.

They manage to look crestfallen in unison.

'If you need to talk to someone . . . ' Mrs Poulter says.

'I'm fine, thank you.'

After a few moments' silence Mr Poulter asks whether I'll keep the child.

'I just said, I'm not sure yet.'

'We mean after the birth,' says his wife. 'You know, if you don't . . . '

'Flush it away? I think that's for me to decide.'

'There's lots of support out there, that's all we're saying.'

'Support?'

'There are plenty of couples out there,' says Mr Poulter, 'who can't have children. They wouldn't be told the circumstances of . . . '

'Conception,' his wife finishes.

'Why not?' I say.

'I'm sorry?'

'Why would that be kept from them?' They look at each other, confused by my question. 'If God loves all his children, why not tell them?'

'It's just easier that way.'

'I'm not giving the baby to anyone.'

'You're going to keep the child, on your own?' the woman says.

'If I have it, yes. Why wouldn't I?'

'It's just . . . '

'You think I couldn't love it?'

'A family home might be better. One where

146

the parents don't know. Where the mother and father love each other.'

'I can't work out if it's the fact I was raped that appals you, or that I'll be a single mother.'

'We just like to think of children having the best possible chance in life, to grow up in — '

'I think you can go now.'

'There's no need to rush into these things. Perhaps nearer the time. You might feel differently then.'

'I don't think so.'

As I show them to the door, Mum appears, her face a mix of guilt and disappointment. They cast her a sympathetic look as they leave.

I stare hard at my mother as we stand in the hallway. 'Did that just happen?' I say.

'Come on, love.'

'Why tell people? Those people?'

'I thought you'd want some options, some support. I was trying to help.'

'By encouraging me to give it away?'

'I didn't think you'd want to keep it, and — '

'And an abortion's too messy.'

'For goodness' sake.'

'Perhaps I could swap it for something, at one of your coffee mornings. A sponge cake. Or some quiche.'

'You're overreacting.'

'Is there a church raffle soon? First prize: an unborn baby. Think how many tickets it would sell.'

We look at each other, my outburst somehow different to every other one she's seen over the years.

'You're my mother,' I say in a more pleading tone, as I touch my hand to my tummy. 'This will be part of me, part of our family.'

She looks as if she might come to hold me, but I walk past her, telling her I'd appreciate nobody else finding out.

★　★　★

Dad is home. There's a tetchy air to him as he bangs about, slamming, mumbling. I haven't left my room since this morning. Mum called up, asked if I wanted lunch, but I ignored her. I listen to them converse but can't hear what is said. The church is a place my mother drags him to from time to time, but I don't imagine he had anything to do with the morning's events. He makes some coffee, then shuts himself in his study. I decide to give it five minutes before going down to share with him the hideousness of the Poulters' visit.

I remember as children we were told to be quiet when he was working, to play outside if possible. My brother and I would dare each other to knock on the door and run away, knowing only the mildest of rebukes would be issued on our capture. The parenting we received was a judicious blend of conservative and liberal, difficult to criticise now as adults. If there were any major traumas, any significant fallout, they were successfully hidden from us. They maintained a unified front, never undermined each other when setting rules. I can hardly remember an argument between them, yet this somehow didn't translate into demonstrative warmth beyond the minimum. They'd kiss goodbye, compliment each other when required, but otherwise it struck me as a companionship; passion, if it had once flourished, had long since withered.

Since returning home, spending hours staring at the same section of carpet or wall in numb thought and reflection, I realise I barely know my father beyond this superficial aspect. I presume there are more layers to him, that there are things that make him sad or despairing or excited, and yet he seems to just tick along, an engine that neither revs extravagantly nor stalls. I consider whether there were lovers before my mother; none was ever spoken of. I'm certain they've remained faithful, but you never know. The thought of either of them cheating both appals and fascinates me. It feels impossible to imagine my parents as anything other than with each other. Loyal, dutiful, unremarkable.

For the first time since I've been back I find myself wanting to talk to my father. His inability to refer specifically to what happened (if absolutely necessary he uses the words *that Tuesday*) has suited me until now. Mum asks daily if I'm all right, the inquiry almost rhetorical, her confusion still checked by the desire to avoid detail. But his silence intrigues me. I haven't seen him cry since I've come back, though that's not to say he hasn't. There was a hint of anger beneath the shock when they picked me up, but I've seen nothing since.

Announcing I was pregnant brought little

reaction; they didn't even ask whether the father might be someone else. Their faces exuded looks of weary acceptance, as if nothing I said could startle them now. Well, whatever you decide, we'll support you, said my mother, looking to my father for agreement that didn't come.

I go downstairs and open the study door. 'Can I come in?'

Dad, sitting at his desk, his back to me, mutters something, reads through paperwork, busily shuffles some sheets.

'Can we talk?' I say.

'Mmm?'

'I want to talk about the baby.' I judge the word baby easier for him to hear.

'I'm a bit busy.'

I go in anyway and close the door. 'I'm going to keep it,' I say. He stops reading for a moment, still with his back to me. 'I'm not letting . . . him . . . be the cause of any more violence.'

Dad writes something on a notepad, contemplates it. I realise he might think keeping it refers only to the birth. 'And I'm going to bring it up. We'll be its family.'

Still nothing, although he's stopped attending to his work, his body utterly still, as if even its breath has been suspended. The space between us feels thick with tension.

'Dad?' He swings his chair round, his face stupefied, taut with anguish. 'Please, Dad.'

'I don't understand,' he says after a pause.

'What happened can't be changed, but it's me who made this baby, my body that will carry it. It's nothing to do with him. I'm not going to kill it or give it to someone else to raise. I want us all to love it.'

His eyes water.

'It's not the baby,' he says.

'What do you mean?' He looks down, his head shaking slowly from side to side. 'Look at me, Dad.'

'I keep going over it in my head. It doesn't make sense.' A tear finally runs down his face. I want to go to him but don't; I can't take on his torment as well. It must be difficult to see the images without knowing whether they're the correct ones. I want to make it easier for him.

'You mean that night?' I say. 'Try not to think about it.' This sounds ridiculous, so I try, 'I'm all right. I'm safe now. He can't do anything else to me.'

He seems to only half listen, distracted by his own thoughts. Neither of us speaks for a while.

'He didn't have anything,' he says finally.

'What do you mean?'

'A weapon. He didn't have a weapon of any kind.'

'What?'

'He wasn't armed, was he? They usually have a knife or something.'

At first I miss his point, thinking perhaps he's angry at the lack of any prosecution so far, at the injustice of it all. But then I'm there, inside my father's head, the illumination absolute. All these weeks, I realise, he's tried to come to terms not with what happened to his daughter but how exactly I allowed it. I tense up, suddenly uncomfortable with the situation.

151

'No,' I say. 'He didn't.'

'You weren't drunk, or drugged?'

'No.'

'Perhaps he put something in a drink, like you read about. Did you leave him alone with your drink? It's easy to slip something in, there was a programme about it last year. Only takes a second. You'd have been helpless.'

'He didn't drug me.'

My father looks beseechingly at me, as if I'm withholding the answer to some tortuous riddle.

'But he's fifteen. I don't understand how . . . I mean the physics of it.'

'The what?'

'I'm just trying to understand.'

I try to take in the implication of what he's saying. Questions I've asked myself hundreds of times seem combative and abhorrent when uttered by someone else. 'You think I could have stopped him?'

'Fifteen. He's a boy. How could he — '

'A strong boy. I can't believe . . . I tried to get him off, Dad. I didn't just lie there.' Seeing that I'm crying, he gets up and walks towards me, softening a little. 'No, don't touch me.' I want this to be clear. 'You think . . . ' I try to choose my words with care, but he interrupts.

'You didn't have any injuries.' A tear winds down his cheek.

'Nothing visible; you know I don't bruise easily. I was sore for ages. He hurt me.'

'But he did force you?'

'Yes! What do you think happened?'

A silence leavens. I tell myself I wanted to talk

about it, to draw some reaction from my father. But not like this. I wonder whether my mother shares any of his disbelief.

'Why can't you accept what I say?'

'It just doesn't make sense. Why did you take so long? To tell someone. The police. Us.'

'I don't know. I was in shock. I couldn't believe it had happened.'

'But you let him in. And the wine.'

I force my voice to remain measured, aware that the truth, my truth, will have to be fought for. 'Why don't you ask me what I was wearing? Go on. How short my skirt was, how much cleavage was on display.'

'Oh, stop it.'

'Once he was there I thought we'd just talk about the work I'd set. I wanted to treat him like an adult.'

'But he isn't.'

'You don't need to tell me that.'

'And you fought back?'

I try to keep the imagery of that night away. I look at my father, at his desperation for answers that will help him understand. I want him to see without me telling him.

'Of course I fought back. I was scared. He was so angry. And strong. There was nothing I could do. I thought I was going to die.'

He looks confused by this. 'Die?'

'It's impossible to explain.'

He looks down, shaking his head, trying to picture the scene yet not wanting to. 'Your mother said he told the police it was consensual, that it wasn't . . . '

'Rape. The word's rape. Why don't you say it? Go on, just once. Say the word. Your daughter was raped. It doesn't matter what he said, I was raped. He pinned me down so I couldn't move — '

'All right.'

'He lifted up my skirt, tore my knickers off and forced his — '

'All right,' he shouts. He turns round and walks to the window.

'He raped me.'

Dad brings his fist down hard on the side of the desk, making me jump. 'Enough,' he says.

We just stand there, both wiping tears from our face. After a minute my mother leans in round the door, but says nothing. I push past her and go upstairs.

19

The man and woman have driven down again, to ask more questions. I watch them park, their plain clothes keeping curtain-twitching in the road to a minimum.

I let them in. They smile weakly. The tracksuit bottoms and T-shirt I wore last time have been swapped for an old bohemian dress I'd forgotten I owned. The man looks me up and down in the way men think women don't see. I offer them tea but they decline. They won't be as long as last time, the woman says. They sit together on the sofa.

'We interviewed Jamie O'Sullivan last week,' she says. 'His parents were required by law to be there.' The scene appears in my mind, his parents' reaction on being told. I'd never met them but knew about the problems at home. 'His version of events differs from yours, though.'

I suppose I'd expected this. 'In what way?' I say.

The man takes out a notepad, opens it and reads. 'He says he came to your flat on

November the sixteenth, the night of the alleged assault.'

The word takes a little while to register, jarring as if it's from another language, or not a word at all. It seems unremarkable in some ways, a police idiom, standard speak. Yet it represents something bigger than itself, the semantics grander than the sound it makes.

I realise that there's a different atmosphere from their last visit, a formality that was absent before. I'd asked my mother to be out of the house this time, to protect her from detail she wouldn't want to hear, detail she'd caught fragments of the last time. But, despite our recent fallout, I wish she were here.

'Alleged?' I say, as if the word has a bitter taste to it.

The man ignores me. 'Jamie says you gave him a glass of wine as soon as he got there.' He says this as if smugly moving a chess piece into a winning position. I hadn't mentioned the wine before. They both look at me.

'He had a glass, yes.'

'And you poured it for him?' he says.

'No, I mean yes. It was already poured.'

'And he drank it?'

I nod.

'Was there any particular reason you gave one of your pupils alcohol, Miss Jacobs?' Unlike his colleague, he prefers my surname. His question sounds melodramatic, constructed by some slick prosecution lawyer.

'I didn't give it to him. I'd already poured it when the buzzer went.' They look at each other

156

briefly, then back to me. 'I thought he was someone else.'

'You didn't mention the wine before, in your statement.'

'I didn't think it important.'

They both frown a little, him more demonstrably.

'Was it a big glass?'

'I don't know. Medium.'

'Can you show us?'

'Show you?'

'Perhaps with a glass here.' He motions towards the kitchen.

I do as they ask, sensing that everything has changed since they spoke to Jamie. What did I expect? That he'd say, yes, I raped her. My teacher tried to help me with work, she let me into her home and I raped her.

They stare at the glass like scientists.

'About two hundred millilitres?' he says to her. She nods and he writes this down.

'And he drank all of it?'

'Yes.'

'And you had the same amount?'

'I think so. Yes. No, I was on my second glass.'

'Second?'

'For God's sake,' I say. 'I tried to stop him drinking it.'

'Two glasses,' he dictates to himself.

We fall into silence. The man makes more notes before continuing. 'You then got Jamie to read from a book.'

'I told you all this last time.'

'I know. We're just trying to clarify a few

157

things, make sure it all adds up.'

'Yes. He'd lost his copy, so I gave him mine.'

'He says after this you watched a DVD on the sofa. A film.'

'No, that's not what happened.'

'He says that when the programme finished he leaned over and kissed you and that you kissed him back.'

'No, I did not.' I feel light headed, the truth spiralling away from me.

'But you let him kiss you?'

'No, not really. I just . . . '

'But you did kiss?'

'He kissed me.'

'Which you let him do?'

'I tried to stop him.'

'You tried but couldn't? How did you try?'

'I . . . closed my mouth.'

'But you didn't move away?'

'No, I couldn't.'

More note-taking.

'And you were on the sofa at this point?'

'No, by the door. He kissed me when I was showing him out. I'd told him to leave, after his comments.'

He flicks back a few pages of his pad. 'About your affair with a colleague?'

'It wasn't an affair on my part. But yes. Jamie was crude. I asked him to go.'

The man turns back a few more of the pages. 'He says after you kissed for a while you undid his trousers . . . '

'That isn't what happened.' I look to the woman, hopeful my disgust is mirrored in her face, but she remains impassive.

'And that you played with him until he had an erection.'

I let out a laugh, the word somehow hilarious. 'He's lying. You must know he's lying.'

'Then you had consensual intercourse on the floor, which lasted about ten minutes, after which he left.'

'God, this is ridiculous. Why would I have sex with one of my pupils?' The man looks at me, as if I'm going to answer my own question.

'The trouble, Miss Jacobs,' he says, 'is the lack of evidence to confirm your account.'

'My *account?*'

The woman tries to repair some of the damage. 'We're not saying we don't believe you . . . '

'What about the examination?' I say.

'There was no real sign of any force,' she says. 'No bruising. None of his skin under your nails.'

'I told you, I washed him off me.' I look hard at the woman. 'Wouldn't you have?'

'An earlier examination might have found something,' she says. 'And if you hadn't thrown the clothes out.'

My knickers, stretched, a little ripped, had gone out with the rubbish two days later. A foolish act, I came to realise, but the technicalities of law, the pragmatics of evidence had been beyond my thoughts. I just wanted the event erased. The rest of what I wore that night, my mother has since disposed of for me — to a charity shop, a clothes bin, the outside bin — I've no idea.

The man coughs an officious little cough. 'Waiting weeks to report it doesn't help your case,' he says. 'Sometimes the memory,' he starts, but decides against it.

The events of that night begin to form in my mind, but their focus has dulled a little with each day, their sound, like a cassette's music that's been recorded over, only faintly heard beneath the notes of my emerging life. Having worked so hard to banish the detail to some remote chamber in my mind, recalling it is like summoning a week-old dream. Reality tainted by the distance I've given it. Reduced to a version.

'But I'm pregnant,' I say. 'That must prove something.'

'Only that you had intercourse,' he says. 'We can do a DNA test on your baby but it won't demonstrate a lack of consent.'

I consider his choice of phrase, how it seems so removed from what I remember happening. 'So that's it?'

'Not exactly,' says the woman. 'Jamie's parents are pushing for charges against you.'

A wave of revulsion sweeps through me. 'Against me?'

'He is underage. They say you abused your position.'

'This is too much. You don't believe he did it, do you?'

'We're not saying that. Just that there's no evidence. If it goes to court, it will come down to who the jury believe. The CPS might not even let it get that far; non-stranger rape is very difficult to prove.'

'So now I'm a suspect.'

'We have to look at everything. If there's no evidence an assault took place, you've already admitted to having intercourse with a minor.'

I should find this revelation disgusting but it's almost a predictable footnote. They tell me I'll be notified of any developments in the case, that I'm to tell them if I'm going anywhere.

As they head to the door, the woman looks at my stomach, managing a sympathetic smile of sorts. 'Are you going to keep it?' she says.

20

When anger rises, I suspect I'm supposed to embrace it, allow it to liberate and empower me. But it just feels like something else he's done to me. To feel anger is to invite him back in, to affirm his existence. I have learned that you can't be angry in a vacuum; hate needs its focus, a channel to travel along, a destination. Feeling nothing is still preferable, something I've become good at.

But there are times I have no choice but to let him in. In my dreams he takes various forms — old boyfriends from college, Nick, my father even — though it's always still him. (It's the familiarity I find the most disturbing on waking.) In these surreal narratives we're less formal with each other at first, no obvious age or power disparity. Sometimes the roles are reversed and he's telling me about the sonnets, or quoting Yeats. We're usually still in my flat, but I might be a girl again, Jamie the older teacher.

We drink wine and he gets me to read, usually from the same Harper Lee, although that too gets distorted, somehow woven into my own life. I become the one on trial as Gregory Peck asks again and again why I gave him the alcohol. All I can think is how wrong it is that the avuncular Atticus Finch has become the prosecution lawyer. At that point I look at my parents in the gallery, their faces rich with disapproval. And then Atticus holds up the book, the novel he's in, asking if it's suitable material to teach a young boy and I stand and say yes, yes it is, and that he's not a boy, not a young one anyway, and gasps fill the courtroom, my father whispering into my mother's ear, and Atticus is shouting now, about Nick and whether I knew he was married and whether he knows I aborted his baby, and I shout that I'm keeping it, I'm keeping my baby, and then Nick's wife stands up in the gallery, her daughters by her side, and she screams that I deserved it, that I'm a slut, before the judge orders her to be removed, and as two men march her away, I mouth that I'm sorry, and that, yes, I deserved it.

And then as the court settles down, an exhibit is introduced, a knife sealed in a clear bag, only when it's passed to me to inspect it becomes the comb from the examination, my pubic hair still caught between the teeth. I'm asked to identify it. Yes, I say, it's the same one, and it's shown to the all-male jury who laugh as they inspect it, pulling at the hairs. The doctor from the examination is called to the witness box, where he stands beside me, snapping on surgical gloves, mint still on his breath. More questions come. Is the comb, now a knife again, the same one Jamie had with him that night? I look around the court, my face desperate, beseeching, everyone waiting for my answer. Just answer the question. No, I say, he didn't have a knife. The doctor confirms this. More gasps. Silence, please, silence, the judge says. And as Atticus repeats that Jamie didn't have a weapon, my father stands and walks out.

Variations on this play out in my sleep, my unconscious mind as creative as it is cruel.

Waking after this, anger can find a foothold. Firstly I'm angry with myself that my mind can allow this dream sequence to occur, then with my parents and their judgements. With the Poulters. With him.

I know the rage won't last, so I indulge it before it fades, crafting my first revenge fantasy. I'm standing in the evening shadows near his house, a week or so afterwards. He walks back from a session in the park with his mates, swigging a can of lager, abusing passers-by. I hear him belch as he nears the alley. An empty can is crushed, then tossed into the road with a deafening clatter. There is laughter. I walk out slowly and stand in front of them, formidable, imposing. As calm as I've ever been. His friends run off, scattering like cowards. My strength is absolute, evoked by everything I wasn't that night. He's shocked to see me, a little embarrassed, before bravado kicks in. All right, Miss? he says. Read any good books lately? There's not a trace of fear in me. The street is empty. In the silence I push the knife in slowly, until the blade is completely in his belly and only

165

the hilt is visible, which I let go of. Our eyes connect and I can see he accepts what I've done as fair. There are no more words. I walk calmly away.

And then, unbidden, I relive the build-up to the real events, as if allowing them to fade would give succour to other versions. I'm able to do this by viewing them from above, an omniscient narrator, detached, impervious.

I recall the buzzer in my flat resounding above the music. I push the small button, weary at Nick's insistence. Turning the latch I hear the communal door bang shut downstairs. I fetch a glass for him, wondering if fatigue will see me soften my stance, wondering whether you can take back someone who isn't yours.

After filling the glasses I turn to see Jamie standing there.

'Hello, Miss.'

'Jamie, what . . . '

He sees the wine and smiles. 'That for me?'

'No, I thought you were someone else.'

He walks over to the table. 'Don't wanna waste it.'

I tell him no, and when he ignores me I try to grab it from him but am too slow.

'Come on, Miss. Not in school now.'

He walks past me, surveying the room. 'This where you live, then?'

'Our session's over for this week, Jamie.'

'Yeah, I know.'

Again I try to take his wine, but he holds it high, just beyond my reach. Inches from him I can smell his unwashed clothes, the cigarettes on

166

his breath. He walks around the room before sitting on the sofa.

'How did you know where I live?' I say. He chooses to ignore this. 'I'm rather busy, Jamie. Is there something you wanted?'

He leans back, scanning the films on the shelf.

'These any good? Not heard of any of them. You wanna watch one?'

There's something absurd about him, sitting there, every now and then taking a gulp of wine. Realising I need to take control, I ask if he's found his book, the one I bought him for our sessions, but he ignores me.

'How long you lived here?'

I go to the bookcase, slide my own copy out and toss it on to his lap. I sit down opposite him. 'I want you to read the trial chapter,' I say.

He huffs, puts his empty glass down and flicks through some pages.

'Chapter eighteen.'

'What now?' he says.

I had meant before next week but think, why not? 'Go on, then.'

He stares hard at me, as if we're back in class on that first day. His voice is mocking as he reads. ' "Thomas-Robinson-reached-around-ran-his-fingers-under-his-left-arm-and-lifted-it-he-guided-his-arm-to-the-Bible-and . . . " '

I lean over and snatch the book from him. 'Slowly. Savour the words — it's not a shopping list. 'Thomas Robinson reached around' comma 'ran his fingers under his left arm and lifted it' full stop 'He guided his arm to the Bible'.' I pass the book back.

167

Anger flickers across his face but passes. 'It's fucking boring.'

'That's because you're saying the words without thinking about them.'

'What's there to think about? It's not real.'

'Try to imagine the scene, see it in your mind.'

He flicks his fringe out of his eyes, takes a packet of tobacco from his pocket and starts to roll a cigarette. 'Not in here,' I say and he puts it away with a grunt. For the first time since the episode in class, a tension grows between us. The lesson with Simon Phillips had gone so well; I sensed a real breakthrough seeing him out of class, a glimpse of someone beneath the bravado. But perhaps I've taken on too much with Jamie.

'Try it again,' I say. 'Picture the people as you read it. And slow down.'

He looks at the page, then back at me. 'How old are you?'

'The chapter, Jamie.'

'Come on, Miss.'

'Old enough.'

He considers my answer for a while, then, 'They say you done it with Mr Ashworth. That he's gonna leave his missus for you.'

Disarmed, I try to formulate a response, but my vocal cords seem paralysed as my mind flashes through all the implications. Images of whispering colleagues in the staffroom morph into a playground of taunting pupils. We'd been so careful.

'Seems you're not old enough to ignore playground gossip,' I say.

He looks around the room. 'Have you done it

here? In your bed? On the floor?'

'Jamie . . . '

'Don't matter, Miss. I've done it loads too.'

'I'm sure you have. Right, back to the chapter.'

He considers the book for a moment before tossing it on the floor and holding my stare. I stand, feeling the wine a little in my head.

'Jamie, you're not helping yourself. Go and pick it up.'

He stands but heads towards the table with his glass.

'No more, Jamie.'

He starts to pour the wine. I walk over and try to take it from him, but he holds the bottle firmly for a few seconds before releasing it. He fronts up to me, a sneer breaking out on his face.

'Are you going to do some work?'

Again he surveys the room, before saying, 'Do you take him in your mouth, Miss? Swallow it?'

'Right, you can go. This isn't going to work. I was stupid to think it could.'

He looks hard at me, as if to say the dynamics are different here, outside the classroom.

'Go on, go home.'

'It's rude not to let a guest finish his drink.'

I raise my voice a little. 'Goodbye, Jamie.'

He swaggers across the room, everything at his pace. I follow him to the door. As we get there he turns, leans forward and kisses me clumsily on the mouth. I jump back, recoiling as if from an electric shock.

'What are you doing?'

'Come on, Miss, just a bit of fun. Nobody will know.'

169

'Just get out. Now.'

I reach for the door latch but he pushes me into the wall and kisses me again, this time harder. He tastes of tobacco and wine and for a second it could be Nick. I try to free myself but his hands, with strength beyond his years, hold my head like a vice. There is a sense of it being a dream, like something I've read or watched. For a moment I don't resist, assuming inertia will lead to embarrassment on his part, but then he forces his tongue into my mouth, wet, probing. I think to bite it, but instead close my lips as tightly as I can. He gives up trying to kiss me, instead putting a hand on my breast, his eyes a study of fascination as they watch his fingers squeeze me. I knock his hand away. He smiles and replaces it. We repeat this sequence several times, almost a battle of wills rather than strength, Jamie smirking throughout.

Some rational part of my mind kicks in, as if pondering a problem that requires solving. I just need to reverse whatever I've done that gave him the wrong impression. Save both our faces, limit the damage. But he grips my breast harder and I call out in pain. I slap his face and there's a pause, as if neither of us knows what to do or say. Jamie backs away, just a step, but keeps eye contact while feeling the side of his face. The mischievous look is gone from his eyes now, replaced by something I've not seen before.

'Get out,' I say and again reach for the door, but I find myself on the floor, my senses trying to re-plot the room. I know that he's punched or slapped me, though I saw nothing coming. A shrill note sounds in my head and I try to focus on something static around me. My mouth tastes warm and coppery and I spit out a mulch of blood on to the carpet. I'm aware of him standing over me.

'Sorry, Miss,' he says. 'You shouldn't have hit me.'

'Please, just go, Jamie.'

In the corner of my eye I see him move away. I hear his steps approach the door and wait to hear the latch turn, worrying less now about saving face. In ten seconds it will be over.

But there's no sound. I want to turn round but I'm frozen, the room silent save for my breathing. I sense him by the door, eyes fixed on me. I consider shouting at him, but remain with my back to the door.

I tell myself it will be fine, that I shouldn't have pushed him so much. This is my fault. I'm the adult here.

'Out,' I say firmly.

He moves across the room in less than a second.

★   ★   ★

Afterwards, once it's over, I hear him in the bathroom. The gap where a flush should sound is filled with the distinctive lighting of a Zippo: click, flick, click.

I'm still alive, I tell myself.

He comes back into the room. I wonder if there's to be more. I force myself not to move. He just stands behind me.

171

'You OK?' he says after a minute, the anger gone from his voice, replaced by a kind of concern.

I say nothing.

'Do you want me to get you anything?'

I turn on my side, bringing my knees to my chest, my back to him. I study the fabric of the carpet, trying to focus on the pattern.

He touches the back of my head lightly and I flinch, shuffling away, towards a corner.

I feel something being placed on me. The throw from the sofa. And then I feel his hand by my face. He's holding a few strands of my hair, which he tucks behind my ear.

Maybe another minute passes before the door to the flat is opened. 'I'll see you at school, Miss,' are his last words. The door is shut quietly. Across the floor, through watered eyes, I can make out the word *Mockingbird* on the book's spine.

21

A letter arrives, from my employer, the envelope tells me. I rang last week to say I was in Devon, that I was still unwell. These viruses can take a while, the woman in admin said, barely able to keep the sarcasm from her voice.

I assume the police would have visited the school by now. Interviews conducted. McKellan, the head, would have been told that the matter was confidential, but it would get out somewhere — like water, always finding a way. And then the pupils will hear. Parents will phone one another, the paper will request an interview with McKellan, the editor excited, the word scandal used. There will be as many versions as those telling them.

Mum is hanging around as I open the letter, so I go upstairs and close the door. I sit on the bed, surveying each wall of the bedroom I've had since childhood. It's been kept vaguely feminine but is essentially a guest room, like my brother's, that easily converts back when I stay. When we moved here as children we fought for this room.

A deal was struck — I can't remember what — and Michael yielded graciously. It was the view we both wanted: I got Cornish hills and a setting sun, he was left with the main road and the nearby Texaco garage. As recompense he was further from our parents' room, allowing a variety of teenage activities that I couldn't possibly have contemplated.

For the first time in my life, I realise I miss my brother. Since being told, he phones once or twice a week and I've come to rely on these chats. He tells me about the country he's in, the people he spends his days with. I push him for every last detail — sounds, smells, colour — straining my senses to experience them also. And when he finishes talking, I fire another question at him, still hungry for detail of a world that isn't this one. He seems to know only the vaguest inquiry about my life is desired. Is Mum annoying me? Am I the talk of the town? We share a joke about front pages of the local paper we grew up with here, the indignity and fervour mustered from comically parochial matters. As we exchange mock headlines — *Rabbit raids allotments; Traffic brought to a standstill by red light* — I realise it's the first time I've laughed since the incident.

He speaks of a girlfriend, something serious perhaps. I'd like her, he says. He always ends asking if I'm OK, sensing that OK is the best I can hope for. Although impractical now, he still renews the invitation to join him. He'll try to get home in a month or so, he says. Please do, I say once he's hung up. You can have this room, I think, then realise he wouldn't want it if he brings someone with him. Picturing this makes me feel like a teenager again, Michael's first girlfriend staying overnight after days of solemn parental discussion. I could hear some of the words my mother and father used as they fretted about it in bed, sensing my father squirm at the need for a decision.

As for my parents, they made love occasionally, birthdays mostly, attempting but failing to render the act silent. As a girl I would put my fingers in my ears, hum, and then share the disgust with my friends the next day in the playground, revolting them with detail they both wanted and didn't want to hear.

But I remember no education — outside of the pragmatics we received at school — no mention of birds and bees, not even childhood accounts of storks that despatched bundles down the chimney. The particulars beyond the mechanics came from our peers — a spectrum of knowledge that ranged from limited but direct experience to a host of fantastical assumptions that both terrified and intrigued. Boys, apparently, given half the chance, liked nothing more than to insert as many fingers as possible inside you. The more the better, as far as they were concerned. It was somehow a coup for them, how many they got in, yet unbecoming for the girl. How did you know, one girl asked, how many they were using? Apart from the pain, you didn't, until you heard about it at school the next week. How many were possible? Nobody knew; the rumours gave no upper limit, though presumably a boy ran out of digits at five, at least on one hand. I remember this terrifying me as a thirteen year old; that it was some essential ceremony to creating a baby, a prelude that paved the way for the enigmatic main event. In class I would look at boys' hands, dirty with bitten nails, gauging the amount of pain I'd feel by the size of their fingers. Nobody contradicted this. And as sex had no other purpose, I assumed it would be my duty one day.

As younger children, perhaps six and four, my brother and I had been curious about the word, enough to run in the kitchen one day, asking our mother what sex was. She fumbled with a few words, before announcing it was when two people pulled their pants down and kissed. So we did. Right there in front of her. A quick peck on the lips, before running off in giggling innocence, shocking visitors for weeks with the declaration that we'd *done sex*.

And now, as an adult living at home again, I listen to my parents' nocturnal movements once again, wondering how I'd feel about hearing them make love now. I presume, perhaps wrongly, that they no longer do. And if they did, that my return and its circumstances have led to a cessation.

I think of my partners, as people term them. Just the two at university, which felt like plenty but probably brought the average down for my year. Despite them being older, I seemed to lead the way in lovemaking, pointing out that speed alone wasn't the pinnacle. Neither frivolous nor earnest, these relationships bestowed my time at

176

college with an innocence and warmth I can now barely evoke. Dreamlike liaisons, tender and languorous. Bodies entwined in the long hours of an afternoon. Holding hands between lectures. Laughing. Lovers unfettered by the squalls of reality. But most of all, I felt safe.

And then Nick, who, despite his sexual maturity, made love as if laying claim to something. Pleasure, rather than something intrinsic, was to be extracted from one another. Our connection was one of flesh alone. Innocence had flown.

$\star$　$\star$　$\star$

I finish opening the letter. Dear Anna, it begins, the informality an unexpected touch. I glance down to see McKellan's signature. I'd only met him a few times. He was a young man for his position. Initially, there was a tour of the school, ending in his office where the door was 'never closed', should I need anything. He'd been less than eager to sanction the extra lessons, stipulating a trial period wouldn't be extended if improved grades weren't observed.

The letter says he has had several meetings with the detectives who came here. The word allegation appears twice, then Jamie's name. He'd been suspended pending the police investigation.

It continues: *On a personal level I am disappointed you did not inform me immediately, instead telling us that you were off with a virus. This has placed both the school and myself in an invidious position.*

And finishes: *I think it best that you remain on sick leave until the police have concluded their inquiry, at which time I will write to you again.*

I tear the letter in two and place it in the bin.

22

As he sat behind the drystone wall, waiting for the last of the light to fade, the man thought about the first time he'd seen her. She had singled him out for attention even then. What she did, with that poem, had made him angry, and it'd taken years to forgive her. He told his classmates that he just went along with it, that he read it because he wanted to, that he knew what the words meant, but he saw they didn't believe him. The teasing had lasted weeks. He made an example of the first boy who mocked him — a headlock allowed half a dozen blows to the face before a teacher pulled him off — but this didn't stop the girls, who seemed to assume they were exempt from such treatment, taunting him, quoting lines the teacher had made him read out. Funny thing was he still remembered some of the words even today: *I have spread my dreams under your feet.* They said you never forgot the teachers who made a difference.

But then she was gone. And the one who replaced her wasn't nearly as young or pretty.

179

He remembered the police with all their questions about consent. It wasn't a word he completely understood at the time, until the woman explained that Miss Jacobs said she hadn't wanted to have sex. Maybe not to begin with, he wanted to tell them. But she soon came round. They said it could go to court, that it was important to establish the truth. After a while, though, they seemed to accept his account of what happened. How they'd drunk wine and then kissed, how she would look at him in class. As they left, he'd heard the policeman tell his parents that the teacher probably made it up as she was worried about losing her job. His father, uninterested in what had happened at the teacher's flat, waited until later to let him know what he thought about him bringing the police to the house. Nothing visible, the marks always hidden by clothes.

She never came back to school, Miss Jacobs. That night was the last he saw of her, until the News the other day, a man with a microphone asking her questions.

After watching it he put her name, the new one, into a search engine, but there were too many results. Adding 'Dartmoor' (where the prison was) narrowed it down, and a few minutes later he discovered she was now some sort of artist. There were even details about an upcoming exhibition, as well as a home phone number. The picture on her website didn't look much like the woman on TV, nor particularly like the last time he'd seen her. He'd copied it to his computer anyway, using two different programs to enhance the quality, but it still became grainy when he zoomed in. At five hundred per cent, the pixels of one of her eyes filled his screen with a grey-green that he left up until leaving the flat to come here.

The woman at the pub had seemed uncertain about letting him have the room on a daily basis. Usually only do weekends or whole weeks, she'd said. He could try the bed and breakfast two miles away if he wanted. The stand-off ended when he agreed on three nights up front. He was told the front door would be locked just after closing time. If he wanted the bedding changed he should be out by ten in the morning. He said that wasn't necessary.

He bought a local paper from the only shop in the small town. There was a post office, a couple of pubs, but little else. He wondered why anyone would choose to live here, high up in the middle of nowhere, battered by rain and wind. Walking back to his room he noticed a large grey building dominating the side of the hill and recognised it as the one in the news report. Fences and stone walls separated it from the nearby houses, which were dwarfed in the foreground. It didn't look like somewhere you escaped from easily.

Looking over the wall at the cottage now, he could see its lights begin to glow in the early evening. He'd set off from the pub just after lunch, a long, circuitous route that allowed him to see the house from a few of the higher hills. The fleece and hat he'd bought lent him a certain authenticity, but he was glad not to have met any walkers today.

There were two lights on upstairs, neither room with its curtains drawn. He wondered how many people lived there with Miss Jacobs. Once the darkness had fallen further, he crossed the garden. As he did, a girl appeared in one of the upstairs windows. She was about ten or eleven, he guessed, her blonde hair in a loose ponytail. He stopped, confident she couldn't see him but still feeling exposed. She looked out into the dark, over his head, before drawing the curtains.

He continued round the side of the house and stood where he could see the kitchen. It was nearly an hour before someone appeared. A man, perhaps ten or more years older than him. He'd seen him coming and going in the Land Rover. He moved about the kitchen, made a phone call, took something from a cupboard. A few minutes later, he was joined by Miss Jacobs, and they sat around a table talking. This time the binoculars focused perfectly on her face and despite her movement as she spoke, he could study her features in detail. Her hair was lighter and shorter than before. It fell to just past her shoulder and every now and then she tucked a few strands behind an ear, like she used to in class. She didn't seem to be wearing any make-up, which made her seem rather plain. Her jumper looked too large on her. It was almost upsetting to see her look so much older. Forty or so, he guessed. He watched as she cupped a mug with both hands, neither drinking from it nor placing it down.

Thinking back to the letter, the one she'd sent his parents suggesting extra lessons, made it all feel so recent. His mother hardly read it once she saw it was from the school. Just left it lying about. He knew it was something to do with the incident in class, that Miss Jacobs felt bad for making him look such an idiot. She couldn't say sorry in front of everyone; that would look bad for her. And so she'd created a way they could meet after school. He waited till his father was out and his mother was three drinks into the evening before suggesting some extra lessons would be a good idea. His poor mother nearly collapsed with the shock.

'You want to do more English?' she said, before scribbling a barely legible reply.

When his father found out, it was already arranged. 'Long as it don't fucking cost anything' was his only comment on the matter.

There were a few weeks at school before the first lesson. It was like their secret. He looked at her without looking at her, something he'd perfected. Little glances. When a friend was talking to him, he looked into the distance, pretended to listen, using it as cover. If her eyes did meet his, he'd shift his stare a degree or two to the side, sense when she'd turned away and move back again.

He would look around at the others to see if any of them were looking at her the same way, but they weren't. When they messed about and she had to tell them off, he wanted to hurt them, make them listen, even if what she was saying was boring, which it usually was, but he didn't care.

He used to try to predict what clothes she'd

wear each day — his favourites were the cardigans that made her tits look bigger and the boots with the buckles on the side. It was strange to both hate her for the thing with the poem yet want to do things with her.

She wasn't the first. He'd fucked that girl who worked in the newsagents, the one in the year above him. They'd got drunk on cider at some party and ended up in the park, sharing fags, talking about how much they hated their parents. She didn't want to do it at first either, saying she had to get back to her friends. But it was obvious: why go to the park with him if she didn't want to get it on? Getting her jeans down took forever as she fought back. And because she wouldn't keep still it hurt like mad and he was sore for days down there. Afterwards he lit them both a fag, but she just sat there snivelling, not smoking hers. He asked if she wanted him to walk her back to the party but she shook her head. A week later he went into the shop but the man said she didn't work there any more.

And he forgot all about her when Miss Jacobs started.

After she wrote to his parents, the days he didn't have English depressed him, and he'd go out of his way to catch a glimpse of her. If he stood behind the basketball court at lunchtime, he could see into the staffroom, where she sometimes went. The male teachers all fawned around her, dirty old bastards. She wasn't interested in old married farts; they were wasting their time. There was a rumour, about one teacher — Ashworth, the history guy — but it didn't matter. It wouldn't last.

Sometimes, in class, she told him off, if he was looking out of the window and not paying attention. He knew she didn't mean it. It was a code really, to let him know she was thinking about him. A chance to say his name, to look at him. She couldn't be seen to have favourites.

And then the time came for the first lesson. The day seemed to last forever, and when he got home there was still an hour to kill. He made himself some tea early, hoping his father wouldn't come back from the pub, then set off on the mile or so walk back to school.

It was strange when he first got there. Awkward. She gave him a can of Coke and they sat at a table. Her clothes were the same as the ones she wore in class, which disappointed him a little. The night before, he'd masturbated to the image of her in a tight skirt and low top. She didn't make any reference to the poem incident, so he didn't bring it up. Instead they went through a book, she talked about the story in it, asked him what stories he liked. It got almost as boring as class. At the end of it, she even set him extra homework. He thought about trying it on with her then — perhaps using his knowledge of the history teacher — but he couldn't bring himself to and she kept talking so much. He walked home across town in the dark, angry, frustrated, vowing that the next time wouldn't be as dull.

But it was because of her that he had something to do in prison, as for the first time in his life he read a book, boring as it was. Several books in fact, perhaps ten by the time he was released. Some, even once he'd finished them, didn't make any sense; he kept reading them anyway, waiting for something to happen, which often it didn't.

Lost in thought, he almost didn't hear the boy come out into the courtyard, the footsteps almost upon him when he realised. It was too late to retreat, so he leaned in close to the wall of the barn, keeping as still as possible in the gloom. If the boy came around the side, he would have no choice. (His probation officer always talked about choices, that everyone could make them — but sometimes circumstances took over. You couldn't avoid all the triggers.) But instead of walking right into him, the boy opened the barn door and disappeared inside. A small gap where the wall had crumbled allowed him to see inside. Just a few feet away, the boy collected some logs from a pile, stacking them in the wicker basket he'd brought out. A large torch had been placed on the surface of an old chest, allowing him to see what he was doing.

A nice little family, he thought, as he watched the boy. It was always unlikely she lived alone, although driving down he'd hoped for this. His fantasies, as ever, had been detailed. Pulling up in his car, Miss Jacobs would see him from a window, at first not recognising him, but once he got out she would smile, like she used to in the staffroom when she spoke to that history teacher, and invite him in. All that business with the police, she'd say, had been forgotten. She thought about him often, thought about that night. How she had to resist him then because of her job, but that really she'd wanted to do it as well. That she'd never done it like that before. Or since. As a bloke on his wing used to like saying, once they get it that way, they don't want it any other.

But when he got here it seemed she had herself a right piece of domestic bliss. A big house with a garden. A family. All the things they'd told him could be his once he was better. Things he should aspire to.

The boy stopped collecting wood for a moment, looking around the walls of the barn, as if sensing someone was there. His breath rose through the torchlight in little bursts. The roof of the barn creaked a little in the wind above them. You can sense me, the man thought, but you can't see me.

The boy placed a few more logs in the basket before he went back in the house and all was quiet again.

23

The exhibition was well attended — forty, maybe fifty people, all milling about in twos and threes. Anna had the gallery to thank for the turnout. There was a time you used to just send out a few flyers, a poster here and there, word of mouth; now every facet of electronic communication and discourse was exploited: email, Facebook, Twitter. Events were pushed down people's throats, built up weeks, sometimes months in advance. Reminders. Reminders of reminders.

Selling herself didn't come easily. We need an artist's statement, they had said. For the blurb. Give people a sense of who you are, your aesthetics. Anna wrote about the moor, the materials it provided, how she drew inspiration from it. It's a little dry, they said. Needs something more of the person, a USP. You've got to package yourself.

She should be grateful. Work had to be sold. What would she do instead? The self-promotion, creating a profile, an image — she knew it was necessary. But why did art make people chase the artist? Why wasn't the art enough? She loathed the attention. People expected talk of creative anguish, the revealing of a muse. They wanted to be able to say to friends who saw her piece in their lounge that they'd conversed with its creator. They wanted a dinner party anecdote.

Anna knew she was being unfair. This was the choice she made when her pots ceased being functional — when she was happy for them to be termed art. And now instead of making things for people to eat and drink from, to cook and store things in, she turned clay that had spent millions of years in the ground into showpieces that sold for several times more than the rustic tableware she began making more than ten years ago. By way of compensation she told herself the Saxons and Celts used to make jewellery as well, but it didn't feel the same. Jewellery drew something out of the person wearing it; it adorned them. A pot on display had something hedonistic about it, about the person showing it. It was attempting to manipulate those looking at it, to affect them. It made her feel pretentious. She didn't want to be an artist, just someone who made things that people could use.

The effusive gallery manager was directing people to the canapés and cheap champagne in the knowledge they'd buy more after a glass or two. The soft lighting, the jazz drifting through the room were all part of the package.

The exhibition's theme was sustainability. Everyone was into it, the manager had told Anna. She thought he'd meant the concept, but then realised he was talking about sales. There would be sculpture tomorrow, photography later in the week. The pieces would be on show for a month. We want art to make people think about the planet, the brochure said. To challenge the way they live. So, her pots were to have a message. Again her lack of gratitude seemed unreasonable.

She looked around the room. Bits of card featured below each of her pieces, describing how the granite plateau the moor sat on turned to clay powder, which she mixed with water from the spring. Then there was the feldspar from the riverbed near the house that she used to make her glazes, recipes carefully worked out over years. Monochrome photographs of her at the wheel and kiln were unnecessarily stylish.

Robert looked at her from across the room and smiled awkwardly. It was hardly his thing either, and he looked incongruous in work boots and a woollen jumper.

'Do you really need me there?' he'd asked.

'No, but I'd like it.'

'I'm not dressing up.'

'I didn't think you would. Treat it like you're going for a pint in the Warren.'

Anna had considered a dress. In the end a long skirt and jumper felt right. A little make-up.

That the prisoner had been captured had allowed her to relax, to dismiss the anxiety that had started to consume her.

She surprised herself by winking at Robert as he shuffled around the room's edge, an innocuous gesture that perhaps signalled a returning intimacy. The lifting of the pressure of tonight might be all it took. Following him around and looking increasingly bored were Paul and Megan. It was an excuse to stay out late for Megan, but Paul would surely rather be elsewhere and he'd shocked them by agreeing to come. He fell behind the others, loitering around the table of wine. Anna caught his eye, letting him know she'd seen him. He feigned innocence and, his guard down, they shared a rare smile.

Further along, Megan was looking proud, stopping at the pots she'd watched Anna make, perhaps hoping a grown-up would ask her about one of them.

Anna's parents arrived late, looking more curious than proud. They'd always regarded it as a hobby, something their daughter hid away to do while Robert worked to support them. Anna would have enjoyed telling them she earned more than her husband last month.

Megan skipped up to her grandparents, narrowly missing a plinth with several hundred pounds' worth of ceramics balanced on it. She flung herself around her grandmother, her grandfather patted her head.

It was simplistic to say they loved her more than Paul. They just loved her differently. Without condition, without prejudice. They understood the process that made her, its beautiful lack of ambiguity. When Robert phoned them from the hospital to announce Megan's arrival, their reaction, the emotions, were easily found. A girl. A little over seven pounds. Her father's mouth, her mother's eyes. How wonderful, as if it were almost a surprise.

They knew Robert didn't know everything. That Anna needed it that way. And so Megan was a relief to them; they could look at her and not feel any sense of shame. They could hold her stare longer, not judge every tiny behaviour as though it held some significance, some insight. They trusted their feelings for her; Megan didn't confuse them. It was hard to resent them too much for this. Dutifully, Paul followed his sister to say hello.

Anna was about to join them when she saw a man across the room browsing the raku display. He seemed to study it intently, as if his sight was poor, or the pattern held some arcane code. Despite his back being to her, she got a sense of a physical presence, as if the space around him was also his. Everyone else in the room moved around politely, almost apologetic with reverence. But his gait lacked any appreciation of what he was looking at, as if he couldn't comprehend it. His clothes added to the incongruity: he looked dressed more for a hike, with a fleece, walking boots and mud-flecked jeans. As far as she could tell, he seemed to be alone. As he moved along the pots, someone appeared in front of Anna, blocking her view.

'Wonderful pieces,' the woman said. 'I love what you've done with texture.'

'Thank you,' Anna said, trying to look round her.

'I'd like to take some pictures of their creator, if that's OK.'

'I'm sorry?'

'I'm from the *Herald*.' She pulled a digital

camera from her bag.

'I'd rather not. Sorry. I can send you a picture to use if you like.'

The woman looked confused. Anna knew she'd think her vain when she sent her the photograph used on the website and other promotion. It was ten years or so old, and made her look like someone else.

'OK to ask a few questions, though?' the woman said.

There was little Anna could say that wasn't documented around the room, but the gallery would expect her to talk to the journalist, provide a quote or two. 'Of course.'

'I was wondering what you love most about ceramics.'

Anna trotted out something formulaic, originality beyond her. She talked about a versatile material, the feel of the clay, the excitement that the uncertainty of first opening the kiln brought.

'And I understand all your materials come from the moor. Is that important to you?'

She was about to answer when she saw the man again through a gap in the crowd. He'd moved along the display on the far wall and was looking at the 'About the Artist' section. He was still only side on, but Anna felt compelled to move to see him better. She heard the woman tut as she moved away.

'Sorry,' Anna said. 'Perhaps later.'

Suddenly everyone seemed taller than her and she struggled to get a good look. When the man appeared again she nearly dropped her glass. Everything seemed to stop: sound, movement, her breathing. Another glimpse, this time the whole of the side of his face. She started to feel hot and sick. The room began to turn a little, the floor seemed to ripple, as if she were on the deck of a ship. Some people passed through the space between them and when she could see him again he was looking up around the room. She told herself she was being ridiculous; it was just a trick of the mind, a doppelgänger. Anna tried to locate Robert, but couldn't. She thought to check the children, but the room was too busy.

'Hello,' a woman she couldn't place said, but Anna ignored her.

Her breathing was shallow now, her exhalation forced, evoking the asthma of childhood. Heat flushed through her. She felt primed for something — fight, flight — she didn't know. Every nerve ending in her body seemed to be vibrating. The thought of running came to her, but felt absurd. Time didn't exactly stop but seemed to lumber as if weighted down. And then the room's voices coalesced into one slow, menacing note, becoming deeper as if she'd been drugged. She was aware she must look strange, and so forced a smile for nobody in particular. Again she looked for her husband.

This had happened so many times, she told herself, though not for years. A face across the street, in a queue, on TV. But it was never him. Just chance throwing a set of similar features her way. Control the breathing and all else would follow.

A gap appeared in the crowd and she could see him walking, not straight towards her, but in her general direction, brochure in one hand, glass in the other. If their eyes met, it was for the briefest of moments, but nothing about his face suggested he recognised her. Inside Anna was screaming; it was so loud, she couldn't believe no one was looking at her. It's not him, she told herself again and again. He was ten feet away now. Eight. Six. Her legs could hardly hold her up. Her hands were shaking, the wine lapping from side to side in its glass. She bit the inside of her bottom lip hard until she tasted blood. She tried to make her eyes look elsewhere but they wouldn't. Standing there she waited for him to do whatever he was going to do.

But he just walked past. He didn't even look at her.

Anna didn't turn round but could sense him getting further away. Finally she forced herself to look and saw the man heading towards the gallery's front door. He put down the things he held and then he was gone.

Robert was by her now, asking if she was OK, saying that she looked a little odd. Anna said she wasn't sure, that it was hot. He said he'd get some water.

It could have been someone else. The senses were flawed, prone to error and faulty processing.

She could see Megan now, showing her grandparents around the room. Anna looked for Paul, but couldn't locate him. She pushed past people, knocking into them, half apologising.

Robert was in front of her with the water.

'Have you seen Paul?' Anna said weakly.

'A minute ago.' He scanned the room. 'Perhaps the toilet.'

She left her husband and quickly headed over to the exit. Along the corridor, she opened the door to the gents. Anna called out her son's name. Nothing. She went in and checked the cubicles, tentatively pushing back each door, but they were all empty. On her way out, an elderly man gave her a bemused look as they passed.

Back in the gallery, Robert caught her eye, pointing out Paul with a nod of his head. Her son was standing in a corner of the room, chewing a fingernail, his face a picture of boredom. Anna, feeling less shaky now, walked over to him.

'Where were you?' she said.

'When?'

'Just now.'

'I went outside.'

'What for?'

'These people are doing my head in. Do we have to stay here all night?'

She thought to say that they needed to talk about the smoking, but was just relieved to have found him. She smiled and put a hand on his arm. 'Just a little longer. Then we can go.'

24

The house moaned as it was buffeted by a south-westerly that swept in from the Atlantic. Above, in the rafters, it creaked like an old man rising from a favourite chair. As the first hint of daylight touched the land, a fine mist rendered the valley ethereal. Anna shivered slightly as she lit the fire; they'd have winter's first dusting of snow in a week, people said. The kindling flared but the logs had too much moisture in them to really catch. She would fetch some dry ones from the barn later.

She was the only one awake, Saturday mornings a slumberous affair for her family. She had two or three hours to herself, to work out what, if anything, last night meant.

These were normally the quiet moments she lived for: sitting in her studio with its comforting smells, watching the weather roll in, the clouds racing overhead as if a film had been speeded up. Her sanctuary, forged on the uplands of a prehistoric outcrop, a hill fort that surveyed all around it.

But nothing lasted. Even these granite walls would one day be weathered to nothing.

As the mist lifted, she saw a lone roe deer grazing on the fringe of Beardown Woods, alert, primed. A minute later the creature was startled by something and it flitted gracefully away beneath the safety of the canopy.

The other window in the room looked south, down the lane to the road, allowing visitors to be seen a minute or two before they arrived. She tried to take her eyes from it, back to the view of the tor, but like the deer she anticipated danger's direction. It was as if that night sixteen years ago had awoken in her a primal aspect that evolution had long since selected out. She had slept lighter ever since. Sudden noises always made her jump now. Her senses were sharper.

The wood burner spat and hissed, issuing only the faintest heat into the room. The central heating would be quicker, more economical, but this had become her morning ritual. It somehow connected her with those who lived here thousands of years ago — people who fought the elements to survive, who worked with the moor, yielded to it. As the small flame danced and licked, she thought of the fire as once being theirs, part of a cycle that — like water — was all joined. And yet unlike water, fire felt fragile. It needed nurturing; everything had to be in its favour, heat, fuel, oxygen — and she could control them all.

Most of her work was done in here, with the electric kiln, but it was the raku firings, out in the yard, that fulfilled her the most: igniting the propane burner; the thrill of the flames as the pots emerged and were carefully placed in sawdust; seeing the crackle in the glaze the carbon had made on each one.

There were new projects to consider, but she wouldn't work today. There would be emails from the gallery, perhaps some orders from last night, but the computer would remain switched off. She should keep busy, though. Perhaps some baking with Megan, an afternoon walk before the sun went down, board games before dinner. Keep everyone close by. She hoped that Robert wasn't called into work, as he was some Saturdays. Nothing had changed, she told herself.

She had tried to hide the unease as they drove back last night, offering fatigue as the reason for her silence. As they left early, people were told she was unwell, to please carry on browsing. Once she'd found Paul, the next voice she had been aware of was Megan's, who was saying Anna had turned into a ghost.

'Mummy's not very well,' Robert said.

'I'll be all right,' Anna said quietly. 'Just need some air.'

They left via a back entrance, Robert telling her parents she'd call them tomorrow and not to worry. It wasn't until they drove through the village of Dousland, and the car climbed the first slopes of the moor, that she felt her breathing return to normal. A yearning to see the wilderness took hold, but she had to settle for sensing it, its spirit lost to the darkness. The low moon gave Sharpitor just enough light to silhouette it on the horizon. Megan and Robert spoke for a while, Anna unaware of the words beyond background noise. Paul coughed a few times, perhaps the cigarettes, but was otherwise quiet. Once or twice Anna checked the side mirror for headlights behind, but there was only black.

In the few hours' sleep she'd managed since, the old dreams returned; scenes she'd forgotten, at least consciously, were played out with vivid clarity. You only knew how far you'd come when something started to pull you back there, giving the present a context. And yet her life before living here happened to somebody else, she was certain. She could recall it, yet only as you can a film or a book.

Voices in her head competed through the night, arguing a case of mistaken identity, or at worst one of coincidence. The alternative had an absurdity to it, a clumsy twist. The new Anna had a different name, thanks to her husband. She looked different to that fresh young woman who was to become a teacher; the moor had weathered her face and hair. Sixteen years had passed. All these things she clung to, yet she knew it was him, his eyes the same at thirty-one as at fifteen.

At 7 a.m. she gave up on sleep, thinking that she could hide from her mind in the studio.

As dawn broke through, she realised the fear had started to become something else. It was as if her body had shut down at the exhibition, opting for freeze rather than fight or flee. And then her mind had got to work through the night. But like a bad trip, a hallucination, she seemed to have emerged into another state — a numbness that wouldn't allow extremes of emotion the fuel they required. Between the long, empty hours of the night and lighting the fire this morning, a calmness descended upon her.

As a child she'd been terrified of injections. General anaesthetics were still regularly used to extract teeth then, and trips to the dentist were a protracted battle with her parents as they chased her between rooms, offering bribes until their patience wore thin. This continued at the surgery with embarrassing scenes as Anna kicked and screamed and bit. Once, they'd resorted to gas instead. But then one day, as they drove there, she knew she'd be fine. There were no histrionics. Her parents maintained a quiet tension, waiting for the eruption. But it never came. She even waved to her mother as the needle went in and she slipped from consciousness. She had, unfathomably, lost the fear. (As an adult the dentist became a source of dread again, as she tried not to gag when someone had their fingers in her mouth.)

And it had happened again. For the first time since he forced himself into her, she realised she was not afraid of him. At least not on a physical level. There was nothing more he could do to her in that regard. And yet his presence was still terrifying, as his power now lay in an ability to reveal, to hurt others, to hurt her son.

25

I saw you for the first time today. You were on a screen. Just a series of pixels, an image, like watching television. You are as long as my little finger, they said. The size of a lime.

I could see your arms and legs, even your nose. Your stomach looked distended. You were like a spaceman floating with the stars.

My father drove me to the hospital, taking the morning off work. I'd rather he hadn't but Mum had a migraine, so we travelled the nine miles in a swollen silence, each bend worsening the nausea.

After we parked he went to get out of the car.

'It's OK, you don't need to come in,' I said.

He looked hurt but didn't object. 'I'll wait here then.'

As I walked to the maternity wing, a waft of fatty canteen food turned my stomach, forcing me to find a toilet. Two flights of stairs and a few corners later, I found the reception desk. As I was directed to a seated area, I thought of the examination three months ago. The wait this time was longer, but eventually a nurse took me to be weighed. As before, blood was taken. In the adjacent room, the chair this time was more like a dentist's, without stirrups.

The man asked the date of my last period, whether the conception was natural. I looked at him nonplussed, wondering if he knew. 'Or IVF,' he said.

More questions came. Did I smoke? When had I last had a drink? This was all in my maternity notes, but I answered anyway.

I was reminded how serious the scan is, that it can detect problems. He would look for the heartbeat first, before measuring the baby to calculate an accurate due date.

The jelly was cold on my stomach and soaked the top of my jeans. I thought you'd be higher up, but apparently you're still in my pelvis, the man told me as he placed the probe just above my pubic bone. The lights were turned out and he nodded to a small monitor where I was able to see you.

'Just had a wee, have you?' he said, looking at his screen. 'There's your bladder, see? All empty.'

As he drew the probe down to my uterus, I could see layers of tissue. And then there it was, your heart, fluttering gently.

The man took some measurements, confirmed the due date.

'Lively little chap,' he said.

I could see you stretching, arching your back. 'A boy?' I said.

'Sorry, just a phrase. Too early to tell.' Next time, he said, they can tell me which you are. I tell myself it's not important; a boy would still be OK, I think. I can choose not to know for now.

The man asked if I wanted to take an image away with me, to show the father perhaps.

As he started taking screen prints, you put your hands in front of your face so we couldn't see you properly. It made you appear either shy or ashamed.

And now we sit together at home, the voices of my parents drifting in from the room next door.

'Everything OK?' Dad had asked on the drive back.

I said that it was. He was trying his best, to repair what had been damaged, but I could give him nothing yet.

I look at the print of you again, wondering how women make the other choice, the one I presumed I'd make, and empathy for those that have grows. It felt straightforward the day you turned the stick blue: I wanted you removed. If I could have done it there and then, I would have. I suspected there were ways, without returning to the clinic and admitting that I should have listened to them. A simple pill perhaps, even days later. Or, further along, a wire coat hanger if desperate. An old medical book in the town's library offered a grim yet at times comic inventory of methods, listing them down the page like a recipe: the lifting of heavy weights; abdominal massage; the consumption of mutton marrow, dried henna powder or carrot seed soup; yoga; hypothermia; acupuncture; receiving punches, kicks or blows to the abdominal area; high quantities of vitamin C; the insertion of a knitting needle; suction through a rubber tube; douching with Coca-Cola. It wasn't research as such, more a way of holding some power over you. Of having the knowledge that such means existed, independent of the more orthodox, medical procedure.

Either way, it was something I fully expected to do. I felt only revulsion that a part of him could remain inside me, like a bee sting or a snake's venom, slowly poisoning my system. I remember that first night in the flat after I knew, hardly sleeping, but when I did drift off, dreaming that you burst from my stomach like the alien in that film, hissing and rasping at me, your face replete with fury and malevolence. The embodiment of evil. You felt like the ultimate crime, an assault where the wound doesn't heal, but instead grows from within, malignant, rapacious. I remember thinking that you were unable to survive on your own, how you feed off me, the host, so that the only way I could starve you was to starve myself.

But then something happened in those desperate and terrible days. I found myself talking to you, or at least the concept of you — the transition from 'it' to 'you' occurred. At first I denounced you, insisted you'd not be inside me for long. But then slowly I began to regard you as mine. The fact that you needed me and not him bonded us; in a sense you *were* me and I was you.

Living at home again, mothers and babies began to fascinate me and I started observing them with curiosity and wonder. Whenever chance permitted and I was close enough, I stole glances, trying to discern a resemblance between them, something that alluded to a link, a bond — physical or otherwise. The mothers themselves, and some fathers, I later noticed, seemed to glow, exuding serenity. Their movements were slower, more graceful than other people's, as if life's pace could now be turned down a notch or two. They appeared fulfilled.

And so the urge to protect you grew a little each day, as if it was diluting the resentment, as if the further you got from the day of your conception, the more nature took over and instructed me how to feel. By the time I saw you on the screen today, feelings other than fear and dread and hatred had formed. Perhaps I could even love you one day.

★　★　★

I should eat well but you make me crave little else but burnt toast and ice cream. In the kitchen another letter from the school waits for me on the table; it's barely a week since the first. I open it in front of my parents this time.

I find I'm able to scan out the pleasantries, focusing on the salient paragraph.

The head says he understands that the police have interviewed Jamie twice and have decided not to pursue charges against him. (The policewoman had told me this on the phone last week, her tone possessing a trace of disappointment as well as sympathy. That there would be no case to answer in terms of my own behaviour barely registered. I thanked her for calling me, grateful it had been her rather than her colleague.) McKellan goes on to say he has written to the boy's parents advising that he can return to school as of next week. I'm unsure which upsets me more: that Jamie has convinced people of his innocence or the head's seemingly callous use of the word 'boy'. But then my eyes go back to the word 'parents', and I realise that I'm going to become one. A parent. A mother. I say the words in my head but they still sound like someone else's.

The letter goes on: *We have no alternative other than to terminate your contract with immediate effect*. I picture him physically terminating it, shredding it, burning the remains. He tells me I am entitled to take legal advice, but that he's been assured he is acting appropriately. He imagines I wouldn't want to return anyway. Lastly he apologises that things have ended this way, that he had much respect for me as a teacher. The last three words of this sentence scream with subtext, but I'm probably being overly sensitive.

The final insult comes with the signature, which he's forgotten. Or his secretary forgot to pass him the letter before posting it.

I look up at my parents sipping their tea timorously. Neither of them has asked to see the screen print of you. Perhaps they think I wouldn't have wanted one. They glance at me, waiting to hear what news the letter contains.

'Termination,' I say.

26

The walk to the far end of the park was no more than fifteen minutes. He saw Megan queuing to get on the bus outside the school gates and part of him wished he was joining her.

'Tell Mum I should be home for dinner,' he said as he passed his sister. She looked confused when he didn't elaborate, but said nothing. Paul thought to tell her he was going to a friend's or something, but the adrenaline was kicking in, focused as he was on the task ahead. With luck he would get the public bus in an hour.

The park was quiet: a few kids from lower years ambling along, a couple of dog walkers unleashing balls from the ends of sticks. With one hand he loosened his tie and placed it in his blazer pocket. He wondered how many would come, how far the word had spread since lunchtime.

To his right the river was high and fast. You wouldn't last long in it at this time of year. Their geography teacher was fond of telling them how it was one of the fastest rising rivers in the country, rainfall from the moor surging down the sides of the great valleys until a trickle became a torrent.

Paul stepped behind a tree, down to the riverbank and sat down out of sight, the water booming past a foot or so away. Rolling a cigarette, he tried to remember when it had all began, when the rumours first started, the taunts he thought were for someone else. There had been something when they returned after the summer break, a word or two shouted from a window or along a crowded corridor. They came from a group of lads you knew to avoid and, until recently, he'd managed it quite well. Every school had them, he supposed. Boys who established their territory, their dominance, a little more each year. If there was any trouble, they wouldn't be far away. So you kept your head down when they passed, let them scrounge a fag from you without protest. You hoped you didn't share a class with them, something that could be achieved with a little academic effort. There were probably one or two lads harder than any one of them, but as a gang they generally went unchallenged, in and out of school.

It was one of them in particular, Adams, who was the most vocal in his goading of Paul, the others laughing along, encouraging him to go a little further each time. He was scrawny in comparison to the rest, probably needing to prove himself more to remain in favour. But his smaller stature was largely cancelled out by eyes that burned with psychosis whenever trouble started to break out.

The first name-calling sounded almost old fashioned, more a word his father would use when he hit his finger with a hammer or the generator packed up. *Bastard*. Paul had to look it up at home to check its actual meaning, which made no sense. His parents were married, after he was born, but that hardly mattered. Other names followed, but still without revealing why he'd been singled out. The verbal assaults grew to him being shoved when he passed Adams in a corridor. Soon the couple of friends Paul did have began to keep away in case they were targeted by association.

He was walking back from the football fields before half-term when it finally kicked off. He was now known as Curtis the Bastard and when Adams shouted it across the road for the third time that day, Paul turned back and walked towards the gang, who cheered with excitement as he approached.

He stood inches from Adams' face, who in turn stood his ground with an aggressive, 'What?'

'That word,' Paul said. 'Why do you call me it?'

'Why d'ya think?'

'I don't know, that's why I'm asking.'

''Cos you're a little bastard,' Adams said, 'who doesn't know who his father is.' The others all laughed. The fight that followed drew a small crowd as they both took a few kicks and punches before a passing teacher pulled them apart, warnings later handed out by the year head. Adams was strong for his size; Paul had caught him with a good swing that must have hurt, but

213

he had barely blinked. There was a repeat the following week behind the canteen that stopped of its own accord, but not before Adams had caught him in the eye with a strong right hook. As Paul walked away, threats were made, the usual names shouted. After the morning's lessons he had walked along the canal, out of town and up on to the old railway line. When it was time to head back he just stayed there, smoking and throwing stones at an old bottle, his hand and face sore. Even as it got dark and the rain came, he just moved into the woods and smoked some more, thinking that he might stay there for ever. Finally, cold and sodden, he headed back down into town. Having missed the last bus he decided to walk the five miles home. He had been trying to hitch the last couple when his dad had picked him up by the pub at Merrivale.

At lunchtime today Paul went and found them in the alley where they smoked between lessons. Adams looked surprised, readying himself for another go. His mates bunched up behind him — Chris Street, Danny Baxter, John Poulter.

Paul had thought to reason with them, try to tease out the origin of their mistake, but their posture suggested this would be time wasted.

He went up to Adams, again as close as he could. 'Me and you,' Paul said coldly to his face. 'Far side of the park, after school today.' A vague insult followed him down the alley as he walked away, but Paul felt some relief at setting things in motion. And there would be no teacher to break it up this time.

Flicking his roll-up into the water, he watched it race away. It was cold in the park now and he thought of his sister on the warm bus, his mum lighting the fire at home. As much as he hated living in the middle of nowhere, it appealed right now: sitting on his bed, learning a few new chords, smoking out of the window with some tunes on.

He'd chosen the far end of the park for the cover it offered. A few trees and the wall meant they wouldn't be seen by the nearby houses or anyone passing, unless someone stumbled right on them. As he crossed the path he could see a few people standing around, the glow from their cigarettes just visible in the fading light. There was something unfair in having to do this alone, approaching a gang who for weeks had been bent on starting something with him for no reason. Even if he fared well against the weakest one, the others would finish the job. That's what they did, hunted as a pack. But, he thought, this at least might put an end to it.

★ ★ ★

They'd obviously kept it quiet as those attending were just the ones from the alley. 'Come for some more, then?' Adams said, walking quickly towards him.

There were no more words, the two coming together at equal speed, arms flailing wildly both as potential strikes and for defence. Inside the school gates such events usually drew excited cheers from onlookers but now Adams' mates

215

remained silent, allowing the fight to play out without attracting passers-by.

The first proper connection was a rising knee into Paul's nose, almost bringing him down. Eyes watering, blood running into his open mouth, he managed to break away momentarily, regaining his balance as he wiped his nose on a sleeve. But Adams was on him straight away, aware the blow had hurt Paul and wanting to follow it up. One of the others was unable to resist a whoop of encouragement, shushed down by the rest. Pulling Adams' jumper over his head and holding him down, Paul was able to get two uppercuts in before taking a blow to the stomach, winding him a little. The two of them fell to the cold ground, the thin layer of mud and damp grass making purchase difficult. They rolled about, neither able to dominate or produce any meaningful strikes. Paul could see flecks of blood across his opponent's shirt and realised it was his own. In practical terms, biting or using someone's hair would give you an advantage in such a fight, but a vague code, presumably based on some forgotten notion of honour, stopped all but the most vicious from doing so, although it was unclear at this stage whether Adams fell into this category.

His arms free for a moment, Paul was able to get an elbow hard into Adams' side, making him flinch and recoil some. And then a punch to the side of Adams' head had both of them crying out in pain — Paul's hand had barely recovered from the same action a week ago. Their heads clashed unintentionally, a dull knock of bone on bone.

There was more scrambling on the ground until Adams managed to get to his feet and got several kicks off, the last crunching hard into Paul's ribs.

He had to get up — you were as good as dead on the ground — but instinct made him curl into a ball. The next lot of kicks had real momentum, raining into his back and arms as he tried to protect his head. He could just make out the feet of the others, standing in a semicircle round them.

Got to get up, he told himself. Fight back. Perhaps he could still win if he got up. But there was a strange sense of calmness about him, as if he knew Adams could do him no real harm, as if he was showing them all what he could take. If there had been something to hand — a thick branch, a piece of piping — he wondered whether he'd have used it, given in to blind rage, unleashing strike after strike, barely aware of anything other than the need to inflict as much damage as possible. Where it came from, this coldly violent impulse, he didn't know, suspecting only that he was capable of it, that one day it would reveal itself to the world. But for now he just lay there, absorbing the blows as if it were his duty.

And then the kicking stopped. Above him he could hear Adams' laboured breath and wondered if there would be more. To his left he heard one of the others light a cigarette. Paul tried to assess if any of the injuries were serious; he hurt all over but he suspected they weren't. Slowly he turned and faced Adams, who was breaking out into a broad grin and looking to the others, perhaps for approval, for a sign to continue. Paul went to get up but was too disorientated and instead fell back down. He was aware of Adams moving towards him, for one last go, but Baxter or one of the others said something. He heard Adams protest.

'Enough,' the first voice said firmly.

'Come on, let's get outta here,' said another.

Paul sensed them walking away, rounding the wall until they were gone, a couple of victory hoots and then silence. He moved again, managing to stand this time. Touching his nose, he smeared the last of the blood away with his good hand and began walking slowly across the park back to the road.

It was possible that that was enough, that a line had been drawn under it, a fresh target would be found. The name-calling would fade. And if it didn't he'd do it again until it did. He wouldn't be a victim, whatever the alternative was.

As he got to the road, Paul saw a bus pulling away, a thick cloud of black smoke belching out behind the vehicle. Free of pain he could perhaps have sprinted and caught it, but it was impossible now. He slumped against the wall, resigned to waiting another hour, and tried to roll a cigarette mostly with his left hand.

With each passing minute, his nose throbbed a little more. There was a high-pitched ringing in his ears, as if loud music had been blasted into them, and a cough produced pain throughout his upper body. He would disguise the injuries as best he could; complaints to the school, investigation, would only serve to undo whatever progress had been made tonight.

Paul thought about what Adams had said before the first fight — about his father — and wondered what it meant. Other taunts had targeted his mother. It was funny to think he'd just fought to defend their reputations. He hadn't, of course — it was more about stopping something before it became a permanent fixture — but the thought amused him.

He turned his mind to girls in his year, ones he hoped heard nothing of the beating. The really pretty ones hung around with boys who had finished school last year, boys who liked to pull up outside the gates on motorbikes, wheelspinning and wheelieing their way into the girls' affections. You couldn't compete with that.

But there was one girl, not long arrived from another school, whom he liked. They passed each other, usually on the stairs in the new block, a couple of times a week. And although she was never alone, there was something different about her, as if she'd never quite fit in or make many friends there. Her hair was short and blacker than anyone's he'd seen and although she'd be described as plain, geeky even, by others, she had this swagger and confidence that Paul thought beautiful. A few weeks ago she'd caught him staring at her, but instead of looking annoyed she gave him a little smile which, after a week of plucking up courage, he'd been able to return. And despite losing the fight, sitting here bloodied and bruised, today had somehow given him the confidence to say hello to her next time.

It was dark now. A woman across the road yelled at her dog which wouldn't keep up. Paul flicked his cigarette into the road and tried to get comfortable.

27

There was a serenity to the house today, a stillness that hung in each room. Even the weather appeared to have halted, the pewter sky low and swollen, its lifeless pallor sickly. Anna vowed to make herself work later, to shrug off the inertia that for now saw her ghosting from room to room, committing to nothing.

Stay at home today, she'd nearly said to Robert first thing. He'd have wanted a reason, but she could have made something up. She'd looked at Megan at breakfast, hoping a cough or cold might be threatening. A day off school, she'd have suggested. Just to be sure. Paul had come in late last evening, heading straight to his room, presumably to hide the mess his face was in. She'd gone up, knocked on his door, asked to go in, but was told not to. He refused to discuss it when he emerged, saying only that he'd sorted out whatever it was. That it was just a stupid argument. Anna fought back tears, saying she'd get the first-aid box, but in her absence she heard the back door slam and the kitchen was empty on her return. In her son's room she'd found one of his shirts stained with blood.

In the end she'd asked no one to stay at home.

Again, she acknowledged that it wasn't simply fear. More a desire not to be alone. The comfort solitude had always brought had, for the first time, vanished. The cottage, for so long a symbol of freedom, now felt like a microcosm of the nearby prison. And who wanted to be imprisoned alone?

In the end Robert had left for work in silence a couple of hours ago, his kiss goodbye perfunctory, his gaze floor-bound. There'd been an unspoken optimism that the exhibition would somehow mark the end of this current fallow spell in the bedroom. The weeks leading up to it were conveniently busy for Anna, as she worked on pieces into the small hours, too tired for anything more than the slightest intimacy. The pressure of the deadline had also been used to justify abstinence. And so, although no direct reference to it had been made, Anna felt the expectation rise following the exhibition. It was only the abrupt way the night at the gallery had ended that had postponed it this long.

The word duty came to mind, as it often did. Robert would never be so facile or chauvinistic to use it, but she knew he regarded sex as intrinsic to marriage. There was a frequency, a spectrum regarded as normal, beyond which it became unreasonable. When his patience and capacity for tenderness were stretched to breaking point, he would look at her almost in a primitive way, as if wanting to point out that what she was doing to him was against nature. She was denying him an essence of himself, repudiating his desire, his masculinity.

When it first appeared, this aversion, she'd ignored it. We have different tempos, contrasting libidos, she'd told herself first, then Robert. Then it was a phase, to do with age, to do with having children. Quite common, she'd read. It would pass. But as it worsened, she began to regard herself as an aberration, as something broken, a malfunctioning mechanism, unable to perform the tasks it had been assigned. Like the ancient, gnarled woods to the north, she was slowly becoming impenetrable.

It was only in the last couple of years, as it worsened, that she had come to fully understand it. As Paul had grown up, the subtle physical similarities, although present, were somehow dismissible, the disparity in age allowing her mind to trick itself. She would shift her perspective, focus on a part of his face that she considered hers alone. But when he reached adolescence, and now that he was about the same age Jamie had been, the resemblance seemed impossible to ignore, especially during the eruptions of fury. It was like seeing a fragment of that night every time she looked at her son.

Discussing her aversion to sex with Robert — its manifestation rather than its cause — only exacerbated matters.

'Has it always been like this?' he asked.

'What do you mean?'

'With other lovers.'

'Not exactly, no.'

'So it's me then?'

'No, it's not you.'

In one of his more progressive responses, he suggested therapy.

'You want to discuss our sex life with a stranger?' Anna said. 'Lay bare every aspect of our relationship for someone to deconstruct, to make notes on, before teaching us techniques to reacquaint our bodies?'

'I thought it could help.'

And perhaps it could have had she been strong enough to consider the notion. There had been times she had almost told her GP — particularly after Megan was born, when depression had regularly flanked her — but who was to say such a phase wouldn't have occurred anyway? 'It always comes back,' she said to her husband. 'Just don't push.'

And when finally she could bear his touch again, and months of frustration played out in a few scrambled moments, Robert would transform into a frenzied being, unrecognisable to her as he gorged himself as a starving man might on food. Afterwards, he would hold her, whispering that everything would be fine now, the subtext being that that wasn't so bad, was it? In her mind it at least meant an end to hostilities for a few weeks.

The evening after the exhibition, Robert arranged for the children to be out. He cooked. There was wine and candles. Music. The scene in the gallery was mentioned. Some sort of panic attack, Anna maintained.

'You haven't had them before, have you?'

'No, I haven't.'

'Perhaps you should see your doctor.'

'I'm fine, really.'

They spoke of plans for Christmas, how to divide the parents up fairly.

'I think we should stay with yours again,' said Anna.

'That'll be three years running. Won't your mother be upset?'

'The children can see them before we go. They'll have Michael staying.'

She pictured her husband's parents, how meeting them for the first time had been cause for disquiet beyond the norm.

I've met someone, Robert would have said to them on the phone, perhaps a few weeks in.

That's lovely.

She has a son.

Oh.

Because however much you respected your son's choices, however open to the unconventional you were, there'd be a tinge of disappointment.

But Anna's concern was misplaced — it had its origin wholly within herself — for Robert's parents were very welcoming, embracing her with warmth and an absence of ceremony. That our son is in love with you is all the affirmation we need, they may as well have said. And so in time Paul had two new grandparents whose ignorance of the truth allowed affection for him to flourish, an affection that with her own parents was always adulterated. Robert's family became like a cleansing surface she could rub

225

herself against, removing the dead skin of a previous life. The arrival of Megan a few years later had merely intensified her fondness for them.

The evening after the exhibition, Robert had cleared the plates away after dinner, poured more wine. They skirted from topic to topic, an edginess creeping into the conversation, the sort of awkwardness that more properly belonged to former lovers meeting for the first time in years. The silences were quickly filled, lest they grew. Later the children were delivered home from friends' houses. Megan went straight to bed and Paul headed to his room.

In bed that night Anna still wasn't sure. It could go either way. Perhaps yielding could distract her from her thoughts.

Robert ran a hand gently down her arm, a test, to see if he could go further.

'I love you,' he said, leaning in to kiss her.

Anna tried, for a few moments kissing him back. Excited by the response, he kissed harder, noisily, his tongue uncomfortably deep in her mouth.

He climbed on to her.

'We'll wake Megan,' Anna said, but he was lost to a passion that verged on fury.

His hand hurried to her thigh, knowing that pauses could prove fatal, that once they'd started it was difficult for Anna to abort. Like an adolescent boy he thrust his fingers underneath himself and between her legs.

'Gently.'

He slowed a little. 'Like this?'

'Softer.'

She attempted to evoke all the times it had felt right, tried to trick her mind, but it was no use.

'I'm sorry,' she said.

Still he tried to work his fingers inside.

'Robert . . . '

'Come on. You'll be fine once we're started.' He slowed his movements even more, using barely any force. 'Am I being too hard?' He moved his fingers further up, trying to find her clitoris. She could sense his panic that the moment would be lost.

'I love you,' he said again.

'I'm sorry,' Anna said. 'Maybe tomorrow.'

There was one last attempt, before her inertia was akin to having another person in the room.

Resigned, he raised himself up on his arms, above her, remaining there in silence for a while. Neither spoke. In the gloom she saw something in her husband's face that reminded her of that night. Finally Robert rolled away on to his side, facing away. She thought she might cry, but didn't.

★ ★ ★

The studio was still in semi-darkness. Anna thought to light a fire but there was no kindling to hand. She drew back the curtains behind the wheel, the day's thin light barely making an impression on the room. Everything was grey — the lane, the sky. The moor could suffocate you on such days.

However she felt tonight, she would give in.

She would give her husband a sign that desire, as well as love, still existed in some form. That it could still be summoned from the darkness. She would forget the exhibition and its aftermath; whatever was to happen, it had taken enough from her.

She sat at the table, looking at colour in the glazes: cobalt, emerald, turquoise, ochre — all foils to the ashen palette outside.

It was still too dark to work. She walked across the room and with both hands opened the other curtains.

His face was just an inch or so from the glass. She jumped back, a yelp rather than a scream coming from her mouth. A small circle of condensation appeared briefly on the window with each of his exhalations. He had a woolly hat pulled down to just above his eyes. For a moment there was a look of surprise on his face, before he smiled. Anna moved backwards, knocking into the table. A small jug fell to the floor and smashed. She stopped by the wood burner and picked up the poker beneath it without taking her eyes off him.

As she held it aloft, he mouthed something. It looked like hello.

28

The poker was heavy in her hand. As a weapon it wasn't ideal, slow through the air, unwieldy, but it was capable of exacting serious damage with just a few strikes. She held it up in front of her, like a sword, so it could be clearly seen.

They stood staring at each other.

Although Anna had been unable to convince herself that a mistake had been made at the exhibition, that somehow it wasn't him, she had hoped it was a matter of coincidence. The fact that he didn't approach or even seem to notice her suggested his presence could have been down to chance. It was unlikely, ridiculous even, but such things no doubt happened.

Or if he wasn't there by accident, then perhaps his curiosity had been satisfied and no more would come of it. He'd maybe seen a flyer and recognised her but had now returned to wherever home was. There would be no need to tell Robert. Life could continue as normal. All this she had clung to.

When the police came, stating someone had

been seen behaving oddly at the end of the lane, she had felt disquiet, her senses pricked. It was as if some part of her knew it wasn't the prisoner. To be seen in daylight, little more than two miles from the place you'd absconded from a week earlier, would be more than careless.

The various woods around them, so long a reassuring protective barrier, had begun to feel threatening, imposing themselves on the cottage. Each day since, as the light had receded, the trees had appeared to encroach a little more, shifting silently down the hills, Anna imagined, until their branches were close enough to scritch against the windows. Despite living virtually on the crest of the moor, it was the slopes of the valley above them that had dominated her thoughts, enclosing the cottage like a cloister. For the first time in years, since the children were young, she had started drawing the curtains in the evenings, something that was soon noticed.

'Do we need to shut them, now that he's been caught?' Robert had said.

'Who?'

'The prisoner.'

'I just want them closed.'

She knew her son never shut his, so she asked him to.

'Why bother?'

'Please, Paul. Just for me.' But he didn't.

Last night, before Robert was in, anger leavened in her. This was her home. She marched outside, pretending to the children that logs were needed. As the security light clicked

230

on, illuminating her and the yard while rendering the moor pitch black, she forced herself to stand there, staring out at all she couldn't see. She'd wanted to shout, a warning perhaps, an acknowledgement that she knew they were being watched.

And now Jamie scrutinised her from a few feet away, studying her face, confirming her identity. After a moment he took his hat off, as if to reveal himself fully.

She broke the silence, shouting, 'What do you want?'

Ignoring her, he looked around the room in fascination, as if it was a cage in a zoo. Finally he said something, but it was lost to the glass. The phone was in the kitchen, Anna thought, and her mobile somewhere upstairs. Neither door was locked.

'What?' Anna said. 'I can't hear you.'

'You make things.'

She followed his gaze again as it moved around the studio, before it stopped by her feet. 'You broke one,' he said.

She held the poker up higher. 'Why are you here?'

He answered but she couldn't hear. He pointed to the side, indicating that he could go around to the door.

'No,' Anna shouted. 'Stay there.'

Again they stood in silence, an absurd standoff. Anna allowed herself to look at him a little more closely. The hair was tidy now, cut short, making it darker. His physical presence remained but looked less awkward in an adult.

The image of his face she'd been forced to live with resembled little the one in front of her now, and yet there was still something about it. It was the eyes. He had her son's blue eyes.

Holding the poker aloft, she motioned for him to step backwards, which he did a little.

'More. Go on!'

When he was ten yards or so into the garden, she crossed the room, lifted the window's latch and opened it slightly.

'Stay there,' she said. He looked at the poker, a grin that could have been from that other time breaking out on his face. 'I mean it.'

'I saw you,' he said. 'On the TV.'

'What?'

'You were on the News. I wasn't sure at first.'

After initial confusion Anna made the connection. Another day she would have ignored the reporter, issued a brusque response to his interview request. It seemed unfair that giving him two minutes of her time had brought Jamie to her home. To her family.

'The escape,' Anna said.

'Yes. Did they catch him?'

Anna's legs felt weak. With her free hand she held on to the window frame. 'Why are you here?' she said.

'You don't need that.' The poker was making her arm ache, but she ignored him. 'You had a different name on the TV. Is that his name, then?'

'How did you know where I live?'

'You can find out most things these days. I wanted to say hello. You left school so quickly. I came around to your flat again — '

'You what?'

'To make sure you were OK.'

His voice had a perverse sincerity to it, nothing obviously threatening.

'You remember what happened, Jamie?'

'When?'

'With us.'

'Course.'

He looked down. Perhaps he felt shame now. Perhaps guilt wouldn't let go of him and this was some pilgrimage of absolution.

Looking up, he said, 'It wasn't all bad, though.'

'*What?*'

'I thought, maybe . . . that we could be friends.'

'*Friends?*'

'Yes.' Jamie stepped forward. Anna thrust the poker through the air a few times and he stopped.

'You need to leave, Jamie. My husband will be back any time now.'

'He doesn't come home until later. Sometimes for lunch, but not usually. And it's still morning.'

'I'll call the police.'

'I just thought we could talk.'

'I have nothing to say to you.'

'It's been such a long time.'

'I want you to go now and not come back.' She said the words slowly, deliberately.

He looked more hurt than anything, affronted almost. Anna struck the poker against the window frame, just once, hard, sending flakes of old paint into the air. He stood staring at her for a few moments, before taking the hat from his fleece pocket and placing it back on his head. As he turned to walk away, he paused and looked back at the house. His gaze moved up, to the bedrooms above.

She watched him cross the garden and walk through the gate at the bottom. She watched as he joined the riverbank, following it back towards the road. And she watched until he was a distant speck that became nothing. Anna thought she saw him turn and look back a few times.

Looking down she saw that the knuckles of her right hand were white but still she didn't release the poker.

29

I want to show you the place you were born. Not the hospital, but where I made the decision that means you are here. Where I came so the only voice I heard was my own.

You've been here so many times inside me, this haven I escape to, but I want your eyes to see its splendour, its majesty. You owe your life to this place.

I feel less trapped today, as if I could drive anywhere, start a life, just the two of us. And yet the moor would always pull me back — whenever danger threatened, boredom struck, frustration grew, I'd come here, as I have for the last year or more.

I only have to move my head slightly to see you in the rear-view mirror. A six-month-old baby, whom I carried and gave birth to, kept as my own despite the advice and agenda of others. Every day you remind me of him and yet you are not him. Everything you become, everything you see, can be shaped by me, not him. This is how I remain sane.

The road undulates, gentle rises and dips. You're so quiet in the car, the rhythm of the engine soothing you more than any rocking in my arms can. You gaze out of the side window and I wonder what you absorb, whether it's just the colour and tones of nature that flash by, or if any detail registers.

The car is freedom, the last of my savings, but I have to get out of the house each day, out of a town with twitching curtains and people whose hushed tones turn to awkward smiles as I push you past. That's her, I imagine them saying. That's the baby. Got pregnant, gave up her job and moved back here. Who's the father? Nobody knows. Have you heard the other rumour?

You've been bombarded by visitors this week, effusive cooing, adults making ridiculous faces and sounds to match. My parents think I don't do enough of that. They say I talk to you like you were an adult, which is why you cry so much.

Last night I stayed up later than my parents. There was a documentary about men who force themselves on women, something I wouldn't have been able to contemplate watching until recently. But a curiosity, almost objective, lured me in and I told myself I could turn it off at any time. In reality it was prosaic, more an anthropological apology. A professor of psychology was interviewed, an apparent authority with several books on the matter to his name. As he spoke — his language functional, scientific — I almost laughed at his arrogance that a man, any man, could write about the subject with the slightest enlightenment.

236

I head out to Princetown, past the prison and Two Bridges. The first allusions to spring grace the land: campion and primrose adorn the hedgerows; lambs caper on sun-kissed slopes. Rooks squabble high in the trees. As I slow down through woodland, the pungent aroma of wild garlic rides the breeze.

As the months pass I search for the first signs of resemblance. There's nothing that chills me outright when I look at you, just hints of someone else. The eyes mostly, but perhaps you have something of his mouth: it turns down slightly at the corners, giving you a faint scowl even when you're not cross. I don't know what you have of mine. Perhaps everything in time. I look long and hard when you sleep, holding my face inches from yours, scrutinising its contours and structure, trying to predict what it will become. You have my father's high forehead; he says your hands are those of a cricketer's. Your hair, still fine and wispy, could be anyone's for now. It's the eyes, though. As blue as mine are green. When you get frustrated, that moment just before the first tears form, a semblance of him seems to appear. This is what I fight every day.

I park opposite the Warren Inn, wisps of smoke rising from its chimney stack. They say the fire inside has never gone out, that it's burned continuously since 1845. I once heard that a group of marines urinated on it for a bet, but I prefer to believe in its longevity. How it's outlived the person who originally lit it.

As I put your tiny gloves on, you study me, your eyes not his today. I put you in the carrier, secure you to my back.

The track cuts down through grass tussocks into the valley where a brook gurgles its way south. Granite ruins are the last remnants of a disused tin mine, its walls evoking ghosts of men who toiled long and hard before climbing the hill to the public house. This is the stillest place I know on the moor. I can spend hours sitting here, watching dragonflies dart and hawk; rabbits, whose ancestors fed the miners, twitch and scurry; gorse flowers, their scent intoxicating. In the distance the trill of a woodpecker echoes in bursts from the woods as it hammers on a dead bough. Wood anemones nod in the breeze.

The tor ahead looks imperious from this low down, but I know it's only an hour's climb, maybe less. I go south along the track for a while, not wanting to head up into the wind just yet. You bounce slightly on my back but never complain.

Ahead, just shy of the forest, a Land Rover is parked. It looks incongruous this far from the road. I'm annoyed at the disturbance to the solitude, but carry on; I want to walk up alongside the drystone wall, up through the heather.

A man my age or a little older is working on one of the wooden gateposts. I've not seen anybody else since the road, yet somehow having you strapped to my back wards off any fear. As I get closer I see the National Park emblem on his vehicle.

Nearer still, I see that his tools are scattered across the path I want to turn on to. He hears my footsteps and looks round. 'Hello,' he says.

'Hello.' I stand there wondering whether to just go straight on.

'Lovely day.'

'Is it? I mean . . . Can I go that way?'

He looks in the direction I've nodded. 'Yes, of course. Sorry.' He starts gathering his tools, placing them in the heather beside the path, dropping some when he tries to carry too many at once. 'You heading up Challacombe?' he says.

'Yes, well, I've not decided. Some of the way. Depends on . . . ' I half turn, revealing you.

'Oh, I thought that was . . . '

'A rucksack. People do from the front.'

He finishes clearing the path and walks towards us. Apart from my father, this is the first time I've been alone with a man since the flat. I scan the horizon, look for walkers, but see none.

'Hello, little fellow,' he says before realising his assumption: 'He is . . . '

'A "he", yes.'

'He's cute. What's his name?'

'Paul.'

'Hello, Paul,' he says, as if addressing an adult. The man's face is soft, peaceful. I suppose he would be regarded as handsome. Talking to you allows him to stand near me without it feeling strange, yet my instinct is to end the interaction.

'Well, we better get on. Bye.'

'Goodbye.'

As I climb the slope I can sense him looking up at us. I congratulate myself on keeping the

239

fear under control, for being capable of conversing with a man I don't know.

My thighs burn with the extra weight of you and halfway up I pause to rest. Turning full circle I take in the great tors to the north, the English Channel glistening southward. The sedge makes a sibilant swish as the wind passes through it. Meadow pipits trill in flight. I place my finger in your hand and you grip it.

The man is still at the bottom working on the gate. What a wonderful job, I think. The moor your office. As I turn to continue climbing, I feel a hint of regret at not prolonging the exchange.

Before long, it's just the two of us. I can see for miles in every direction — north to Okehampton, the Cornish hills westward, the Tamar Bridge to the south, shimmering like a mirage.

I hardly spend time alone with you, the house is so often full. They know not to ask about your father as they fuss over you. They know only that he occupied little time in my life. A one-night stand, if you like. He wasn't interested in you. Or me. This is our story. A simple tale to hide a family secret. One or two at church know, which probably means they all do. But I will protect you from the truth as best I can.

Perhaps I will tell you one day, though I am unsure how such a conversation begins. You'll ask questions, about him, your father, as you'll call him, though he's not in my mind. I'll be vague, play down our involvement with each other. Or perhaps I didn't know him at all, a stranger at a party. We were drunk. I don't

240

normally behave like that; a one off. Better you believe you were an accident, which I suppose you were. But you'll push and push. I'll say I tried to find out who he was, this man I knew for one evening. I'll pluck a name, one you'll like — I only knew his first name; he'll be handsome, charming, irresistible, the sort women flock to. It was a beautiful clear night. We talked and talked. He was a musician, travelled the world. Played the piano in dimly lit cellar bars across Europe. You can't hope to tie down those tortured artist types. Not that I tried. Why didn't we swap numbers? I don't know; we just didn't. We shared a moment, a wonderful passage of time that resulted in you. Someone must know where he is, you'll say. They don't; I tried when I found out about you. He was just a friend of a friend at some party. There one minute, gone the next. I'm sorry. So he doesn't even know I exist? No, he does not.

Did I love him? I'll try hard to picture him when you ask this, picture the man neither of us will ever know or meet, the face you'll try to imagine all your life, I'll bring it into my mind, expelling the other one, the real one. I'll see his beautiful features, the ones that he gave to you; I'll see his smile and I'll tell you that, yes, I did love him that night, your handsome father. And that I could tell he felt the same. And then you can let him go. Let him travel and play his songs. Accept that he gave you life but nothing more. I will be enough for you.

And if I can't lie to you? If in some moment of cruelty or by accident you hear about him and question your right to exist? I don't know. I don't know how you live with that. I can only tell you that *I* did. That I survived it, when I thought I wouldn't. That I chose you; what he did was the smallest part in your creation. His was an act of hatred, of anger, mine one of hope. I made you, carried you, brought you into the world. I will bring you up, protect you, hold you. You are not part of him. I will show you my love is enough. You were not forced on me, as he was. I could have given you to others; for a long time I thought I might. That way you could never know. But as you grew inside me, that became less and less an option. I hope you see that one day. I hope you will never have to.

At the summit I unstrap you and sit on a rock, you on my knee. The wind makes you blink a few times until you get used to it. Here we are, I say. On top of the world. In the valley below, the man is little more than a black dot.

30

I have to learn to live again, to reclaim some of what has been lost. Or replace it with something new. I hate to leave you, even for a few hours, but I have to discover what I'm going to do with the rest of this life. I thought I was going to teach, to inspire, show others the importance of things greater than ourselves. Maybe I'll teach again, but not now.

Not wanting to drive in the city centre, I take the bus to Plymouth, remembering trips there as a teenager, hating it even then: great concrete structures that loomed overhead like battlements; the fervour of shoppers, traffic that charged at you.

But I can't hide away for ever.

The fug of carbon monoxide in the bus station joins the heat from the midday sun, hitting my face like a sirocco. The roads choke with motionless cars; horns blare above the generic urban drone. A group of bare-chested men leer at passing women, calling after them, congratulating each other on their bravado. I keep my head down until I'm beyond them.

Teenagers, rapturous that school has broken up for the summer, converge on the city in reverberant clusters. Further along a group of workmen are sitting guarding a hole in the pavement, smoking, pouring tea from a flask. Their Day-Glo vests barely cover skin that's been so sunned over the years it looks reptilian.

'All right, love,' one of them says. I stiffen, focus my gaze ahead, try to look uncaring. Another says something about no need to be grumpy on a day like this, that they were only being friendly. Once past them, their stares still perforating the back of me like a shower of arrows, I want to ask them why passing men aren't subject to similar salutations, if that's all they are.

And so I spend the next five minutes occupying a detailed fantasy where I calmly stop and humiliate them into silence with slick put-downs. In reality any engagement would see me unravel in a tearful verbal assault, confirming their stereotype of some women as unhinged, overemotional. By walking on in silence I no doubt live up to their other image — aloof, prudish. Or perhaps the categories are broader than this. Maybe there's a whole subset to each, which they filter us into for convenience. Woman as harpy or siren, as bitch or courtesan. The witch, the hag, the matriarch. The good wife. The virgin, the prude, the slut. Always woman *as* something. Wife, lover, mother.

I remember at work walking past groups of pupils, older boys, hearing fragments of their exchanges, boasts of what they'd do, or had done, to girls. Coarse yet bizarre terms, sexual euphemisms that conveyed both immaturity and aggression: *I'd give her one; I'd love to ruin her; I could do that some damage.* That. (Always what they could do *to* them, not *with* them.) And these, presumably, were directed towards the attractive girls, ones who maintained a sense of respect, or at least allure, in these boys' eyes. If you were more ordinary looking, you fell into two other groups. Those who had supposedly been sexually active were said to be up for anything, always putting it about, taking it in various places. Dirty little bitches. Tarnished. Yet an overly virginal reputation was subject to equal, though less detailed, scorn. These chaste young women were somehow sullied because of their supposed purity. They were eternally frigid, their vaginas sealed up, the skin grown over, incapable of yielding to the good times such boys thought they could show them.

I tried to recall which group I most likely fell into during my own school days, presuming that things were no different then. I was neither beautiful nor ugly, so attracted minimal attention. Did boys leer at me? Did they brag about the things they'd like to do to me? We just saw them as harmless, silly and annoying — a different species, if you like. The boys a year or two older seemed different, more aloof, more mature, but when I came to teach them, I realised they weren't particularly.

★　★　★

245

The Jobcentre is cool inside. Blinds keep much of the day out, the light anaemic, artificial. People mill about with varying degrees of despondency on their faces; others wait in queues, listing from side to side, huffing with indignation. Keyboards clack away, phones drone. I try to walk with purpose. Around the edge of the main room, boards list jobs by kind. I look at the options. Again I'm forced to think in categories: woman as barmaid, nurse. Secretary. Dinner lady. Hairdresser. Carer. Cleaner. Dentist's Assistant. Receptionist. Nanny. Beautician. Chambermaid. Others come to mind: air hostess, midwife. Perhaps the boards should be divided by gender.

I join one of the queues.

'Do you have an appointment?' the woman at the main desk asks.

'No, sorry.'

'You'll have to make one. I can go through today's boards with you but you need an appointment.'

'OK.'

She types something as I sit down. After taking some initial details she asks whether I have any qualifications.

I hesitate. 'A degree. English.'

'Anything vocational?'

'Teaching. I teach. Taught. But I don't want to do that.'

She looks over the top of her glasses at me, as if her typing has been wasted.

'What sort of work are you looking for?'

'I'm not sure.' Her stare suggests it's still my

turn to speak. 'I'd like to work in the countryside, perhaps on Dartmoor.'

'I see. And do you have any experience in the environmental sector?'

'No, I don't.'

'Some volunteering, perhaps.'

'No.'

A huff. She clicks her mouse a few times, then reads a list of jobs. I don't really understand what they entail, their description an array of baffling words, newspeak. I interrupt her. 'Something that doesn't involve people really.'

She takes the rest of my details, tells me again that I need an appointment, to go to another desk to make one, where a claim for benefits can also be made. They'll need to know the details of my last employment, how it ended. Meanwhile, they'll call me if anything suitable comes in. She's unable to resist an emphasis on the word suitable. I leave without speaking to anyone else.

Lured by the smell of sea air, I walk up to the Hoe. I'd forgotten how the city unfurls into its sprawling harbour, somehow redeeming itself, the transformation immediate. A throng of boats small and large basks in the waters, the sky cerulean, cloudless. Royal Navy vessels, now the only visible grey, are assembled further out aside the breakwater. I sit on the grass and let my hair ride on the breeze. An array of flags flutter atop a line of lofty poles, one of which is being used by a family as cricket stumps. All around me gulls hover and wheel before landing, walking brazenly up to anyone with food. I recall coming here on a school trip, being told how Drake had watched the Spanish Armada rise over the horizon, a 130-strong fleet bearing cannons and Catholicism. There's peace to be found here, but a group of boys playing football nearby leave me a little self-conscious and I head back across the putting green.

The road arcs down to the old part of town. I feel calm again here, the water gently sloshing between a trawler and the harbour wall. Rigging clinks lazily on the masts of yachts.

Narrow, cobbled streets wind behind the shops and cafés, old buildings with fascias that offer antiques, second-hand books, curios. I find myself inside one. It opens out Tardis-like into a sprawling mass of old furniture, forgotten toys and military memorabilia. Traditional jazz issues weakly from speakers at either end of the long room. I weave between totemic piles of musty books that lean precariously, wondering how you'd go about browsing something near the bottom. Locked cabinets line many of the walls, each devoted to assortments of model cars, coins and miniature glass bottles, plus ceramics, old tools and knives ranging from pocket size to a couple of machetes. Further along, a mannequin stands proud, imperious in its grey German army uniform. On a table at the back there are boxes of postcards, black and white photographs. I flick through some. Men with weather-worn skin unload the morning's catch on to the quay. Another shows Victorian children in dainty bonnets and long socks skipping around the statue of Drake. Several catalogue the rebuilding of the city centre after the Blitz.

I scan a tall bookcase — literature I'd studied, deconstructed, fallen in love with. I run a finger down the spines, realising that I've not read a novel since. Almost eighteen months. I no longer own any; my father, at my request, took two boxes full to the charity shop once I moved back. Something else Jamie has taken from me. Suddenly anxiety rises and I realise a title has reminded me of *that* book. The one I was using for the lessons. I see, though, that this one's something else, a different sort of bird. Not one that mocks.

The musty scent, unique to old books, soon comforts again. I want to buy one, as a test. As reclamation. I slide a Jeanette Winterson out, brushing and blowing the dust off the top.

Edging round a corner, I'm greeted by a sinister-looking ventriloquist's dummy, sitting malevolently on a chair. It evokes memories of a forgotten childhood fear, a terror even, yet I find myself unperturbed by it now.

I make my way back to the door, the corridor of books guiding me full circle. I realise I haven't seen anyone to serve me; there's not even any obvious counter. I call out, but nobody answers. I put the money on the dresser by the door and leave.

A few doors along, a window of oil paintings in ornate frames draws my attention. Women with tousled hair and few clothes seems to be the theme. They lie theatrically on a chaise longue or sit back to front on a dining chair, sombre or sensuous, I can't tell. Behind, at the back of the room, a bearded man with long hair attends to a large canvas with lavish strokes. I'm about to walk on when I notice a sign, the words 'Assistant wanted' scrawled in a careless hand. I open the door, perhaps to ask the man what he requires assistance with. Without looking up he tells me I want upstairs, seemingly knowing the sign was my interest rather than his art.

Two flights later, I find myself in some sort of ceramics workshop. Shelves of variously styled pots, plates, jugs and bowls line three of the walls in assorted stages of production. Another large unit in the centre of the room is littered with pots from floor to ceiling. Space on the floor is minimal, as buckets and bowls lie filled with coloured liquids and powders. As with the antique shop, I can't see anyone, but a low whirring sounds from the back of the room, an occasional splash of water the only other noise. Standing there I notice a warm, dry aroma to the room, like someone baking biscuits.

'Hello,' I call. Nothing. I walk round the central unit and see an elderly man, his hands caressing wet clay on the wheel in front of him.

I go to speak again but he says, 'One minute'. He's shaping some sort of vessel, wetting his right hand before gripping the clay and bringing a rim up until it thins out. He gently pushes the top in and I realise it's a vase. An awkward minute or so later, he's finished.

He sits back, contemplates his work, then slows down the wheel with a lever to the side, before switching it off. He takes what looks like a wire garrotte and pulls it under the base of the vase to free it from the wheel. Delicately, he lifts

250

it off and places it to one side.

'What do you think?' he says without looking up.

'I'm sorry . . . ?'

'Deserves a reaction, I think. Clay's been in the ground for millions of years; now it's a vase. Who knows what's in there? Old forests and mountains, a civilisation or two. What do you think?'

'It's . . . nice.'

'Nice? Nothing else?'

'I wondered about the job.'

'Mmm, it has potential,' he says, ignoring my statement.

I imagine him to be in his early seventies, his few strands of white wispy hair strewn wildly about his crown. His skin is almost leathery; the parts of his large hands not coated in clay are liver spotted. He turns to look at me for the first time. His eyes burn with something I can't place at first; obsession maybe. They belie his age.

'See the sign, did you?'

'Yes.'

'Fancy getting your hands dirty, do you?'

'I'm not sure. What would I have to do?'

'No glamour involved, I'm afraid. Weigh the clay, mix some glazes, pack the kiln.' He scans the room. 'Tidy up a little.' As if reading my mind he then says, 'Can't pay you much.'

'Oh.'

'Not money, at least.'

There's something absurd about my interpretation of his remark. It should make me anxious, upset, but doesn't for some reason.

251

'You could learn,' he says whilst continuing to work.

'Learn?'

'Like an apprentice. Use the wheel at the end of the day, when we've finished.'

'I need an income really.'

'I can show you techniques. Teach you to throw. Up to you. What you doing at the moment?'

'Nothing.' I look around again. The smells excite me. 'I have a son.'

'So do I somewhere.'

'I mean, I can't be here full-time.'

'How old is he?'

'Eleven months.'

'Bring him in.'

'In here?'

'Why not?'

'I . . .'

'Look, have a think. Nobody else has been up. There's a card over there. Give me a call by Friday.'

With that he starts the wheel again. On a small table by the door I find a pile of cards. I take one. *Jack Reynolds — Studio Potter* it reads.

'Goodbye, then,' I say, but he doesn't hear.

31

'Mugs,' Jack says as he searches for something agreeable on the radio.

I weigh out ten lumps of clay, each one eight ounces, and pass him one. He holds it, moving it up and down slightly — distrusting me or the scales, I'm not sure — before issuing a hum of approval. He then slaps it from hand to hand several times, like a child playing with Plasticine, before throwing it on to the wheel head. He pushes the button that starts the rotation, wets his hands and begins centring the clay. I place the box with the rest on the table beside him, before packing the kiln with last week's bowls.

For two weeks now I've driven to Plymouth and walked along the waterfront to the studio. I spend the mornings mixing slips, pugging and stacking the clay. We take turns making green tea in a pot Jack made in the eighties. Has to be Japanese, he says, and never blended — sencha his preference. The leaves look like the grass we used to smoke at college. I expect it to taste bitter but the flavour is delicate and clean.

'It smells of the sea,' I say, which makes Jack laugh.

He tells me about the tea ceremony and its significance, how raku pots evolved from this. Like a child, I fire off questions, happily rapt in this new world.

I kiss my son goodbye each morning, my mother grateful for a reason not to return to work for now. They can manage without her, she insists. She stands at the door holding Paul, waving his hand for him. An anxiety gripped me for the first few days, that somehow the Poulters would come round, make her see sense, and she'd hand Paul over like a pet whose owner could no longer cope. There'd be an It's-for-the-best look on her face and I'd rush out of the door searching frantically. Irrational, but motherhood has evoked a fiercely protective vein from within me. But each day, when I arrive home, they'd just be playing, or she'd be reading to him or watching him sleep.

'It's OK,' she'd say, as if sensing my fear.

My father continues to work for my forgiveness, without referencing directly either the night in my flat or his confusion surrounding it. I manage to find a balance between appreciating his financial support and holding something back emotionally. There's genuine sadness in his face these days, times when I catch him staring into nothingness, lost to an unremitting torment. In time I'll be able to hold him again.

There's an affectation when he plays with his grandson, though I can't know whether there would have been in more typical circumstances. I want to ask my mother how he was with us as children. (Perhaps he's keen not to be viewed as a father by Paul, being the prominent male in his life.)

I recall him neither as an authoritarian nor tender parent; he administered as few smacks as he did hugs. My enduring images always come from childhood holidays, scenes glimpsed, piqued by a smell or sound in adulthood. Once, we were walking back from a day spent on a Cornish beach, the car still a mile or so away. Michael had cut his foot in the sea — not badly, but enough to render the trek tense. I needed to wee badly but there was nowhere to go and we were on the road by now. I remember Mum saying I should have gone in the sea, but I'd never been able to. After half a dozen times of telling them I couldn't wait any longer, my father scooped me up, carried me to the edge of the pavement, pulled my knickers down and told me to go in the drain. Every few seconds a car would pass and I'd try not to look at the driver. Dad didn't shout but I could feel his anger.

★　★　★

Jack works his thumb down inside the clay to create an opening, before bringing the sides up with his fingers.

We signed no contract. There are no terms and conditions. See how you get on for a month, was all he said. This informality, together with his age, somehow allows me to do this, to spend hours each day alone with a man. Perhaps if he were younger, this wouldn't work.

My attempted small talk is, if not ignored, then not indulged either. Nervous on my first day, I'd asked him about a television programme on the night before. He didn't have a TV, he said.

He hasn't spoken of a family and so I haven't asked. It would be construed as rudeness or indifference in others, to not inquire about somebody, their background. But it's as if we know not to. Something is emitted from each of us, a signal that wards off intrusion.

Between the hum of the wheel and the background voices on the radio, there are never awkward silences that need filling. His head lowered, eyes studying the clay, I'm able to watch him. To invent a life, a past. Occasionally, I nearly lapse and ask him something. How did he end up here, doing this? There are no clues around the room. No photographs of a wife or the son he spoke of briefly. A pile of CDs are the only visual hint at an interest beyond ceramics. When we do talk, the conversation is filled with abstractions and I sense a frustrated philosopher, an academic who didn't study long or hard enough, who found the system impregnable or abhorrent. I sense other careers were tried, half a life lived before any artistic calling. It's all speculation, but focusing on another life suits the need to escape my own at times.

He gives the mug a rim, pinching the clay to a point then lightly pressing down. There's less precision than I thought. I imagined delicate movements, surgical in nature, but he reminds

256

me this isn't really art. You make it, get on with the next; twenty mugs an hour, his aim. Jack senses my interest and without looking up talks about his teacher, one of the last English country potters. The man sounded both generous and uncompromising. 'He could turn out a hundred and twenty pots an hour,' Jack says. 'Usually with a hangover. You had to be quick to earn a living in those days. They weren't artists; things were made to use.'

Jack smoothes the mug's wall with a rib, an old credit card cut to shape. Finally he picks up a knife with the blade cut to an angle, which he gently places on the wheel's surface, as if sharpening it, Cutting into the mug's base, he removes the waste clay.

'The man would throw a ton of clay a day sometimes,' Jack continues, 'all dug up himself from the nearby hillside. Some of his pots were so big, he'd use cows' ribs to lift them off the wheel.'

The image is both comical and remarkable.

As Jack talks, I drift off a little, reflecting on this new life I've somehow forged. Or been given, for surely the things that happen to us are, for the most part, beyond our control. And yet we still bring them upon ourselves with the choices we make. A million outcomes whittled down to the life we know. If I hadn't walked past Jack's sign. If I hadn't applied for a job at that school. If I hadn't been late for my class.

Counting the days I've been here, I realise it's a Wednesday. Somehow, for the first time since, a Tuesday has passed without resonating. Without its usual jolting. Along with everything else, he had even claimed a day of the week from me.

Jack dabs a small sponge on the end of a stick into the bottom of the mug, soaking up the excess water. He stops the wheel, looks over the mug once more, before undercutting the clay with a cheese wire, releasing it from the wheel and placing it on a board. Once they're leather-hard and had handles applied, I'll dip them in slip.

Thirty minutes later, he's about to start the last one, when he looks up. 'Come on. Your turn.'

I fumble for reasons not to, but before I know it Jack's stood up, looking expectantly at me. 'Go on.'

'I've never . . . ' I start to say as I sit down.

He hands me the clay. 'Let's see what you've learned in a fortnight.'

I throw the lump, which lands somewhere near the middle of the wheel head. 'Hmm,' Jack says in a non-committal tone. I push the lever forward and the clay races round. 'Ease back,' he says. 'You want it to stay on there.'

I slow the wheel and cup the clay with my palms and fingers as I'd seen him do.

'Water,' he says.

I dip a hand in the bowl and start again. The clay feels cool and slippery as I start to apply gentle pressure.

'Don't be afraid of it,' he says. 'Now, try to centre it, so it doesn't wobble.'

I'd imagined this to be the easier part.

'More water,' Jack barks. 'Keep it wet.' He points to my right hand. 'And get that bloody finger out of the way.'

'Which one?'

'The one that's ruining it.'

Once I feel there's no movement I take my hands away. Jack looks down at the lump of clay. 'It'll do. Now open it out.'

I push a thumb in but the side collapses. Jack tuts and moves in behind me. He leans over and puts his hands around mine, bringing the clay back to its starting shape. The weight of his chest against my back should feel domineering but doesn't. His arms run along the outside of my own, encasing me. There are notes of the sencha on his breath, his face inches from mine. It's not simply the years between us that renders it unthreatening; the intimacy is somehow channelled away from us into the activity itself, so that our connection is part of the process, removed from us as individuals.

This time he guides my thumb gently down into the centre, our hands entwined, coated in liquid clay. The contact is both gentle and firm. 'Now push in and up.' As he speaks saliva clacks in the side of his mouth, his breath on my ear. Together we draw the clay upwards, extending the walls of the mug. Jack wets his fingers some more. I let him guide my hands until, the basic shape achieved, he allows me to carry on alone.

'Ease off now,' he says as the mug thins out. 'Don't jerk away at the top. We're after soft edges.'

I push down with one finger, creating a drinking edge. Finally I undercut the base and turn the wheel off.

We both study it, this unremarkable piece of clay clumsily fashioned into something resembling a mug. With my palms only I lift it gently, placing it with the others.

'Tomorrow,' says Jack, 'we pull the handles.'

32

'I think we should tell him,' Anna said.

Robert brought the axe down, splitting the log in two, one half rolling along the barn floor to her feet. Each subsequent chop was accompanied by a theatrical grunt, the effort put in excessive for the size of the log, as he jettisoned his frustration.

'Who?' he finally said.

'Paul.'

He was about to raise the axe head again when he realised what she meant and a quizzical look became one of incredulity. It had been years since they'd discussed it seriously: the subject, perhaps like a discovered affair, gradually disappeared to a vanishing point, yet could still be recalled with a phrase, a glance.

The first time Paul used the word, he was two. (Anna had said it playfully a few months after moving in, teasing Robert, who didn't baulk at the label.) It could have been something else, a word with similar timbre, perhaps not a word at all. But a minute later he said it again.

They had looked at each other. Why not? It was just a word, an epithet that kept everything simple. Mummy and Daddy. Egalitarian, orthodox. Mummy and Robert would always provoke inquiry, from friends, at school. And if Daddy was established, it would endure any attempt to revise it; they had to make a decision then. Robert had shrugged, as if to say, it's up to you. Anna nodded, smiled, and Daddy it was.

They wondered if Paul would remember the year or so without his new father, a sense of his absence lying beneath the surface, unseen yet felt. And there was more than a year of photographs Robert was missing from that might require an explanation one day. But they would deal with that if it arose. A story of Robert working away perhaps. Or the time for truth chosen for them. Of course people would know. Family, for one. But that was for another time. When Paul was older. Anna would sit him down when he was six or eight or eleven, and tell him. She'd say as far as she was concerned Robert was his father. He only missed out on the first bit. He did all the things a good father did. The comforting, the nurturing. Always one more story at bedtime when Anna would have firmly drawn the line. The patience when chickenpox saw Paul cry all night.

Watching them bond, seeing her son not only accept this new person in his life but become dependent on him, had drawn from Anna unrivalled happiness. Within months of living together, whenever Paul stumbled into the living room late at night, bleary eyed, woken by a bad dream or a fever, it was Robert he'd go to, curling up in his arms while Anna fetched a blanket or medicine. Splinters and cuts were predominantly paternal matters as far as Paul was concerned, Robert's administering of first aid somehow gentler, fostering a mollifying trance in the patient, his touch itself a salve. And this father by default would look at her as if to say, sorry, what can I do? But she felt no envy, no sense of possession when this occurred. They were merely the loving gestures of a father.

Anna observed as milestone events seemed to be savoured as much by Robert as they were by her. Paul's first day at school, standing in fretful silence by the car, watching this fragile boy with his cumbersome satchel walk gingerly across the playground. Then later, picking him up together, sharing proud glances as they listened to the day's account. And the first time father and son went out alone for the day — a fishing trip, Paul's rod a birthday present the week before. Nothing was caught, but his smile had lasted a week. Or when Robert built him a sledge and they trudged up the valley through the snow for its maiden descent, Anna and a year-old Megan watching them from an upstairs window. And without the knowledge of Paul's conception, Robert was able to dismiss the mischievousness, Paul's occasional cruelty towards his sister, as harmless.

Looking at them together, seeing her son flourish in Robert's presence, Anna had been forced to revise her sentiment that children didn't need a father. Perhaps they didn't, but it was hard to ignore these scenes of bonding as they played out.

And so, she thought, when the time came for honesty, they'd be so close it would hardly matter. They would hug, their love stronger for the revelation. Blood, it appeared after all, did not carry everything.

But with each passing year it became easier not to tell him. Plenty of children barely resemble their parents. Robert lost touch with most of his friends from the time before he met Anna. The few that were still around, plus parents, were taken aside, the situation explained. And everyone new to their lives accepted the reality in front of them. Robert and Anna and their son. Later a daughter.

Anna always feared that the disclosure of one truth would soon tease out the other.

'Why now?' Robert looked hurt. Not the anger of sexual rejection, but a vulnerable, crestfallen pain.

'I don't know. I think he suspects something.'

'What do you mean, suspects something?'

She told him about the photographs on his computer, the one of them in bed.

'So he takes unusual photos, so what?'

'There's something about them, like he's searching for something.' She wanted to tell him about the obscene sites Paul had visited, but he'd regard it as irrelevant, which perhaps it was. 'And the skipping school, the withdrawal.'

'I'd worry if he wasn't withdrawn at his age.'

'It's more than that. He's so angry at times. And the fighting . . . '

'He said it was nothing much, that it was worse than it looked.'

'And you believe him?'

'He doesn't want to talk about it. Anyway, you shouldn't go on his computer.'

'He's not going to volunteer anything.'

'And this is your reason for blowing his world apart?'

'We always said he should know one day.'

'Don't you think he has enough going on at the moment?'

'We'll always find a reason not to.'

'I'd thought . . . '

'What?'

Robert stacked another log, hefted the axe above his head.

'That we might never tell him,' he said before another powerful chop, a log scuttling past Anna's feet with more force this time.

She didn't say she had hoped for this also. That until the exhibition she had started to believe they wouldn't discuss it again unless their hand was forced.

'He'll find out one day,' Anna continued. 'He'll need his birth certificate for something. It needs to come from us.'

Robert shook his head. 'It's your call. He's your son.'

'Please, Robert. Just stop a moment.'

He flung the axe down in a corner and gathered the loose logs into a pile.

'You'll still be his father; he'll not see you any differently.'

'You believe that?'

'Yes.'

'So why do this?'

'Because we're lying to him. We could justify it when he was younger.'

'He's still a boy.'

'Who's becoming a young man.'

'Why now? You've said nothing for years.'

'I don't want him to hate me.'

'But it's OK for him to hate me?'

'Nothing will change. He loves you.'

'Everything will change. Megan will have to know.'

'Why?'

'You can't expect Paul to keep it to himself.'

'We can ask him not to tell his sister yet.'

'She'll pick up on something, you know that.'

'But he'll still be her brother. They'll get used to it.'

'Half-brother.'

'Children don't care about such labels.'

'What's a half-brother?' said Megan. She'd wandered into the barn, unheard. They'd been careless. Paul was out, but they'd broken their rule, knowing their daughter was in the house. Robert cast his wife an accusing glare.

'Megan! What have I said about creeping up on people?' said Anna.

'I didn't creep up.'

'How long have you been there?'

'I don't know. I just came in. Why are you shouting?'

'We're not shouting. Were you listening to our conversation?'

'No.'

'Then why were you standing there?' There was anger in Anna's voice now.

'I just . . . '

'*Answer me*. Did you hear what we were saying?'

Megan's eyes watered.

'It's OK, darling,' said Robert. 'What is it?'

Megan sniffed a little. 'I came to tell you there's someone at the front door,' she said before running back inside.

33

Anna heard the voices but couldn't discern what was being said. It didn't sound like the police again, the tone was informal. Robert said something about the weather on the moor and then she heard the front door shut.

'Someone wants to buy a pot,' Robert said as he came into the kitchen. Behind him Jamie walked brazenly in. He looked tired and was unshaven, but still something glinted in his eyes.

'He was at the exhibition,' Robert continued, 'but didn't have his chequebook. As he was passing, he thought he'd try here.'

She did sell pieces from home occasionally, though only by word of mouth. There was no sign at the end of the lane that suggested a pottery could be found along it, but Robert didn't seem to consider this.

Jamie held his hand out. 'James,' he said.

Anna ignored the gesture. She tried to keep her voice steady. 'I've nothing for sale here. You need to go into town.'

'Nothing at all?' said Jamie. 'That's a shame, I really liked them.'

Robert looked confused by her tone, but she could see his thoughts were still with their conversation in the barn. He left them to it, went to the other side of the kitchen and washed his hands in the sink.

Jamie looked around the room. 'So you make it all here, up on the moor?'

'Yes.'

'That's not a bad way to earn a living.'

'It's OK.'

Robert turned round, perhaps sensing something was wrong. 'You local, then, James?' he said.

'No, just visiting the area. Searching for fresh air. Just me and the open road. Came down this way once on holiday, with my parents, long time ago, when I was a child. Trip down memory lane, I suppose you'd call it.'

Anna held his stare. Jamie's vocabulary struck her as odd, as if another education had occurred since the one she'd briefly witnessed. 'I'm sorry you've had a wasted journey,' she said.

'Not to worry. Like your husband said, I was passing. Perhaps I could try another time, maybe the next batch you make.'

'You'll be gone by then,' Anna said, a little barbed.

'Oh, I could come back this way.'

'I'm sorry, you have to go to the gallery. They'll get their commission that way.'

'Well, I might do that.'

Jamie was turning to leave when Megan came

270

down. The rebuke outside clearly forgotten, she asked what was for dinner, stopping on seeing the stranger.

'Hello,' Jamie said.

Megan stood by her mother, who pulled her in close.

'Don't be rude, Megan,' said Robert, his back still turned. 'Say hello.'

She managed a muffled response.

'And how old are you, Megan?' said Jamie.

'Eleven.'

'Eleven, wow. And are you good at making things, like your mum?'

'We're quite busy, I'm afraid,' said Anna, her daughter silently protesting at how tight she was being held.

'I was hoping to buy one of your mum's lovely pots, Megan, but she doesn't have any ready.'

Anna sensed Megan was about to correct him. 'I'll show you out,' she said.

In the few seconds they stood there in silence, Anna felt sure he was going to reach out and touch her daughter. Maybe ruffle her hair or pat her head in an avuncular gesture. It would signify an immediate end to the ridiculous and torturous exchange; she would be compelled into action of some kind. Perhaps he knew this, because instead he allowed her to usher him out of the kitchen.

In the hall Jamie paused by the dresser, noticing the rows of pottery on the upper shelves. These were pieces from the last ten years or so that Anna was unwilling to part with. Not out of any artistic pride or profound fondness for them aesthetically; but each one had been fashioned during a period of terrible darkness. The process of making them had allowed her to transcend the mechanics of doing so, enabling her to banish the old life as it once again threatened to take hold, and emerge back into the equilibrium of her current one.

Jamie reached out and picked up a small bowl. 'They're not for sale,' she said.

He looked at it for a few seconds and then placed it back.

At the front door, the two of them alone, Jamie turned round. His clothes smelled damp and musty. 'It was lovely to meet you and your family,' he said, his voice carrying through the downstairs.

Anna looked hard at him, hoping to convey fury at his presence in her home, in her world. She wanted to say this was the worst thing he could do, but it wasn't true. They stood there. Whatever I have to do to make you go, Anna thought, I will do it. Finally he turned and left. As soon as he was over the threshold, she closed the door and leaned into it. From her studio she watched him walk along the lane, back to the road.

She checked the time; Paul wasn't due back for a while. She sent him a text message, asking if he needed a lift home.

The bedroom window offered a slightly longer view, but she couldn't see Jamie on the road. Perhaps he had a car. Perhaps he had doubled back away from the lane to the other side of the house. She went into her son's room, but a low mist in the valley spoiled visibility. Megan was still downstairs, so Anna stole a look from her daughter's bedroom window. Nothing. She checked her phone: Paul was going to be late home, his tardiness for once bringing relief.

She listened at the top of the stairs. Robert and Megan were chatting, something about school, about the frog dissection. For a moment it seemed quite reasonable to take the car, the Land Rover even, and drive, looking for him if he was on foot. And if he was still on the road, it would be easy, barely a movement at all to bring her hand down through a few degrees of the steering wheel, a firm contact, decisive. Visibility could be so poor up here. Anna tried to focus on her breathing.

'Mum, come down,' called Megan. 'Dad's showing me how to make a fire.'

'In a minute.'

She went back into Paul's room and sat on the bed. She studied his possessions. Fourteen years the room had been his, just a few months after Robert suggested she stay the night in it and she'd climbed the stairs to rid herself of the past. The day they moved in had been the gift of a second life and she could scarcely believe it. Her parents helped to move her stuff, their faces full of resignation. They'd only met Robert a few times, once on the moor, a couple of times at the house. He seems nice enough, was all her mother said at dinner, perhaps knowing their right to give parental advice had been exhausted. Her father merely commented on how cold the cottage would be in winter. That first night here, in her new home, had felt like reclamation; everything he'd taken, she believed for the first time, could be salvaged. Even Paul slept through that initial night, not crying despite several teeth coming through. They awoke to the sounds of birdsong and the river in the valley.

She picked up one of Paul's tops, flung over the back of his chair, and brought it to her face, breathing in its scent.

34

How soon is too soon? An encounter on the moor becomes a date a year later. A first kiss goodnight, on the cheek, numbers swapped. Don't be the first to ring. A film? Yes, that would be nice. A warm feeling I'd forgotten. A vague awareness something is happening. What to wear, what impression to give? The longer skirt. I have no short ones any more. A little make-up. Heart beating faster driving there. Don't seem too keen. Will he see through me? Do I give off an aura, a stench of damaged goods? Can men tell?

There was a girl I used to hang around with at school. Claire. We were fourteen when rumours broke of her having a sexual encounter of sorts. She denied it, told me nothing had really happened, but the damage was done and her reputation became embellished into something heinous. People then forgot the original story; she was just 'that girl', her name used as a synonym for anything licentious. I tried to defend her initially but it was clear I would become tarnished by association.

The persecution lasted until she left a year or so later, by which time we'd drifted apart. The only thing you can do is move away, start again, hope your reputation doesn't follow you.

The film was terrible, facetious, though we laughed anyway. It hardly matters when you're that nervous. You let me pay, which I liked. And then a drink in a nearby pub. A longer kiss, less awkward. Tender, even. Yes, I'd like to see you again. I'll make dinner, you said.

This house is beautiful. That you both live and work on the moor fascinates me. Before you started cooking, we stood outside, the sky cloyed with a million stars that left me unable to speak. That's Orion's Belt, you said, your arm extended over my shoulder, guiding my gaze. Looking west you tried to find Venus but couldn't. Too early, you said — whether meaning this evening or the time or year, I wasn't sure.

You told me about standing here at dusk in autumn, when, if fortune is with you, the sky darkens with a million starlings preparing to roost in the larch plantation to the south, their aerial dance balletic, rippling and wheeling like a living sculpture.

I look around the lounge as you cook in the next room. Sparse, humble. I run my hand across the stone wall, the warmth from the open fire deep within it. You call through: wine? I hesitate. OK. Your parents judge me from their picture on the mantel; they wonder if I'm good enough for you, whether I'm going to tell you. They look nice, but I still want to turn them to the wall.

You bring the drinks in. We chink glasses and I have to stop myself kissing you.

'How can you afford this?' I say clumsily. You seem only a few years older than me, which makes you too young for all this.

'It sold at auction. I was lucky. You should have seen the state of it when I moved in.'

'How long have you been here?'

'Three years. Bit more. It's a labour of love, a long-term project. Friends helped get it this far; a traveller stayed for a while, in exchange for labour.' You look around the room. 'Damp's a big problem.'

'Don't you get bored out here? Or lonely?'

You smile, as if my question is absurd. 'There's always something that needs doing. And people pop by. I'm not one for crowds.'

You talk about a dislike of cities, how they all look the same to you, that you're allergic to their clamour. Parents who took you on endless walking holidays as a child gave you a love of what they called the last wilderness areas, which you say are slowly vanishing. You refer to the moor as the uplands, which I hadn't heard before. It makes me feel even further away from everything else.

'I like living where nature dominates man rather than the other way around,' you say, and I reflect on your words for a moment.

I try to drink slowly.

You talk about the different winds, how the one from the west is the warmest, the most forgiving. Others are more malevolent, seeming to blow right through your bones. And the rain, how it drives in for days at a time, soaking you to the marrow. You think it'll never stop, that you'll soon sink into a quagmire. But then you wake up to a windless, cloudless day, a sky that's cyanic blue. The granite walls of the cottage sparkle in the sunlight, the moor's primeval beauty alive again.

'Some people only know the Dartmoor of Conan Doyle fiction,' you say. 'The bleak, bog-ridden wilderness, shrouded in mist.'

You tell me there are a hundred and sixty tors, that the granite plateau beneath runs all the way through Cornwall to the Scilly Isles. I could listen to this all night.

'The soil is acidic. That's why there are so few human remains and tools found.' I listen as you tell me how the molten granite flowed into the south-west peninsula hundreds of millions of years ago. Encroaching ice sheets to the north then created the Dartmoor tundra. 'The freezing and thawing levered huge granite blocks down the tors, so it looks like an eruption.'

'Clitter,' I say, then blush at the word.

'Yes, clitter.' You worry you're boring or patronising me, that I'm humouring you. No, I say, please carry on. 'As the ice to the north retreated, plants from the south were able to flourish. Almost the whole of the moor was once wooded — birch and hazel, alder and the stunted oaks. The first settlers here were nomadic hunters, who had little impact on the land. But agricultural settlers came later, living on the higher treeless slopes until the climate cooled, forcing them down, causing deforestation.' As you talk you tend to the fire. There's a hint of annoyance in your voice

278

as you describe the blankets of planted conifers that alter the moor's ecology.

'It's not ours to change,' you say.

'Isn't it protected?'

'It's not easy. Some people look at it and see only austerity, a cruel landscape that's battered by the elements. It doesn't evoke the romantic idyll of the Cotswolds with its pretty cottages and quaint villages. I mean there is that, but mostly it's barren. But if you look, I mean really look, you see curlews and golden plovers, even peregrines. There are rare butterflies, kingfishers and otters. In the woods further up the valley, there are more than a hundred species of lichen, some of which aren't found anywhere else in the country.' Your passion is intoxicating.

We lapse into silence. The wine, rich and spicy, warms me.

'Tell me about the myths,' I say.

'Which ones?'

'Have you ever seen the hands?'

'The Hairy Hands? That steer your car off the road?' You affect a sinister tone, then laugh.

'What, you don't believe in ghosts?' I say.

'No, not really.'

★ ★ ★

The food is uncomplicated, restorative. You keep apologising for the absence of a particular flavour. I don't care. I'm thinking about the kiss after the film. The first since the night in the flat. You were gentle, even as you pulled me into you, gripping my arms. The thing I feared the most was your smell, in case it was similar, but it wasn't.

'Some more wine?'

'No, I've got to drive back.'

'You could stay,' you say. I look down, embarrassed. 'There's a spare room, I meant. If you wanted another drink.'

I didn't want any more wine but here I am anyway; not in the spare room, but in yours. You showed me the other bedroom, an old futon the only furniture. Or you can share mine, it would be warmer, you said. I ask if you can put some music on. Anything, I say. You leave me alone and I fight the nausea. My chest tightens. I hear some music start up, then stop, replaced by something softer. I turn off the lamp by the bed so that only a silvered light from the moon prevents the room from being in darkness.

I picture my son at home, hoping he doesn't wake to find my bed empty. I'll drive home before dawn.

I have to do this no matter how much my body rebels. Part of me wants to rush, to hurry through it, so that you're the most recent. I crave some different memories to be etched into place.

You're back. We undress, folding clothes on to chairs as if we've always done this. We both keep our tops and pants on and get into bed. The sheets are so cold, forcing us together.

'Sorry, I haven't got around to heating up here.'

'It's fine.'

We start to kiss, but I pull away. 'Can we just talk for a minute?'

280

'Of course.'

You tell me about your job. I tease you about the day we first met, how you dropped all your tools in the heather. That was almost a year ago, yet you still recognised me two weeks ago in the market. It took me a moment or two. Something in your cheeky grin. You asked where my son was, even remembering his name. Had I walked on the moor much recently? You said you hadn't seen me out that way since. I mistook your small talk for just that, said goodbye, only for you to catch up with me a few rows away. And then I realised you were trying to ask me out.

'What made you think I was single?' I asked you later. 'You knew I had a son.'

'I don't know. I just couldn't imagine you being with someone.'

We kiss again. I wonder what you'll think of me tomorrow. You ask what exactly I do at the workshop in Plymouth. I tell you about mixing glazes, weighing clay, making my own pieces sometimes. What did you do before that? you say. I kiss you, longer this time. No more talk. You lift my top over my head, take off your own. Warmth from the fire is still in your skin. You smell of outdoors. The moonlight is sufficient to make out the line of each other's bodies. I fight to keep the panic away as you touch me. It would be easy to float away, leave behind only my body, a receptacle. I'll want a bath afterwards, but not here.

Your hand parts my legs. His angry words from that night return briefly: *I can't make it wet.* Your tongue moves gently in my mouth.

281

But then you pull away. At first I think I've done something wrong. That somehow you know, that your fingers inside me could sense it. But I realise you're putting a condom on. That dramatic pause, the fumbling. I remember Nick, how he hated to wear them, how he spoke of being inside his wife without one. I've read that some rapists wear them, to avoid detection. That same dramatic pause, the fumbling, even then. Wishing that Jamie wore one is wishing the non-existence of my son, so I don't do it any more.

As soon as you're inside me, I realise I'm crying, the tears sweeping down in a silent cascade. You don't notice at first. I will myself to do this, it doesn't matter how it makes me feel. The sensation is strange, like the very first time but without the pain.

'Hey, what's up?'

I pull you closer. 'Don't stop, please.' But you do. 'Please, carry on,' I say.

You continue and I stifle my sobbing to a tremulous whimper. Again there is the urge to remove my attention, to escape into fantasy, but I force myself to stay. Don't stop, I whisper. Why are you crying? Don't stop.

I realise I'm just lying there. Without my arms around you, I could be a corpse. Isn't there something I should be doing? You must think me ridiculous. Small groans of pleasure come from your mouth, rhythmic, unthreatening. I wait for you to do something that renders the terror unconquerable, but you don't. Gentle to the end.

And then it's over and he's not the last person to be inside me.

The weight of your body on mine pins me to the bed. It should be oppressive but isn't. After a minute you move slowly off me. We lie in silence facing each other, our exhalations fusing in the space between our mouths. You brush the last tears from my cheek, sensing not to ask again. I am already in love with the scent of you. The watery light filters through the curtains, shadows undulating on the walls through the night. I don't care that sleep won't come.

It's strange to hear almost nothing. No cars or sirens. No drunks stumbling home. Occasionally an owl hoots, an old beam moans in the wind above. But otherwise silence.

I think of my old flat, wondering who lives there now and how we know nothing of the acts that occur in homes before us, the ghosts left behind. I wonder what has happened in this room over the years and whether I'll be here again.

The need to wash heightens until I can no longer ignore it. For a moment I imagine walking naked down to the river beyond the garden, where we stood before dinner. Deep enough to immerse myself in, I picture myself lying there, shivering violently as the icy water purges me. And then the same thought as earlier: I wonder what you'll think of me in the morning. How soon is too soon?

It's still dark when I get dressed.

'Don't go yet,' you say across the room.

'I have to get back to my son.'

35

'Why not?' you say, as again I prepare to flee before the sun comes up.

'Because.'

'Because what?'

Because everything. 'You don't just move in with someone.'

'Why not?'

'I don't know you.'

'Last night suggests otherwise.'

I smile like a child. 'I want to go slowly.'

'Why?'

Because each time you hold me I think I'll break. 'Anyway, it's not just about me.'

'I did mean both of you.'

I look hard at you, scrutinising the words for sincerity.

I'd brought Paul here a week ago and you made us lunch. He seemed to like you, as much as one year olds are discerning. I watched you play with him, looking to see whether it was for my benefit. I've made no plans for anyone else, I want to tell you.

'What about his father?' you say. You've asked so few questions until now. Please don't. 'Is he around?'

'There isn't one.'

'That's impressive. Unique, I'd say.'

'I mean he's not with us.'

'Oh, I'm sorry.'

'Not that. Can we just . . . ?' It is the first time any tension has risen between us. 'I'm sorry,' I say. 'I hardly knew his father. Can we leave it at that?'

It's starting to get light outside. The urge to wash each time has eased, but your feelings scare me.

'So, can you imagine living here?'

I've thought of little else. This house in the heart of Dartmoor, once two dilapidated barns, converted with love and sweat into a home. You showed me photographs taken after you'd bought it. Two shells of mud and stone, roofless, held together by little more than a giant ivy tree. Ten-feet-high nettles almost hid them from two sides. You talked about the foundations, packing giant stones underneath the walls before they could be restored, and how you rendered inside. As you worked you lived in an old caravan in what would become the garden, its roof held on by rope and a block of granite as the elements pummelled you. You managed without running water for the first few months, until you found a spring, rising a few hundred yards away.

Your little project, you call it. A lifetime's work, and yet in some ways it's perfect now. Comfortable enough to live in, bare enough to nourish the soul, removed from the world that still overwhelms me.

I imagine the seasons enveloping you. I picture you finishing work in the winter, lighting a fire, reading by its light. In the summer you work all evening before walking the mile or so to the Warren, drinking beer by the perpetual fire. Friends visit at weekends and tease you, calling you a hippy, calling you mad. Even colleagues leave the moor behind after work, heading for towns, even cities. But you stay because, like me, you need to.

So far you know that I left here to study, that although I finished my course, an academic life wasn't for me, and I returned, pregnant. Respecting my privacy you probably fill the gaps in once I've left, assuming Paul's father was what I ran away from, which I suppose is a version of the truth. I wonder what else you will extract from me.

From the bed you watch me dress in the half-light, your head propped up by an arm. I haven't cried the last few times; it feels like I suspect it should. An ache manifests in my chest when we're apart — for you, for this place — feelings that both thrill and terrify me. I ponder for hours what connects people, where it comes from, where it goes. You might be the first person I am in love with.

My father knocked and came into my room last night, perhaps sensing my newfound joy. He'd had a few pints after work, his complexion suggested. Paul was being read a story by his grandmother downstairs.

'Can we talk?' he said.

I shrugged my shoulders, which he took to mean yes, closing the door behind him. I wondered if this was going to be it, the grand apology, redemption sought. Unsure whether I wanted it eighteen months after it was due, I asked him about his day, but he ignored me.

'You know I don't always show my feelings?' he said.

'Dad, please.'

'That doesn't mean I don't have any.' He sat on the end of the bed, almost falling off at first. 'And you know I love him.' I wasn't sure who he meant for a second. 'He's my grandson. He means the world to me.' He put a hand on my leg, patted it, our first physical contact since before the row. Even when I pass Paul to him, I make a point of avoiding touching him. Even after the birth, he knew not to attempt to hug or kiss me. We hadn't been particularly tactile before, so the transition required only a slight adjustment.

'I will always love that boy,' he said, as if this might not have been a given.

And that was it. His outpouring. No shameful regret; no dormant rage. Not even a craven reference to *that Tuesday*. For him, saying he loved Paul had needed a couple of hours in the pub first. He went downstairs to his study and I wished I was here.

You make a last plea for me to come back to bed.

'Do you mean it?' I say.

'Yes, I want you in this bed.'

288

'You know what I mean.'

'Yes. Of course I mean it.'

I look out of the window. The first covering of daylight graces the top of Crockern Tor as the sun spills on to the land. Dew glistens at the sides of the lane that leads up to the road.

A person could hide here for ever. People wouldn't stumble upon you, they wouldn't just be passing. The first thing you see each day is one of the great tors that gaze serenely down on you. Or the ancient, opaque woods to the north, the stunted oaks, twisted by the wind, gnarled and otherworldly. At weekends you might not see another person. You could just walk down to the stream, immerse your feet in the cool limpid water and let the uplands heal you.

I kiss you on the mouth, say that I'll call later. That I'll think about it.

'Give me a reason why not,' you say as I'm halfway downstairs and I know that I can't.

36

Robert asked Paul if he had put the chickens in for the night, as he was asked to do an hour earlier when the last of the day's light remained. He hadn't and moaned at the prospect.

'It's OK, I'll do it,' said Anna, leaving the room before Robert could object.

Outside, the chilled air tingled in her nostrils, the absence of cloud cover promising a frost overnight. Her steps across the yard resounded in the silence of early evening, each one a flagrant announcment of her presence. Down in the bottom corner of the garden the cottage felt distant, as if great effort would be needed to get back there. The torch was comforting, more for its weight than the light it gave off. Anna shone it into the pen where eyes met its beam like pairs of stars.

She hoped she had been the only one to hear the phone in the night; no one had mentioned it at breakfast. There'd been five or six rings, just after 4 a.m. She had been awake for an hour anyway, listening for the sounds of someone trying to be quiet. One more ring and she would have gone downstairs, perhaps unplugging it; there was nothing to gain by answering it. But then it stopped. Robert's breathing, lighter for a few seconds, returned to the rhythm of deep sleep. No more sleep came for her, though, as she waited to see if it rang again. She would go to bed last tonight and disconnect it, making sure she was first up tomorrow, her caution undetected.

Earlier Megan had complained that some of the specimens were missing from her collection in the barn. A badger's jaw, an adder's shed skin. Others had been moved around, spilled on the floor. Robert had teased her, saying the fox had probably taken them, but nothing was made of it. She was probably mistaken, they agreed. When she was alone with her daughter, Anna had told her not to go into the barn again on her own for now, as another fox might end up in there, and, if cornered, could be dangerous. Megan looked at her with almost mocking disbelief but, perhaps due to the tension of the last few days, decided against a protest.

Inside the pen Anna started to corral the chickens into their coop, a few clucks of protest riding the breeze up the valley. Even in the dark, she sensed one was missing. Once they were all in, a sweep with the torch confirmed this. Robert had extended the height of the mesh in the summer when a few got out and a comical half an hour had been spent catching them. Perhaps it still wasn't high enough. She walked along the perimeter, shining the light across the heather,

292

down to the stream. Two eyes looked back at her, still as the moon, before the creature scurried away, too fast to be a chicken. She pointed the beam further out, until it faded to nothing, before walking on.

It felt like a clod of grass underfoot. Or one of the soft mounds of sphagnum moss you found down by the bogs. She pointed the torch at her feet. There were no wound marks, no blood as far as she could tell. Its neck curved back on itself, suggesting it was broken. Megan had names for the chickens — characters from *The Simpsons*, regardless of gender — but it was impossible to see which one it was. Anna nudged it with a boot. She fetched an old hessian sack from the shed, dropped the bird inside and placed it in the composter. She would bury it tomorrow and think of something to tell her daughter. A disease perhaps. Best keep an eye on the rest, she would say. With it buried, its broken neck out of sight, Robert might accept this too.

She forced herself to remain outside a little longer, watching the moon rise, its quiet majesty lanced by a lone cloud.

★ ★ ★

Back inside Anna washed her hands. She allowed the water to run hot, evoking a forgotten obsession with hygiene. She worked the soap into a generous lather, rinsed, and then repeated the action. The stench of death removed, she looked in the mirror. Her eyes were tired, perhaps defeated.

Living amid this virginal landscape with its

untamed slopes and rarefied air had always felt like being in the remotest corner of the world, removed from any reality she'd known. She had created not only a different life, but another person. A metamorphosis. There was the Anna before the attack, the Anna of today, and a veiled year or so that sat in between like a vacuum, a murky portal that she passed through only after the birth of her son. It was hard to conceive of that young woman, the one whose figurative death somehow led here. For years Anna, the new Anna, remained angry with her, at times hating her for being so credulous, so trusting and naïve. If there was blame, it lay with her. But Anna now regarded her with forgiving scrutiny.

Healing wasn't a word she used — the residue of that Tuesday would always be part of her, like the moon on the seas, exerting its abiding influence. But that wasn't to say happiness had finished with her after that night: she had two children, a loving husband, the art that, until recently, stirred her each morning. And there was always contentment to be found in nature, a peace that lifted her above individual concern, connecting her with others who felt the same. The moor had cleansed her. But healed, not quite.

The act itself, its brutality and violence, no longer had any hold on her; it had long since been deposited deep in her mind, so that it resembled a childhood nightmare, one you could, with effort, recall. But what it had done to her, the filter it left, through which all the future had to pass, had the permanence of granite. It

294

shaped everything: the fallout with her father, the dislike of crowds, that moment when Robert was more forceful than usual, perhaps entering her too quickly, or holding her arms down. It would be simple to tell him not to, that she didn't like that. There would be no need to elaborate. But instead of anger or alarm, she merely became cold, disassociation the habitual way. Robert had called her a corpse once. He waited until he'd finished. They'd even laughed about it the next day, as she mocked his necrophilist potential. They could still do that sometimes, render it farcical, tragicomic. Perhaps these had been the times to unveil. Ha, ha, yeah, the reason I'm a corpse is . . . Why hadn't she? A few dates in, when there was nothing to lose? His reaction would have been transparent: either masked revulsion or quiet concern. Any response between the two would soon have crystallised into one or the other, with only the latter allowing a relationship to flourish.

But it was easier to avoid judgement of any kind. With acceptance would come a certain curiosity, as the images sharpened in his mind. An initial pledge of understanding would soon be corroded by his imagination, dripping like acid on to thoughts, until eventually he would, if not ask, then consider the questions her father had put to her. One day he would ask about the force used, whether she'd done everything possible to stop him. Whether a boy, unarmed except for his temper, could do that. If he didn't ask Anna, he would ask himself. Who could blame him?

And then for a few years she told herself that telling him would only increase the likelihood of Paul finding out, although Robert was more than capable of pretending to be his father. No, it was something else that stopped her. Something more than feeling unclean or sullen. More than the fear he would see her as someone else. Something even more than the shame.

Certainly words felt an inadequate form of revelation, failing to capture anything beyond mere cataloguing. But even if they could, she probably wouldn't have uttered them. She owned that night. For all its horror, she felt possessive of it, protective even. Ownership imported a sense of power over it, which would be diluted by dissemination.

And yet even without these recent events, the weight of the lies had begun to match the legacy of the attack. Perhaps the truth could be borne. The fantasy of a new start beckoned, like the nearby farmers swaling the gorse and scrub, burning it so that new shoots could grow through.

★ ★ ★

In the lounge Paul was asking for a lift into town after dinner. Anna would mention the chicken to Robert later, telling Megan tomorrow that Bart or Homer or Marge had died.

'It's a school night,' Robert said. 'Don't you have revision to do?'

'Not really,' said Paul.

'That means yes, then.'

'I can do it tomorrow.'

'Where are you going?'

'Just round to Chris'. Watch a film or something.'

'And will Chris' parents give you a lift back?'

'I'll get the last bus.'

'There isn't one that late,' said Anna.

'I'll hitch.'

'No you won't,' she said. 'I don't want you going out this late.'

'It's not late. Jesus, they've caught that guy, who wasn't even on the moor.'

'Just ring if you can't get back,' said Robert.

Anna tried to hold herself together. She could say nothing further without giving something away.

'James said it's not easy to escape from prison,' said Megan as she packed her school bag for tomorrow.

'Who's James, darling?' said Robert.

'That man who came to buy one of Mummy's pots.'

Anna and Robert looked at each other.

'When did he tell you that?' snapped Anna.

'When we got off the bus after school. He was going for a walk. He said there was nothing to worry about and that they wouldn't let anybody else break out. He said we were safe living here.'

Anna fought to keep the panic from her voice. 'Were you there, Paul?'

'What?'

'After school, when Megan was talking to the man.'

'Yeah.'

'What did he say?'

'I dunno. Stuff.'

'You shouldn't talk to strangers, Paul,' said Robert.

'I'm fifteen.'

'Well, Megan shouldn't.'

'I can't stop her.'

'What did he want?' said Anna.

'God, why the interrogation? He was just some nerd walking the moor.' Paul got up and stamped upstairs. Base from his speakers soon resounded through the ceiling.

'Megan,' said Anna slowly. 'What else did the man say?'

Megan's face tightened, unsure how much trouble she was in. 'Nothing.'

'Nothing?'

'He wanted to know how old Paul was.'

37

Anna chose a fallow part of the garden, up behind the barn, the ground still hard from the overnight frost. Robert had said they should take the chicken to the vet, in case it was infectious; she told him she would call them later, for advice. *I advise you it's dead, I advise you its neck has been broken.* More lies.

Once the hole was deep enough, she emptied the bird from the sack. It landed with its neck corrected, coiled round the earthen wall, like a cat asleep. She looked up to the conifers, to the old woods upstream, the tors behind. Her breath, rapid from digging, hung in the air, dispersing slowly like a smoke signal. Winter had crept up. She took the spade and began replacing the earth.

Megan was at a friend's tonight. Anna had asked her husband and son to come home straight away after work and school. There were things to talk about. Robert had looked cross that she'd made up her mind, chosen a moment without further discussion. She had today to decide how much truth could be endured, and in what order the revelations should be delivered.

The thing with a lie, she thought, is how lonely you become. That Robert knew Paul wasn't his son changed little, given what he didn't know himself. There were her parents, but when you try so hard to distance yourself from the truth, you don't choose to revisit it in order to share the burden. Least of all with a father who had once doubted what had happened and a mother who cowered each time the night in the flat was mentioned.

And Anna had two lies. Separate yet inextricably bound, they followed her everywhere, like shadows on an X-ray, unseen by others, but always there, filed away. Tonight she could reveal them, hold them up to the light: *Look at my disease. This is what I'm made of. I am not what you think I am.* Their power would be stripped. His power. His ability to shatter their lives, gone in a sentence or two; Anna would do the devastating before he could. Scorch the earth between them. What was left after that, she couldn't control. The police could be called, the chicken dug up if necessary. A warning would be issued; he would be told there were no secrets to expose, to leave them alone. They would escort him from the moor. New shoots would emerge.

★　★　★

She had a good fire going. The studio could have felt foreboding since his appearance at the window, yet it retained some comfort. She allowed some of the past to form at the edges of her mind, the first days and weeks after that night, how she started walking the moor, letting it envelop and soothe her. She remembered an entire day spent here, traversing the tors, struggling with a decision that would echo throughout her future. Higher and higher she had climbed. There was a bird, a wagtail. Forgetting it was autumn, for a moment she'd interpreted its staccato dance along the wall, its frenetic trill, as an attempt to lure her away from its young.

★   ★   ★

Anna drove through Princetown and headed south. Looking across the moorland to the prison, she imagined the man who'd tasted freedom, now back in his cell, tales of his escape to regale. The roads were quiet; a few walkers were scattered at the edges of her vision.

The road wound down, over Devil's Bridge before opening out on the long straight towards Sharpitor. She turned off before Yelverton, heading down to Meavy, keeping a steady speed, the road narrow and serpentine. At Cadover Bridge she parked and got out. A long walk was needed, away from the cottage, to rehearse tonight in her head.

The cloud had thickened. A stillness lingered, the only sound the flow of the nearby river. She began walking south along the west bank of the Plym. The water, initially calm, began to surge as the banks neared one another, cutting between the moss-coated boulders, white with fury. After walking for a few minutes she changed course, climbing up through the woods, only occasionally looking back down towards the river, where she saw only trees. The ascent steepened, the roar of the water below grew fainter, soon fading to nothing. It was difficult to maintain a good rhythm, as networks of roots, partially hidden by fallen leaves, conspired to topple all but the most cautious of walkers. When she stopped to rest, blood pulsed in her ears, her thighs burned. A break in the cloud allowed dappled sunlight to create a mosaic on the ground around her. Holding her breath to listen, she heard the occasional branch crack in the mid-distance. She spun round but couldn't locate its source. Silence returned.

Further on, through a gap in the canopy, the escarpment rose proudly, a few small trees clinging to its face, as if a giant might use them to reach the top. Free from climbers, the Dewerstone's rocky crags soared imperiously. Ivy bedecked its surface, as if binding the fissures like wounds. A pair of ravens soared above its crest, issuing throaty gronks as they performed playful tumbles.

Anna climbed further.

Finally the ground began to level off into pastured fields, leaving the woods behind. She slipped through a fence, catching her leg on the barbed wire. Her trousers tore and a trail of blood rose, as if drawn on in ink.

The recent rain meant the earth was soft here, each step requiring effort to lift her foot from the mud. Beyond the hedge at the far side of the field, the moorland returned, a granite stack rising up ahead. When she reached it, Anna climbed the least steep side, and sat down at the top, breathing heavily.

The Cornish hills were visible in the distance. She followed their contours down to the sea, the sun glistening off Brunel's bridge. Plymouth sprawled along the coast, but could still be covered by a finger. She thought of Jack in his studio, though she'd heard he had retired years ago. An invitation to the exhibition was sent to him but she'd known he'd baulk at the idea. I just make things for people to use, she could hear him saying as he closed the workshop for the day and headed to the Dolphin for a pint.

The wind made her eyes water as it blustered in from the west. She pulled back the torn flap of her trousers, the blood now congealed to a deep burgundy.

He'd been quiet but she could sense him behind her. She'd presumed there would be walkers but she could see none. There would be no signal on her mobile either.

'That's some climb,' Jamie said. 'I could hardly keep up.'

Anna fought to keep her fear in check. 'Worth it, though, don't you think?' she said.

He moved round so he was in front of her, eight feet or so below. He looked out into the distance, his back to her. 'Beats me why people live here. There's nothing for miles.'

'Some like it that way.'

'Do you, Anna?'

It was strange to hear him use her name; in that other time, after school, she'd asked him to, but he had kept to Miss.

'I need the space,' she said. 'Everything needs its space.' He turned to look at her, but she didn't meet his eyes. 'Why are you here, Jamie?'

'I told you. I think we should be friends.'

'*Friends?*'

'Yes, friends. We go back a long way.'

'And do you usually kill your friends' animals?'

He let out a little laugh. 'It was making a noise, giving me away. Your husband might have heard me.'

Anna followed a plane as it tracked the horizon in silence, its contrail breaking up. Forcing herself to look at Jamie, she saw a wildness in him. His clothes were filthy, his face unshaven, and an intensity that suggested derangement burned in his eyes.

'You need to leave us alone,' she said, her voice tremulous. 'You need to go home and not come back here.'

'Oh, come on, you can do better than that.'

'What do you mean?'

'I come all this way to find you, after all this time, and you want me to leave straight away.'

'I'm not afraid of you.'

'See, that's something to build on.'

'There's nothing here for you.'

'Nothing?'

'No.'

'I wouldn't say that.'

'Well, I'm saying it.'

He moved a little closer, forcing her to look at him. 'How old is he?'

She recoiled inside, but managed to show none of it. 'Who?'

'The boy. Your son.'

Anna looked away.

'He looks the right age,' Jamie continued.

'I was seeing someone then, having *consensual* intercourse with them. He's Paul's father.'

'How do you know?'

'They did a test. Do you think I would have had your child, after what you did?'

'I don't believe you. Does he know?'

'Know what?'

'About me?'

'There's nothing to know.'

'I could ask for my own test.'

'There wouldn't be any point.'

'And does your husband know about us?'

'There isn't an "us", Jamie.'

'I can tell him if you like.'

'Tell him you raped me?'

'That's just a word. You don't remember it like it was.'

'It's what you did.'

Her words seemed to bring a trace of shame to his face, she couldn't be sure. He jumped up a level so he was only a few feet below her now. She flinched, but remained where she was.

'We could be a family, all of us.'

'You're crazy. Why would I want to be with you?'

Jamie thought for a moment. 'Perhaps I'll just tell the boy.'

'This is what's going to happen, Jamie. I'm

305

going to go home to my husband and children, you're going to drive to wherever you came from, and we're never going to see each other again. I'll call the police if I see you near the house again.'

'And say what? That I've been trespassing?'

'They'll have records on file.'

'Of charges that were dropped.'

'Goodbye, Jamie.'

She stood up to walk away, but he grabbed the bottom of her leg. 'I *want* us to be friends,' he said. 'What's wrong with that?' She shook free, her boot striking him hard in the face at the same time. He grinned and brought a hand to his mouth. Blood seeped between his teeth, before he spat it to the ground.

'Just go!' Anna screamed. 'Leave us alone.'

She scrambled off the stack and marched down the slope, into the treeline. The rudimentary path snaked back into the valley, the woods thicker here. She could hear him following. Anna broke into a run, trying not to topple over, grabbing branches at every opportunity to steady herself.

She was off the path now, skidding, half falling. The river could just be heard, a low boom echoing up from below. Her momentum finally pulled her over and she landed hard, scraping her face and palms along the ground. She rolled a couple of times, knocking against the trees, their roots digging into her body. A boulder stopped her progress and she lay there until her breath returned. Twenty yards above, Jamie clambered down.

When he reached her he spoke. 'Just accept it. Some things are meant to be.' He smiled a bloody smile. 'Tread softly because you tread on my dreams,' he said, again affecting a thin laugh.

Lying there, Anna thought of her son. Nothing about him was part of Jamie. Robert was his father. Megan his sister. What happened that night happened to the old Anna, the one who died shortly afterwards.

She looked around. There was still nobody else out here.

He went on talking. 'I read that book in prison,' he said.

She focused on the end of the sentence. 'There were others, then?'

Jamie grinned back at her.

'What book?' Anna said.

'*Kill a Mockingbird*. Can't say I thought much of it, other than the connection with you. It reminded me of that night, you trying to get me to read it.'

Anna stood up. Hatred propelled her towards him, screaming, swinging. He looked surprised, moving only to protect himself. They fell to the ground and for a moment she was above him. She launched blow after blow but, as in that other time, they fell harmlessly, his arms and hands covering his head. And then he was laughing, as if she were a child, her punches and slaps dismissed with contempt by an older brother. His physical dominance was even greater than before. She stopped, exhausted, defeated.

She got off him and sat on a rock, her

breathing deep and laboured.

'I like it when you fight back,' he said. He got up, dusted himself down and came and sat next to her. 'All that anger, though, it's not good for you.'

Anna wanted to cry. It had been so long since she'd wept, when she just let everything out. She tried to picture Robert tonight, his reaction. Whether he'd hold her, or storm out into the darkness. Paul, she thought, would break things, shout, which in some ways was easier to deal with.

She'd built a family, something that struck her now as incredibly difficult to do. That you could lose it with a few words seemed unfair. The lies had been sustained by stability; she'd been happy to see the truth disappear into the past, where it became just a story, a version known only to a few.

Anna stood up. 'Goodbye, Jamie.' She would find the path, head down to the river and walk back to the car. Later she could call the police.

As she began to walk, he held her arm. 'This is just the start of us,' he said. 'You know that too. I know it was wrong, that night. It wasn't how it's supposed to be. But I'm better now. They showed me how to get better, told me how it should be.'

She shook her arm free and continued down the track, but he was behind her in seconds, turning her towards him. Anna looked at him, wondering if it was possible to feel any pity. 'Just go home,' she said.

His grip was tighter this time. As she struggled

to get away, they fell sideways on to the start of the rock's ledge, rolling a few almost comic turns together. Coming to a halt, faces inches apart, Jamie let out a small laugh, his brief frailty now maniacal.

Sensing his arms loosen, she shuffled backwards, up the slope a little, before standing. Looking up at her, he managed another grin of disdain. As he moved to stand, his boot slid on the moss, sending him a few feet further back. He did this several times but, without anything of substance to grip on the rock, could get no further up. Realising the slope fell away to nothing behind him, he flung both arms out, clutching at the branches above. For a moment it seemed they would hold, despite his weight, and again there was the grin of bloodstained teeth. But the main branch began to crack above him, the smaller ones around it fraying. And then there was nothing holding him but the gradient of the rock. Slowly, inch by inch, he began to slide backwards over the edge. His fingers dug in, slowing the movement so it was barely discernible. Anna took a pace downwards but began to slip herself. There was panic in his face, almost a plea. And then the slide gathered momentum, a few more kicks, some desperate clawing, and he was gone.

Apart from a few branches snapping, there was no noise. Not even a distant clump a few seconds later.

Anna ran up to the track and around the rock stack, found a gap in the trees and leaned over where it was safe. Seventy feet or so below, Jamie

309

lay on the ground, face up, unmoving except for an occasional spasm. One of his arms lay beneath his head, contorted, forced back on itself. It wasn't possible to see if his eyes were open. After a minute the twitching ceased.

She looked frantically up and down the river, but there was no one on the banks. Her heart pounding, she stood there watching him, half expecting him to get up, to come after her, but also knowing that he wouldn't. To his side, the river raged, oblivious, hurrying to the coast. Her legs trembled violently as she tried to walk and she leaned into the bough of a tree for balance. Bending forward she was sick a couple of times.

★   ★   ★

It was cooler now, the cloud banking in from the west. Anna shivered, realising she could have been standing there for ages. Or just a few minutes, she couldn't tell. A walker should have come along by now. She should be answering questions, making a statement. She tried to remember the order of things, so that people understood. There would only be her version this time. The nausea had passed but she felt dizzy, disorientated.

She blew into her hands. Someone would come along soon. If not she could call for help, perhaps anonymously, when her phone had a signal.

Looking down again, she thought that his head had shifted slightly, facing the rock now rather than the river, but she could be imagining it. You couldn't survive a fall like that. She stared hard, looking for any movement. The ground around his head looked darker. If she went down, there would be a pulse to feel for, the rise and fall of his chest to observe. Vital signs. Ten minutes, it would take, to walk along, pick up the path that led down to the river. Perhaps another ten to walk upstream to the point below.

38

Despite the thunderous roar it made, there was something soothing about the noise. He seemed to be able to hear it, not just inside his head, but within his entire body, as if it were part of him, with no beginning or end. And within the thunder lay a thousand separate rumbles, each one consuming him before being replaced by another.

He could make out a white light all around him too, dimming to black before returning again. A thought rose in him, that he should move some part of himself, but when he tried, pain, hot and fierce, shot through his whole body, and so he focused again on the booming.

He was unimaginably cold, like that time his father shut him out in the snow in just his pants because he'd broken the television by spilling juice down the back of it. Poor bastard, he thought. That once colossus of a man, the only person Jamie had truly been afraid of, now barely able to make it upstairs on his own. Something to do with hidden fibres in the walls of the factory where he'd worked. A lifetime of inhalation, and now a slow death, reliant on the woman who'd endured even more of his cruelty than Jamie.

He recalled his last visit there, a week or so after leaving the prison, arriving in the middle of the day, so he could ask his mother for money while his father was out at work. But he was there, this once tyrannical man, imprisoned in a room, in the house where unspeakable things had happened.

The temptation had been huge. To inflict some small revenge on this cripple in front of him. Instead he'd bent down in front of his father, their faces inches apart, listening to the shallow wheeze, his chest rising and falling as if bound by one of the belts he'd once wielded with quiet rage. They'd held each other's stare for a minute or so while Jamie's mother kept up small talk from the kitchen. Look at you now, Jamie thought to say. All your power and brutality quietened for ever. Reduced to a rhythmic rasp. Undone by the tiniest of substances. His father's eyes still burned with a hint of the man he had been, as if he knew part of him would live on through his son.

As he stood, Jamie patted his father's knee and winked at him. In the kitchen he took the roll of notes his mother was fumbling with and kissed her on the cheek, her tears like brine. You'll stay and have some tea, won't you, she'd said, but he hadn't.

And as he listened to the water roar past him now, he thought about the things you couldn't escape, the parts of you that would have their way, that were beyond control, despite the techniques they'd taught him inside. He was what he was; there seemed little point fighting it or running from it, this dark corner of his mind, this voice that had been with him for as long as he could remember. It could be suppressed, perhaps ignored for a time, only to rise again, the impulse, the urge, searing inside him like an inferno, raging until, finally, it was dowsed.

The light around him dimmed once more, but this time he remained conscious. Again he thought to move but some deep pain made itself known at the contemplation of this. He realised then that someone was standing over him, regarding him. And then he felt something, a touch of some sort, on his neck. He thought of Miss Jacobs and coming here to find her, watching the house, her family coming and going, knowing nothing of his presence. And after days of looking at them, seeing their lives silently play out through the house's windows, he'd felt a small part of it all, as if he belonged in some way, that there was something here for him. Even when he was inside the cottage, wanting to buy something she'd made, seeing her anger, he thought some good could come of it all.

He sensed the person moving away, their footsteps lost to the rushing water.

Again he pictured his father, considered the evil the man had somehow given him. At least, Jamie thought, his own demons would play no future part in the world, the line halted with himself. It had been cruel to let Miss Jacobs think he might be the boy's father. Once he'd worked out the dates, he'd thought he'd try his luck, in case she wasn't sure, to see if such a lie held some leverage. And he could see that she wasn't certain, despite what she said at the top of the rock. She didn't know. All this time, she didn't know.

But he hadn't come in her that night in the flat. Not even close. He never understood why — it was the only time he hadn't been able to — but something in her pleading, her attempts to reason with him rather than continue fighting back, even once he was inside her, had put him off.

The pain seemed to have stopped now. Or at least it had become something else. The white light faded and did not come back, and with it the noise of the rushing water.

39

The cottage was empty, cold looking. Anna put the heating on, then lit the fire in the studio. There was still an hour's light left, but she drew the curtains throughout, including her son's. The children would be waiting for the school bell to sound, Megan off to a friend's for homemade pizza, Paul trudging home for some talk his mother wanted.

Again she pictured her son, so beautiful beneath his anger, the world waiting for him to embrace it once adolescence had finished with him. His sister, fascinated by everything she saw and read. And their father, this wonderful man who'd shown more patience and love than she'd thought possible. She'd borne the truth for them so that they didn't have to live that night as well. It had always seemed a selfless act, to protect them.

Tonight, she now realised, could be whatever she chose. More lies, half-truths. Or words that changed everything.

She showered, taking longer than usual, but

not excessively. Enough to remove him again. Looking in the mirror was still something she rarely did beyond necessity. There was never a pause to regard herself, to really *see* herself. For months afterwards her reflection had disgusted her, so that like an inverse Narcissus she had become expert at avoiding it. Even at the hairdressers her gaze would be cast to the side or downwards, just a few degrees, so as not to appear peculiar. That's fine, Anna would say, even before the woman had held the mirror up behind her. And when necessity determined she wore make-up or tidied her hair, she learned to blunt her vision, as if regarding herself through mist; looking but not really seeing.

As she wiped away the last of the condensation with her hand, she let the towel drop. It was easier to look into her eyes than to study the naked body below them, and yet the longer she stood there, the more tolerable it became. She supposed she was still regarded as slim. Her breasts sat lower these days, but not unreasonably so for her age. Her pubic hair seemed profuse since looking at the images on Paul's computer. The graze on her forehead from falling throbbed and she took a finger to it, touching it lightly. She gathered her clothes and got dressed.

Outside, the temperature had quickly dropped. In the gloaming light Wistman's Wood was just a clump of black further up the valley. It was always hard to imagine the snow covering everything, until, as most years up here, it finally did. She pictured the fox tearing across the side of the

318

hill and wondered how much of its escape was calculated, how much consideration, or at least intelligence, went into the route it chose. Perhaps it just fled, instinct doing no more than attempting to put distance between itself and the hunt. Or perhaps it, too, had tried to lead the dogs away from its young.

The scene a few miles away formed in her mind. A walker would have found him by now. There'd be a piece on the local news at teatime. A man found. A body found. She thought to call the police before anyone got home but decided against it. At the very least they would take her away for hours, document a story that began more than sixteen years ago, before the issue of culpability arose. It could wait until later; her family should be allowed the truth first.

Turning back to the cottage, an orange warmth glowed from the downstairs windows, looking like a scene someone had painted.

She was supposed to feel something, she was sure of that. As she put the chickens away for the night, the same thought occurred again and again. That she was supposed to feel something.

★   ★   ★

Anna opened one of the windows in the studio and sat there hoping to hear the bus traverse the cattle grid beyond the hill. A soft wind ushered in, hints of the snow to come riding on it.

The studio felt like a room in a stately home, its contents untouched, preserved as a reminder of another time. She had not thrown any clay for

319

more than a week. Nothing had been made. There was danger in these fallow spells, she knew. A risk that creativity would abandon her, that she'd return to the wheel with nothing to offer but inertia. If you didn't understand the forces inherent in what you did, how could you hope to summon them if one day they were absent? All you could do was keep faith that each time you began again it would still be there.

And yet, right now, it seemed unlikely she'd make another pot. Her work felt ridiculous against all the worthy endeavours others did (not to mention the day's events). It was self-indulgent and decadent. It helped no one, it contributed to nothing. Art seduced you this way, espoused its worth until you believed it yourself. It encouraged you to hide within it, to regard all else as inferior. But its value was illusory. It now sickened her how art drew out judgement, how it encouraged discrimination and hierarchy. Aestheticism, it seemed to her, meant elitism. She'd always wanted to be an artisan, not an artist. She'd wanted to be removed from the profusion of male potters who adorned their work with the naked female form, thinking it was something to be marvelled at, as if its only value was visual.

★　★　★

The home phone rang.

'Is he back?' Robert said.

'Not yet.'

'I'm stuck at work. Some walkers have been

320

reported missing; we're going to help look for them. Hopefully done in an hour.'

'OK.'

'You'll wait until I'm home, won't you?'

'Of course.'

'I love you.'

'See you in a bit.'

Back in the studio she stoked the fire. It would have cost nothing to tell her husband she loved him too. But she could not have matched the intensity or sincerity of his words, instead merely batting them back in reflex. She would say them if they got through this. She would use them if they made love again.

The phrase lingered in her mind. Making love. A gentle euphemism, almost quaint, repudiating the more harsh terms: to copulate, to fornicate, to fuck — even the words sounded barbed. To make love. To produce it, as if it didn't exist. We need to make some love. Assemble it. Construct it. And when it's depleted, we can just make some more.

The kitchen door opened and then closed.

'Paul?' she called.

'Yeah.' He said it wearily but without annoyance. Anna went to meet him but he'd gone upstairs.

'Do you want some tea?' she called up.

Music came on, not loudly but enough to stop him hearing her. She boiled some water anyway, tried to keep busy. Looking into the garden, she thought about the chicken in its shallow grave. She wondered how long decomposition would take. Strangely, her daughter would probably

321

know. A gradual putrefaction, a fusion with the earth.

Perhaps she could have buried him too, dropped the body in a hole so that it also lay coiled as if asleep. And if the earth was patted down enough, covered with branches, it might be unseen, undiscovered for months, years. She could check on it regularly, repairing any damage animals and weather had done, like tending a grave. How long would it take to dig such a hole?

There had been three hours of daylight remaining when she'd left his lifeless body by the river and walked back to the car; perhaps dusk had fallen on the path as she'd left it, Jamie still there. Deep in the night, the house cloyed with slumber, she could slip out, drive back to Cadover Bridge, where Jamie's car would still be parked. In the moonlight she would follow the river south. The spade, still dirtied with garden soil, would become heavy, but adrenaline would push her on. As she neared the spot, shadows would play tricks on her, a body would become a fallen tree or a clump of earth, the woods alive with sound. And if he was still there, she would drag him along, a few hundred yards perhaps, an hour or so, and up into softer ground. His weight would make it difficult but she'd have all night. Three feet down would do, maybe four. She'd stop for breaks, rubbing her hands to warm them, listening to the lament of a nearby tawny owl. There would be no fear. In a week or so heavy snow would fall, the ground would freeze around him, entombing him.

But even were she capable of this, the thought

that he'd be for ever buried here sickened her. Spring would come, the ground would thaw. He'd rise each year with the sap. The soil itself, the rivers, would be polluted. His voice would ride the wind as she walked the tors. Even in death he would claim some part of her.

So she'd left him to be found, if not today, then tomorrow. An accident, would be the conclusion. Or the final act of a man who realised what he was. A leap to death.

But he hadn't jumped. Anna thought again for a moment about her culpability, her failure to act, to move a few paces down the slope and reach out, albeit endangering herself. Inaction, it seemed, could hold as much significance as any act. There had been a choice this time. A few short moments when instinct was supposed to govern how you behaved, when your humanity, the quality that marked you as different from people like him, took over.

But then she thought about the others, the women behind the prison sentence he spoke of. In those few words, he had, unwittingly, given her something remarkable: that there had been at least one other exonerated her entirely. All the guilt, the endless minute scrutiny and doubt, fell away as she realised the implication of this. Without meaning to, he had confessed. She hadn't led him on that night. She had done nothing wrong, in school, at the flat. It was who he was.

Had she been the first? Were there women afraid to come forward, girlfriends who sensed something of his nature, who tolerated a milder version? Perhaps it was hidden from people close

323

to him, if such people existed. A secret life, much like her own. This they had shared.

She went upstairs. Her son's door was ajar.

'Can I come in?'

'Yeah.' Paul was lying on his bed, composing a text message. She turned the music down, sat by his feet.

'Good day?'

'OK.'

'I thought we could have chilli later, if you like.'

'Yeah, don't mind.'

'Dad'll be a bit late.'

'What happened to your face?'

'I fell over on a walk.'

He looked at her, as if to say, I came home on time: what now?

'We need to talk about something later, when Dad's home.' Paul rolled his eyes a little. 'It's not a lecture; you're not in trouble.'

Again she tried to picture the reaction. If necessary, she could call Megan, speak to her friend's parents, ask that her daughter stay the night. In her mind Anna rehearsed telling her son now that she loved him, but it would sound awkward. She wanted to reach out, play with his hair, twirl it around a finger. Perhaps, afterwards, he'd let her hold him.

The music stopped.

'Shall I put something else on?' Anna said.

'It's OK.'

He pressed a button on his phone, sent the message. She stood to leave, but instead said, 'We could move.'

'What?'

'Nearer your friends. Anywhere. All of us. We could start again somewhere.'

'Why?'

'Because you hate it here. And it's just a place. Would you like to? After your exams, perhaps.'

He looked at her, confused, a little suspicious. 'It's not that bad here,' he said.

Anna smiled at him. 'No, it's not. And you'll be able to drive in a couple of years. Save up for a car. Dad can give you lessons.'

Paul lowered his gaze. Anna put a hand on his arm. 'Come on, I'll make us some tea.'

'We don't have to wait until Dad's home,' he said.

'For what?'

'We can do this now. If you want.'

'The talk?'

Her son looked at her, suddenly older than his fifteen years, a maturity and wisdom in his voice that made Anna feel like a little girl.

After a pause he said, 'Is it about that man, the one hanging around?'

Anna felt sick, scared. She tried to speak but words wouldn't form.

Paul continued. 'The one at the exhibition and outside school?'

'Outside school?'

He nodded. 'So who is he?'

Anna wiped tears away. 'We should wait until Dad's home.'

'Tell me.'

Her son looked more vulnerable than ever. She wished Robert were here.

'I think you know,' Anna finally said.

'That Dad's not my dad?'

Anna pulled her son towards her, holding him fiercely. She stroked the back of his head as he sat there, impassive. 'We can talk about it later,' she said.

'So is it that man?'

Anna found the word from somewhere. 'Yes.'

Paul tried to pull away but she didn't let him.

'It'll be OK,' she said, her voice breaking up. 'I promise. There's nothing we can't deal with.'

This time Paul released himself from her grip. He opened a drawer by the bed, took out some tobacco and started rolling a cigarette. She could see he'd started to cry.

'Please, Paul.'

His hands were trembling, the tobacco spilling from the paper. He picked it up and started again, a flash of anger rising in him.

'Here, let me.' Anna took the pouch and papers from him, rolled two cigarettes and passed one to her son.

'How do you know how to . . . ?' Paul said.

'Just don't tell Dad.'

After lighting them she opened the window and they sat on the bed smoking, Anna coughing with each inhalation.

A minute or so passed, then Paul spoke. His voice was measured now, almost resigned. 'Something always felt wrong.'

'Your dad loves you more than anything.'

'Like there was you and Dad and Meg. And then there was me. Like I was a guest or something. Someone who didn't laugh at the same

326

stuff, or talk about the same things. A code that you all knew, little looks between you, games, nicknames. I try to join in with it, but I sound stupid.'

'You're our son, as much as Megan's our daughter.'

'Except I'm not.'

Anna's gaze found the floor. She gave up on the cigarette, throwing it into the yard.

'So who is he, that man?'

Anna tried to look up, but couldn't. A warm tear ran down her cheek.

'It doesn't matter. Robert's your father now.'

'I always thought I didn't really look like Dad.'

'You don't look that much like me either. It doesn't matter.'

'Dad doesn't know it's that man, does he?'

'No. I'm going to tell him tonight.'

'Why's he only tried to find me now?'

'He's not a good person, Paul. It was just one night.' Her son got up and went over to the window. 'We can get through this, you know. I know you're angry, that we kept this from you.'

'That you lied.'

'Yes. Because we didn't want to hurt you.'

'What does he want? Do I have to go and live with him now?'

'No, of course not. This is your home, we're your family. Your dad and I love you so much.'

'How do you know it's him?'

'What?'

'If it was just one night. How can you be sure? Did you have a test?'

'No, but — '

'So I could be Dad's.'

'I didn't know him then. Your father and I met after you were born.' Anna heard the absurdity in her words.

'And there was no one else?'

Anna wiped her eyes on her sleeve. 'There was someone.'

'So how do you know it's not him?'

In the fog of recent days Anna had thought once or twice about Nick, perhaps clutching at some fanciful notion that she'd been wrong. They'd made love without protection once, a week or so before, both drunk. Nick had convinced her he could have no more children — whether by design or not, she hadn't asked him. His word had been enough at the time.

So her son was right; there was little certainty about it. Why hadn't she checked? Nick would have co-operated. Just to be sure, to rule it out completely. It seemed ridiculous that she hadn't. But she hadn't needed to. Her son's features, his temper. That they could be nothing more than her own projections had never seemed worthy of serious consideration. But she should have checked. At least contacted Nick. She pictured him in her flat, that last time, getting dressed, going home to his wife. Her handsome, older lover. Eyes bluer than the sky.

And yet it hardly mattered now. Paul was Robert's son. She felt that more than ever tonight.

'Dad's home,' said Paul, as the sweep of headlights arced across the ceiling. He threw his own cigarette from the window.

'I love you,' Anna said. 'We love you.'

They listened to the Land Rover park.

Anna stood. 'You coming down?' she said, but got no reply.

★　★　★

She put the kettle on to boil just as Robert came in the back door, the early evening chill following him in. He managed a half-smile, which Anna returned. She had a sudden urge to tell him she loved him, to kiss him.

'I got back as soon as I could,' he said.

'Did they find the walkers?'

'Not yet. Probably in a pub somewhere, having a pint by the fire.'

Anna made some tea while Robert told her someone had fallen from the Dewerstone, that he'd just heard it on his radio. An amateur climber or some unfortunate walker, they weren't sure. There'd been a suicide a few years back, which was another possibility. She found it surprisingly easy not to focus on the image of Jamie falling, landing. Even once she'd scrambled down to the path below, walking back to his body, feeling his neck for a pulse, she'd begun to feel a sense of calm. Blood had trailed from his mouth and one ear, darkening the earth around his head. She'd sat on a nearby rock for a few minutes, watching him, listening to the rushing water behind her. Walking back to the car, an image had come to her. It was a few years ago and the children had just got in from school. They were being unusually quiet so she had looked in the lounge, where

329

the two of them sat on the sofa listening to the same iPod, sharing a single set of earphones, the music or whatever bringing smiles to their faces. Just brother and sister, as it should be.

'Is he home?' Robert asked.

Anna nodded. As he crossed the kitchen she met him, burying her head in his shoulder, holding him tightly. He hesitated before responding, perhaps smelling the tobacco on her breath, perhaps fearful of what tonight would bring. For the second time tonight she whispered in someone's ear that it would all be OK. That they could get through anything.

Behind they heard Paul coming down the stairs.

We do hope that you have enjoyed reading this large print book.

Did you know that all of our titles are available for purchase?

We publish a wide range of high quality large print books including:
Romances, Mysteries, Classics
General Fiction
Non Fiction and Westerns

Special interest titles available in large print are:
The Little Oxford Dictionary
Music Book
Song Book
Hymn Book
Service Book

Also available from us courtesy of Oxford University Press:
Young Readers' Dictionary
(large print edition)
Young Readers' Thesaurus
(large print edition)

For further information or a free brochure, please contact us at:
Ulverscroft Large Print Books Ltd.,
The Green, Bradgate Road, Anstey,
Leicester, LE7 7FU, England.
Tel: (00 44) 0116 236 4325
Fax: (00 44) 0116 234 0205

NO WAY BACK

Matthew Klein

Every time Jimmy Thane has been faced with a crossroads, he's taken the wrong path. But after years of drinking and womanising, he has been given one last chance to save both his marriage and his career. He has seven weeks to transform a failing company, but from the moment he enters the building there's something wrong — the place is too quiet, too empty. When the FBI comes calling about the disappearance of the former CEO, Jimmy starts to wonder what he's got himself into. Then he discovers surveillance equipment in his neighbour's house, looking straight into his own. And his wife isn't just tired, she's terrified and trying to hide it. Jimmy's not living his dream — he's been plunged into the worst kind of nightmare . . .